ENTERING THE FAIRY KINGDOM

After Mrs. Hubbard and the Vicar had been walking about an hour, as far as Ian could judge, they had penetrated quite deeply into the forest. Suddenly the Vicar halted, letting his torch illuminate the ground around him for some time. Then he stooped and picked up something from the ground at his feet, handing it or part of it to Mrs. Hubbard. Without ado, they raised the things they were holding to their lips and disappeared.

Other Avon books coming soon by
Linda Haldeman

STAR OF THE SEA

The Lastborn of Elvinwood

by

Linda Haldeman

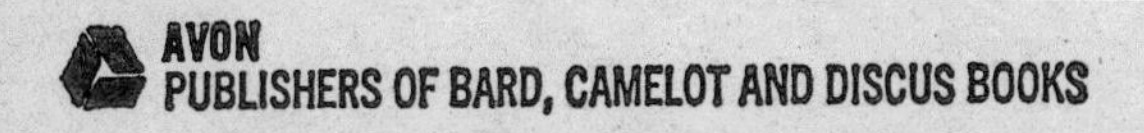
AVON
PUBLISHERS OF BARD, CAMELOT AND DISCUS BOOKS

All the characters in the book are fictitious, and any resemblance to actual persons, living or dead, is purely coincidental.

Cover illustration by Elizabeth Malczynski

AVON BOOKS
A division of
The Hearst Corporation
959 Eighth Avenue
New York, New York 10019

Published by arrangement with
Doubleday & Company, Inc.
Library of Congress Catalog Card Number: 77-27704
ISBN: 0-380-47985-0

First Avon Printing, May, 1980

Printed in the U.S.A.

To Gene, John, Ruth, and Elaine

I would like to express my gratitude to William Lafranchi, David Kaufman, and the staff of the Rhodes Stabley Library of Indiana University of Pennsylvania for all their help in researching this book.

Contents

Chapter 1

The Forest and the Town

Please to remember the Fifth of November
Gunpowder, treason, and plot . . .

It was the perfect time of year for bonfires, although the gunpowder conspirators were not likely to have taken that into consideration. Winter, insofar as winter occurs in the South of England, was more than a month away, but nights were chilly enough to make pleasurable the heat generated by the remembrance of treasons past. On the hill above Elvinwood, Surrey, a vigorous bonfire blazed in the dusk, kindled and tended by the young husbands and fathers of the hilltop housing estate. By the time darkness came a mountain of spare kindling, building scraps, and old furniture was blazing, sending sparks into the clear night sky. Fireworks were set off at judicious intervals by one of the fathers whenever he suspected interest among the spectators was lagging. The bonfire was a community project ostensibly for the children but marked by that undercurrent of tribal fellowship that prevails when otherwise isolated people work together. The men had built the fire from the discards of their wives' autumn housecleaning while the children supplied refreshments in the form of chestnuts gathered from the woods behind the estate, enough of them to fill an old perambulator found unsuitable for burning. There was something vaguely primitive about the scene, reminiscent of some ancient Druidic rite: the inconstant orange glow of the fire spluttering hungrily as another victim, a pale green kitchen chair rung, was cast on the altar, the fire god answering with a shower of green and gold stars spurting from a cardboard cone labeled "Trafalgar Fountain." The lacquered blue pram sat cool and unconcerned in the background like the womb of an earth goddess distributing largesse without fanfare or fireworks.

The American family was coming to see the bonfire, a matter of some satisfaction to the inhabitants of the estate, who were more than mildly curious about these visitors from abroad. A university professor with his wife and four children had leased the house at the top of Church Hill, an area of unattached houses with private gardens between the estate of council-owned townhouses and the row of elaborately landscaped stockbrokers' mansions that ran down the other side of the hill. Not many Americans came to Elvinwood except for brief visits. But this family was staying a whole year. The professor was supposed to be doing research, and his wife was writing a book or something. The children, the ladies of the estate reported in scandalized whispers, were not attending school, but living in merrily unproductive idleness, which was what the hard-working residents of the estate suspected the adults were doing as well.

The family hurried now toward the mounting bonfire in their customary formation. The two boys, near enough of an age to be sometimes mistaken for twins, forming the vanguard, with Ned, the younger, carefully keeping half a pace ahead of his elder brother, Brian, as if to compensate for the loss of primogeniture. The father, dressed rather too casually by hilltop estate standards, kept an even pace directly behind his sons. The females made up the rear guard, though probably more from their own natural slowness than from any feeling of subservience. Anne, who was struggling through the uncertainties of the kindergarten adolescence between babyhood and girlhood, walked in front of her mother, but not very far in front, inspiring a monotonous running encouragement from behind. But the scandal of the estate was the baby, Penny. She arrived shoeless, capless, and pramless, riding her mother's back like a red Indian papoose. Nothing like that had been seen in Elvinwood before. The mums of the estate, like those in most parts of England, paraded their plump, well-wrapped infants in large, elaborate perambulators as valuable for prestige as for function. Small wonder they blanched at the sight of that apparently underfed and under-clothed child observing the world with round blue eyes over her mother's shoulders from a flimsy canvas backpack.

The strangers were made welcome and offered chestnuts. Someone inquired about the baby's age and whether they minded the dampness. The Americans knew themselves to be outsiders, observing but not participating in a community ritual, but they accepted their role with good grace. If truth be told, they did not much miss the ebullient welcome they would have suffered at the hands of such a party crashed in their own country. They were outsiders and were content to be, observed and observing on the periphery of the magic circle of fire, like anthropologists at a potlatch. The baby stared open-eyed and open-mouthed at the mountain of flame before her, smiling in wonder and delight at the fountains and whirling wheels of multicolored sparks, following the path of shooting stars that soared over the hill and disappeared in green-and-gold explosions into the blackness of the woodland beyond.

In the forest itself there were other observers of the ritual, observers unknown to the people of the hill, observers who had often witnessed and wondered at the human magic that manifested itself each harvestide in recent centuries.

"Every year it diminishes," remarked Garumpta the Fernlord to his aged mate, Aneelen. "I wonder if their powers are diminishing as well," he added, a faint spark lighting his deep-set green eyes.

"Not likely," Aneelen retorted. "They are probably just losing interest in the ceremony, whatever it is. Humans have a shockingly brief attention span."

Garumpta nodded melancholy agreement. "I rather hope it remains awhile longer, though. It's one of the few attractive things they do."

The wood stretching perhaps a hundred acres behind the hill belonged in these latter years to the National Trust, a society that bought and preserved in its natural state as much of undomesticated Britain as it could get its grip on. The American family took long and frequent walks along its cool, well-kept footpaths. They entered the woods by means of an alley that passed behind a brick block of flats built to resemble vaguely an uninspired Roman viaduct. The alley piddled out into a dirt path which, after passing a couple of isolated homesteads, unconcernedly traipsed across a pasture before entering the wood itself, an ancient forest of chestnut, oak, and birch, kept ever green by a dense undergrowth of ivy and great bushes of holly and glossy-leaved rhododendron. There were few weeds or wildflowers, as the floor of the forest was covered with a thick carpet of decaying leaf matter. Sunlight, more abundant in autumn than the usual descriptions of soggy England would lead one to believe, passed here and there through the leaves above, occasionally spotlighting a fine woven lacework of spider web suspended between two large yellowing fronds of fern. Mushrooms were numerous and in great variety. feasting off the rich garbage of the forest.

"It deserves to be a magic wood," the American mother remarked one afternoon not long after the Guy Fawkes' Day celebration. They were walking through a section of the wood they had not visited before, slightly downhill single file along a scarcely definable ribbon of a path that led through tangles of creeping ivy and blackberry briars to an impassable thorny thicket that sent them struggling back up to the main path.

"I could do without that sort of magic," the father grumbled.

The sun glistened only palely through the trees, warning of the lateness of the hour and the nearness of winter. The wood was loud with numerous bird cries. The baby, contemplating the world from the elevated perch of her mother's shoulders, smiled at the sun and the glistening leaves and at the cacophonous concert of birds. She sucked her two middle fingers; her head slowly dropped until it rested on her mother's shoulders and she slept.

Anne, as was her habit, was lagging behind. At least that's what the grown-ups called it. Actually she was exploring. Big people missed so much because they rarely looked down or slowed their everlasting long-legged rushing, dragging after them whole worlds of protesting children torn between fascination with the wealth at their feet and the fear of being deserted. Anne had just come upon a large leaf, something like ivy. She paused to lift it carefully, discovering under it a shiny black beetle complacently cleaning its antennae. Interrupted by her father's impatient admonition to "keep up," she answered automatically with a cross "I AM!" The baby momentarily raised her head, then dropped it again with a sigh. At ten months she was already fairly immune to familial racket.

Anne hesitated, looking about, absent-mindedly picking up a large chestnut burr near her feet. Her father called again, his voice edged with irritation, and she started forward. The chestnut burr in her hand seemed to move, ever so slightly. She stopped, startled, and then quickly pulled it apart. Inside sat a very cross-looking, cross-legged, cross-eyed man no larger than her thumb. He was dressed in ragged and faded clothes of the sort she had seen in story books: a patched brown leather jerkin and puffy, bloomerlike breeches that had probably once been green, but were now more like gray; his hair and beard were long and thin, the color of wet sand. His face was lined and brown, but his cheeks shone out from it bright red, like apples in a paper bag. His ears were pointed at the top, but it was his eyes that were the most remarkable. It is hard to say what color they were—a little green, a little brown, even a suggestion of red, like the forest. And most remarkable of all, they stubbornly focused only on each other. She stared open-mouthed at him for close to a minute. Anne was still too young to be afraid, and the sight before her was no more strange or wonderful to her than was the shiny beetle or the star spurting rockets of Guy Fawkes' Day. Fairies in her world were no more exotic than robins.

"I'm sorry," she whispered at last. "I didn't know you were there."

Gently she replaced the other half of the burr, laid it carefully in the shelter of a protruding tree root, and hurried in pursuit of the impatiently receding backs of her family.

Chapter 2

Midwinter Night

It was well into December before winter came, not that winter in southwestern Surrey is all that bad. It snowed occasionally, but the snow rarely stayed on the ground more than a day or two. The neat, well-tended gardens of the hilltop estate were never bare of some kind of flowers or greenery. With December and the approach of Christmas came the annual pantomime season. In London the theaters made various gestures in the direction of the traditional Christmas pantomime, but as often as not they were token gestures only. After all, the pantomime was an entertainment geared to the tastes of another era and not likely to attract contemporary audiences, which always contained a fair number of visiting foreigners unfamiliar with the language and conventions of such a peculiarly British exhibition. There was even a rumor that *Peter Pan* was not going to be put on due to lack of interest. Interest immediately awoke, manifesting itself in irate letters to the *Times*, and *Peter Pan* was forthwith produced.

In Elvinwood, where tradition was strong and box-office receipts of little import, the local amateur theatrical society put on a "real" pantomime, just the way it had always been done. There were patter songs, jokes ancient and topical, a fairy scene involving the children of the local dancing school, and a great deal of good-natured audience participation. The villain was played, as all local villains were, by Ian James. With his face and profile Ian James was destined to be an actor. His dark eyes glinted just enough, his long nose hooked downward just enough, his black hair receded from his forehead and curled at his neck just enough, and his beard was trimmed to just enough of a point to give him a memorable appearance, sometimes majestic, sometimes sinister, sometimes both simultaneously. Were his features further exaggerated even slightly, the result would have been caricature. As things stood he had the advantage of being able to do both comic and serious villains with ease. In private life he was unspectacular; a bachelor in his early forties, he lived alone on a small inheritance, which enabled him to devote a good deal of time to his greatest interest, the local theater.

Indeed, he could almost always be found at the old brick building that housed the Elvinwood Auditorium, a haphazard affair that would have been peremptorily rejected by any self-respecting American small-town junior high school. The stage was too small and too high; the rows of removable seats squeaked, rattled, and occasionally fell apart during performances. The heating system was all but nonexistent, and the hall so drafty that audiences at winter productions were wrapped up like a convention of Laplanders. For all that, the little hall was filled for every performance of the pantomime, for things were done properly at Elvinwood.

The American family came, of course. They came to everything interesting that went on in the auditorium. When they trooped backstage after the Saturday matinee, Ian James greeted them warmly, for being a reticent person himself, he enjoyed their high-spirited enthusiasm.

As the parents herded their children out of the dressing room they very nearly collided with their next-door neighbor, Mrs. Hubbard, a grandmotherly widow who also came to everything and always thought to stop backstage and congratulate the players. She responded cheerfully to the children's effusive greeting and suggested if they liked Christmas activities they attend the carol service to be held at the parish church the following evening. She stood a moment by the open dressing room door watching the parents maneuver their little crowd out the stage door.

"Not a bad lot, I'd say," commented a voice next to her. Mrs. Hubbard turned to see her old friend the retired Vicar of a nearby country church.

"Why, good afternoon, Thomas," she exclaimed. "How

have you been keeping? I don't believe I've seen you since Midsummer last."

"So you haven't, my dear. So you haven't. I've been keeping as well as I have a right to expect, and I'm looking forward, of course, to tomorrow night."

"Oh quite." Mrs. Hubbard glanced around quickly as if to be sure they were not overheard. "I say, why don't you stop around at my place for a bit of supper after the carol service. Then we could walk over after it gets late."

"Jolly good," the Vicar beamed.

He thrust his head into the dressing room where Ian James was creaming the thick villain's makeup from his face.

"Splendid job, as always, James," he called gruffly.

"Thank you, Vicar." Ian's voice was muffled by the large facial tissue he was using to blot his lips. He did not turn to greet the old man, for he felt slightly ashamed at having listened to this private conversation. It wasn't like him to do that sort of thing. He knew Mrs. Hubbard only to speak to, but he had in the past had dealings with the Vicar. He was an interesting old fellow, if a bit eccentric. He claimed to be eighty-five, but certainly didn't look it. He appeared to be in ruggedly good health, walked a great deal, and swam, it was rumored, every day that the temperature was above freezing. He traveled a good deal too, especially in the Orient, and was by popular report quite a scholar in astrology and other sorts of Eastern occultism. It had been on account of that reputation that Ian had consulted him the previous year for assistance in an article he had been writing for the parish paper on the three Magi. The Vicar had been helpful, but like most scholars had offered more information that was required or even desirable. Ian had indeed been rather shocked by some of his more unorthodox views. He had not thought about that interview for some time. It had been a strange one for sure. And now there was this queer conversation with Mrs. Hubbard. What about tomorrow night? It was the Sunday before Christmas, which accounted for the carol service being held then, but what else could be going on? He drew his wallet from his trouser pocket and examined the small calendar inside. There it was, Sunday, December 21, eve of the winter solstice. Strange. Very strange.

The carol service always took place on the Sunday evening before Christmas, replacing the usual choral evensong. Ten bells pulled in harmony by ten skilled bellringers sent their merry falling chords through the chill air drawing the faithful and those who simply enjoyed singing carols toward the church. Yellow light beamed through the open door onto the stone paving leading through the ancient churchyard with its Celtic crosses and fungus-stained gravestones. The interior was bright with many candles, wreaths, and ropes of festooned greenery.

There were no empty places in the well-polished pews, at least none that Ian James could see from the rear choir stall, the place where he sat every Sunday of the Christian year from First Advent to Last Trinity, as often as not the lone bass, lending all the support he could to the row of well-scrubbed boy altos in front of him. He was not alone tonight, though, for the carol service was popular with choristers and congregation. During the reading of the lesson he had leisure to take stock of this season's assemblage. The Americans were there, and so, he noted, were Mrs. Hubbard and the Vicar. Well, he reminded himself, wherever they were going after the service was none of his business.

Ian had no further opportunity to think about the Vicar and Mrs. Hubbard until the service was over. He then disrobed quickly, not quite knowing what the rush was, and burst out of the vestry door wrapped in his coat and scarf before the last of the congregation had disbanded their cheery little caucuses on the paths and in the road.

"Happy Christmas," one group called.

"And to you," answered another family-sized company entering a large black automobile parked somewhat illegally on the sidewalk across from the church.

Here came the American children, herded by their mother like rebellious young sheep being urged home by a nervous collie. He watched them cross the road and start up the hill. A slow, chill drizzle was setting in.

"Good night, Mr. James. Happy Christmas."

"Happy Christmas to you, Mrs. Hubbard."

He stood awhile watching the departure of the last of the churchgoers, not knowing why he did not himself head for home before the weather got worse. But stay he did, standing in the shelter of the little pagoda-shaped roof that stood over the churchyard gate. The worshipers had all departed by motor or, soggily, on foot. One by one the lights in the church were extinguished, leaving all in silence and darkness save for the misty streetlamp across the road. The verger, having completed his locking-up duties, hurried through the churchyard and out the gate without taking any notice of Ian in the shadow of the gate roof.

That amused him for some reason, and he stood for a few more minutes chuckling in the darkness before he also started walking up the hill. The prospect of being virtually invisible intrigued him, and he proceeded on his way in such a manner as to continue the illusion, though later he could in no way explain his reason for doing so. The walls and hedges that surrounded most of the houses that fronted Churchill Lane, houses that celebrated their proximity to the church by bearing saints' names—St. Catherine's, St. John's, St. Anne's—helped shadow Ian from any eyes that might unaccountably be seeking him out.

At the crest of the hill he encountered a problem, for there, set a bit back from the road, was young Dr. Elder's house, a modern American-style dwelling with a modern American-style open front yard in place of the usual walled garden. A cheery porch light dispelled any protective shadows that might dare to hover about the periphery of all that wholesome openness. Ian crossed the street, reminding himself all the while how absurdly he was behaving, for he would just have to cross back over again at the top of the hill in order to turn left onto Southdown Road, where his flat was located. His present course would lead him directly into the grounds of the Oak Haven School for Girls. A mental picture of those dear lumps of girls in their dull green skirts and wide-brimmed hats marching down to the church two by two, a pair of thin, nervous mistresses leading the procession and the great, square battleship of a headmistress bringing up the rear, caused him to change his course at the top of the hill, not to the left, however, but to the right, down Buckingham Avenue.

On the corner was Mrs. Hubbard's attractive brick cottage with its perfectly manicured garden. A single dim light shone from the sitting room. Next loomed the large, ponderous square house surrounded by its overwhelming twenty-foot hedge which the American family had leased. Most of the lights upstairs were shining. They're probably getting the children to bed, Ian thought. He stood around the corner of the hedge, protected by it from the worst of the rain and wind, listening to the music that drifted through the large bay window of the lounge. Radio Three, he surmised. *The Messiah*, he knew.

The upstairs lights went out. The front door opened slightly, and there was a brief rattling as milk bottles were set out. Then the door was closed and locked. The rain continued steady and chilling; the wind rose, rustling through the hedge and wailing around the house, rattling loose windows, forcing its way past ill-fitting doorjambs and down chimney flues. Ian huddled against the hedge wondering why he was not warming his numb feet before the electric fire in his flat, sipping a glass of port. Somewhere a clock struck ten. *The Messiah* marched to its climactic "Amen."

Ian sank deeper into the hedge as he heard quiet footsteps coming along the sidewalk next to him. Two figures sharing a large, black umbrella approached and passed into the light of the streetlamp: Mrs. Hubbard and the Vicar, just as he had expected. Still not knowing what moved him, he fell in a few feet behind them, staying as quiet and as much out of sight as possible. All this was quite uncharacteristic behavior for him. He was by nature reticent, more than willing to let every person live according to his lights, with his curiosity kept well in check. Yet here he was, risking pneumonia to tail two old people in the rain, simply to find out where they were going.

They turned, much to his surprise, down the alley behind the council flats that led into the National Trust forest. Ian hesitated at the edge of the ink-black woodland path. Light was behind him, and the sleepy town bright with Christmas lights. Before him was a black abyss, or perhaps a dark curtain closed before a stage whose set and action he had never seen, nor was ever meant to see. The leaf-crushing footfalls of the pair in front of him were starting to fade into the distance. Ian hesitated a second, looking back over his shoulder at the amber streetlamps twinkling like small bonfires down the hill into the valley below. Then he plunged forward through the dark curtain, trying to keep step with those ahead of him so his own crackling footfalls would not be heard.

The wood was not the sort of place Ian would have chosen to come to on a cold December night; yet once inside, he found it a surprisingly comfortable place. The trees kept out most of the wind and a good bit of the rain. It was wondrously dark, though. Alone Ian would never have been able to keep to the path. However, the Vicar, some twenty feet ahead of him, was lighting the way with a small electric torch. Ian followed the thin circle of light as a driver in deep fog might follow the lights of the car ahead. He could follow their voices as well, for the two old people were carrying on a lively conversation. Ian was unable to make out most of what they were saying, but he resisted the urge to walk a little closer, although they might not have noticed his presence. He had already stumbled a couple of times over unseen stumps and once nearly slammed into an indignant birch sapling, but Mrs. Hubbard and the Vicar took no notice and simply hurried on past the cow pasture and the darkened farmhouse below it.

After they had been walking about an hour, as far as Ian could judge, they had penetrated quite deeply into the forest. They struggled along a narrow path, getting deeper and deeper into a thicket of dense underbrush. Suddenly the Vicar halted, letting his torch illuminate the ground around him for some time. Then he stooped and picked up something from the ground at his feet, handing it or part of it to Mrs. Hubbard. Without ado, they raised the things they were holding to their lips and disappeared.

Ian James staggered back against the trunk of a great old beech. He was shaking so, he could hardly keep his feet. His hand had gone quickly up to his mouth in the first instant of shock and now refused to return to his side. He remained as though paralyzed, able to absorb nothing except that his heart was beating loudly and rapidly. Then his hand dropped, and he sank to the ground amongst the gnarled beech roots. He felt himself to be alone and was terribly afraid. The forest was a stranger to him now, cold and terrible, and he longed to be out of it. His mind urged him to flee, but his feet would not.

Slowly he forced himself to move, creeping forward on his belly, groping with numb fingers in the soggy mat of dead leaves toward the thicket where the Vicar and Mrs. Hubbard had vanished. His mind again told him that he ought to be going in the opposite direction—away from, not toward, the mystery. His mind had had enough of spying in the rain, but his hands and feet continued to grope toward that thicket. Presently his left hand touched what seemed to be a round, smooth stone. He took it in his hand and sat up to examine it. Even in the darkness he could make out what it was: a chestnut. Holding the nut gingerly between his forefinger and thumb, he slowly raised it to his lips. He felt himself falling rapidly, as if he were going down too fast in a lift. He landed with a thud and a crunch in the middle of a large brown paper carpet. Looking up, he saw with wonder that he was surrounded by a dense jungle of thorny vines as thick as tree branches. The carpet crackled under him as he shakily stood up. It was certainly a lumpy carpet, for all through it ran a pattern of bony ridges, as though someone had run electric cables under it. It was an odd shape too he realized on making a cautious reconnaissance. The part behind him seemed to be round, while that in front came to three distinct jagged points. My God, he realized with a start that sent him flying off onto the ground, it's a maple leaf.

He lay in the dampness staring up at the network of branches armed with lancelike spikes that twined above his head. A large boulder rolled by him, stopping a short distance away. Ian crawled over to examine it and was not greatly astonished to recognize the chestnut that apparently had brought him to these straits.

"Well," he said aloud, pleased to hear that his voice at least was not noticeably altered, "well, well, well."

He touched the side of the chestnut thoughtfully. His mind was now quite clear, as minds tend to become when crises reach overwhelming proportions, and his feet were once more willing to take orders. If one took a lift down, it stood to reason that one might take the same lift up again. Ian leaned against the smooth wall of the chestnut and bent forward to press his lips against it, bracing himself for a possible jolt. It was then that he noticed out of the corner of his eye light flickering through the branches. So occupied had he been with his own transformation that he had failed to observe that he was no longer in darkness. The light appeared to come from a fire, and a quite healthy one at that. Ian James looked at the chestnut—his way out, he hoped, to his own prosaically comfortable world. Then he got up and walked toward the fire. After all, had he come this far in the rain and cold only to turn back unsatisfied, his questions unanswered? He crept forward, keeping half an eye on the chestnut to be sure it did not go on without him. Perhaps he would have to make a quick getaway. One more step and he was out in the open in the midst of a most remarkable scene. He slipped back into the shadows where he might observe it undetected.

A large circular clearing had been made on the ground surrounded by a wall of intertwined thorny branches that met in a domed roof high overhead. A fine roaring bonfire blazed in the midst of this circle. A number of gaily dressed people roamed about the area. Ian thought at first glance that there were about twenty of them, but he later realized there were not nearly that many. They all seemed rather old, and many were grotesque in face and figure. He had come, it seemed, upon a feast, for there were pots hung over smaller fires in the background, and even as he watched, two white-bearded old fellows carefully carried between them over to the fire a chestnut larger than the one he had descended on, and laid it gently on a pile of burning embers. Fascinated, Ian moved slowly around the walls, clinging as closely as he dared to the shadow of the thorn-armored branches. A stooped old woman in a lace cap and scarlet apron stirred a large pot from which exuded the unmistakable odor of mushrooms. Beyond her another group of women arranged high piles of puffy-looking rolls and steaming berry pies on a long board laid across two lumps of a gnarled root.

On the far side of the fire from the place where he had entered, Ian came to what appeared to be a sort of throne room. In its center stood a sapling stump carved out to form a double seat, decorated with beautiful and intricate carvings. On this throne sat a very old and bent person with white hair and beard, both of which fell below his waist. He wore a plain gold circlet on his head, and over his shoulders a worn purple cloak with frayed gold trim. Beside him sat a shrewd-looking old woman, thin and dry as a winter leaf; yet her eyes were bright and full of life. Standing around the throne in conversation with these notables and conspicuous in their twentieth-century mackintoshes were Mrs. Hubbard and the Vicar. Beside them Ian saw with some surprise another Elvinwood citizen, and certainly the last person he would expect to see at a fairy feast, Marian Crawley, the estate agent. She was one of those crisp, tweedy, no-nonsense English career women who could with equal ease substitute for an ailing duchess at a court function or take over for the governor of a Borstal institution. At the moment she was listening intently to the conversation the Vicar was holding with the old chief. Ian strained from his hiding place to catch the drift of it.

"I don't in truth know what it means, reverend sir," the old fellow was saying in a dry, grating voice. "But I can sense it, the presence of some great force in the air around the forest. It, whatever it is, is most probably searching for us."

"Aren't you afraid, my lord?" the Vicar asked.

"Afraid of what?" the old fairy snorted. "I can think of no evil that could befall me or my people that has not been visited upon us already. And yet by a thread we survive. Though how long we can continue as we are I don't know. The chance of any sort of contact with outside forces would be in a way welcome. We have been isolated for so long. But," he gave the Vicar a dry smile, "though we are diminished, we are not yet demolished. And we still manage to hold a reasonable feast at the change of seasons."

The old woman Ian had seen supervising the setting of the board approached the throne, bowed deferentially, and whispered something to the wizened old lady. She nodded, the other bowed and moved back from the throne, keeping her face carefully toward it until she was out of the room. Her ladyship turned to the company, her wrinkled face struggling with the memory of a smile.

"You see us, dear friends, at the height of our present power. We are ever smaller and weaker, barely fit for feasting most of the year. But fortunately your Christmas celebration closely coincides with our Midwinter festival. Inadvertently your people lend us strength. For through your holiday shows—what is it you call them?"

"Pantomimes," the old lord growled, obviously displeased with the turn of the conversation. His lady smiled sympathetically.

"My lord does not approve of the manner in which your people depict our people," she explained.

The Vicar nodded. "All that blue tulle and butterfly wings."

Ian winced; he had been in charge of costumes for the pantomime.

"And *Peter Pan,*" the old lord growled. "Blasted Tinkerbell!" He turned with sudden fierceness on the Vicar. "Why are your fairies always silly dolts of females?"

"There now, my lord," his lady interposed, placing an affectionate but surprisingly firm hand on his arm. "They mean it as a compliment. They consider their young women handsome. Besides, if it were not for all that Tinkerbell nonsense you would be tucked in bed shaking with ague right now, supping on warm fern tea instead of leading your honored guests to a full and merry feast."

The lord rose slowly, supporting himself for an instant on the arm of his throne. "Come, most honored guests. Forgive my outburst. I am weighted with many troubles. But tonight they will not interfere with our pleasure."

He offered an arm to each of the ladies and led them toward the hall. The Vicar took the fairy lady on his arm and followed. The lesser folk gathered around the great fire bowed low as Garumpta and his guests entered.

Suddenly there came from above a sound, distant but

clear, like a fanfare of rasping trumpets. The revelers halted, startled, staring at one another in confusion and fear.

"It is the King," the old lord cried. "Do reverence!"

Chapter 3

The Exchange

All the company fell forward upon their faces as the trumpets sounded again, very near at hand. There was a humming flutter on the briar roof above them. Two large dragonflies, nearly twice the size of the prostrate fairies, each carrying proudly a golden horn that twisted most remarkably in miles of tubing ending in a large bell, forced an opening amongst the thorn twigs, then leaped easily to the ground, raising their instruments for a final blast. As the fanfare died, Oberon, King of Fairies, accompanied by his Queen, Titania, his Puck, and a small coterie of courtiers, floated through the opening like seed pods on an autumn draft. They were in full regalia, and a magnificent sight they were. Oberon, who stood considerably taller than the wood fairies, taller even than his six-legged guards, wore a shimmering doublet and hose of an elusive shade that was neither white nor silver, nor any other clearly defined color. They looked, indeed, as though they might have been made of woven spider webs. His cloak was green, trimmed with white down such as one finds surrounding the seeds of dandelion and milkweed, decorated throughout with small drop-shaped jewels, brilliant as diamonds yet warm as pearls. These same jewels adorned the many-pointed crown, elaborate, yet delicate as lace, that rested easily on his black, curly head. His Queen's crown was smaller, but similar in design and material. Her hair was also black, falling in a rippling cascade down her back. The skirt of her gown, which was made from the same cobwebby goods decorated with the same raindrop gems, did not reach quite to her ankles, falling in gathers from her narrow waist like a classic ballet skirt, revealing small, narrow feet that came to a sharp point at the toes.

Indeed, all the features of the royal couple seemed to come to a point. Their fingers were long and thin, ending in long, sharply pointed nails. The tops of their ears, their eyebrows, their noses, their chins all were endowed with the same sharp point. Even their eyes seemed more slanted than round. They were hardly beautiful by human standards despite their finery, for all those points gave them a somewhat wasplike appearance from which men instinctively shrank.

The Puck, though, was a different sort, looking a bit more like the pixies depicted in storybooks. He wore homespun motley in the warm colors of autumn leaves. He was brown-skinned, red-cheeked, pug-nosed, and was constantly hopping about in comical poses winking and making wry faces. Yet when he did pause in his caperings, allowing for a moment his ever-changing face to relax in thought or wonder, the brightness of his green eyes took on an unsavory aspect, scheming, malicious. Slightly smaller than his royal masters, as were all the courtiers, he walked a few paces behind them, sometimes hovering at the King's side as if ready to respond quickly to a whispered order.

Oberon's voice was high and thin, yet unexpectedly strong:

"All rise."

The prostrate group rose and stood, heads bowed, before him, not moving even to brush off the debris of the ground that clung to them.

"I seek the tribe of Garumpta the Fernlord."

"Garumpta and all his folk are before Your Majesty," the forest chieftain replied with a deep bow.

Oberon frowned as he looked over the company. Then he gave a small sigh.

"These are all your people?"

"Yes, Your Majesty. We are much diminished. These three humans are here as honored guests at our festival."

"Let them come before me."

The three stepped forward and bowed deeply as each was introduced.

"The Reverend Dr. Heaton, an honored student of the Old One; Mrs. Hubbard and Miss Crawley, old and honored friends of this tribe."

"Rise, human guests of the Fernlord. May your people live in peace with the land."

"May the stars ever light your path, Master of the First Folk," the Vicar, who seemed well versed in fairy etiquette, replied. "And may your subjects prosper and increase."

"Would that they could," Oberon said. "But you see before you in this remnant of a tribe the largest and most prosperous community in all my kingdom."

This was news indeed, and not just for the guests, for there was a rustle and a murmur throughout the company. Garumpta raised his hand for silence.

"And how has such a thing happened?" Marian Crawley exclaimed with a show of distress. "Surely there are yet thriving enclaves in Ireland and Wales where there is still belief in the 'wee folk.' "

"What living creature can hope to prosper long in the world of men?" Oberon replied, his eyelids narrowing until only a thin slit showed, and his hand tightened around the ornately carved staff he carried. "They have driven us from our land and deprived us of our power until we are diminished and depleted to near extinction."

The Vicar, who had by common consent become spokesman for the humans present, made haste to assure the King that Garumpta's tribe lay in no danger, being protected by the National Trust.

"So I have judged," Oberon agreed. "It is indeed because of your safe situation here, Lord Garumpta, that you may be able to perform a great service for our people. Are these the only men who know of your existence here in the forest?"

"Yes, Your Majesty."

"What of the one who picked up Mompen?" Aneelen asked.

"Oh I had forgotten about that," Garumpta exclaimed. "Mompen, our lastborn, claims to have had contact some weeks ago with a creature we believe to be human."

"Ah," Oberon lifted his voice in apparent interest. "Your lastborn." He spoke as though to himself, then turned briskly to the Fernlord. "Let your lastborn come before me."

There was an anxious murmur and flutter through the

company, and considerable confusion. At length the smallest and most miserable creature in that small and miserable band was urged forward into the open. Garumpta laid a firm but kindly hand on his shoulder and led him to Oberon's feet. Trembling so that his legs were wholly out of control, he dropped to his knees with an awkward thud.

"Your Majesty," Garumpta announced. "I wish to present Mompen, our lastborn."

The Puck, who had been discreetly helping himself at the festival table, turned, strode up to the kneeling fairy, and stood over him, hands on hips, examining him like a farmer at a horse auction. Suddenly he threw back his head and laughed, a fierce, rude, barbarous laugh.

"Great earth, air, fire, and water," he gasped, making a show of trying to control himself, for Oberon was glaring at him. "Is that the best you could do? The bandy-legged, pigeon-toed, pot-bellied, mush-faced Lastborn of the Firstborn. Ah we are doomed indeed."

Mompen looked up at him, roused by the brutality of the attack from his own fear and embarrassment at being singled out in the presence of the King. The Puck recoiled from his gaze in visible consternation.

"High stars," he whispered. "On top of everything, he's cross-eyed! But," he added, looking at Oberon with the trace of a grin, "he's also male."

"The more grief to you, Robin," Oberon retorted, his voice low and grating with suppressed wrath. "So he is, and that leaves us with but one alternative to extinction, and that one not entirely to your liking, I think."

The Puck turned on his heels throwing a sullen scowl over his shoulder, and retreated into the shadows.

"If you do not care to feel the weight of my staff on your impudent shoulders, you will stay far from that table," Oberon called after him. Kicking at the ground like a sulky child, the Puck wondered back in the direction farthest from the food-laden board.

"Do not mind my Puck," Oberon addressed Mompen. "He will be properly paid for his rudeness in time. Come, rise and tell us your tale."

Mompen stumbled to his feet as awkwardly as he had left them and stood fingering his patched stocking cap and staring at his pointed one, which insisted on pointing only at each other. He took a deep breath, swallowed loudly, cleared his throat, and at last began to speak, or rather mumble hurriedly in a peculiar, high-pitched voice.

"It was close to a month ago, Your Majesty. The sun was shining and it was warm, very unusual so late in the season, Your Majesty. I was resting in my chestnut burr pram near the foot-path where the sun beats down strongest." He stopped, struggling to turn his disconcertingly unfocusable eyes on Titania. "Have you ever taken the sun in a chestnut burr, Your Majesty?" he asked in an enraptured whisper. The Queen, smiling, shook her head. "Ah," Mompen murmured. "It is the most delightful sensation, all warmth and softness and comfortable smells. You must try it." With great effort he returned to the present business. "I was just dozing when I felt the ground beneath me tremble under heavy footsteps. 'Men,' I thought, and pulled the top of the pram over me. I might have rolled away, but I was so frightened I forgot how to make the thing work. So I just lay there as still as I could, listening to the heavy thuds and the loud voices passing by. They seemed to be going away, and I was starting to relax when I was moved very quickly and far." He forced his eyes toward Oberon. "Were you ever picked up like that, Your Majesty? When you couldn't see where you were going? I wasn't sure if I was going up or down. I was very frightened, Your Majesty. I'm easily frightened, don't you know, being the lastborn and all. I was so frightened I couldn't move. Have you ever been that frightened, Your Majesty? I often am. I am now." He giggled a little hysterically. Garumpta laid a steadying hand on his shoulder. He shuddered, gulped twice, and continued.

"I was like that when it opened my shell. All I could see was its face looking at me. Have you ever seen a human face at its regular size, Your Majesty? Well, of course you have, haven't you? Its face was so big, and it stared at me with great balls of eyes the color of summer sky. I liked its hair, though," he smiled a bit self-consciously. "It looked like two flaxen ropes hanging down on either side of its face. It looked so soft. I think it might make a lovely eiderdown."

"Oh," Miss Crawley exclaimed. "It must have been the little girl in the American family I'm letting the brick house on the hill to. She has braids—her hair in ropes."

"Oh yes," the Vicar said. "Aren't they the ones at the theater yesterday, Sybil? That carry the baby in some sort of camping gear instead of a proper pram? I've seen them at times near Great Pond."

Mrs. Hubbard nodded. "They should certainly present no problem. It's most likely that the child will say nothing about the incident, for children are most fearful of the scorn and disbelief of their elders. In any event she has said nothing to me, although we frequently chat over the garden hedge."

"What did the human do, Mompen?" Oberon urged with a touch of impatience.

"She stared at me for some time and I at her. I don't think she was at all frightened, just a little surprised at seeing me. Then she said, 'I'm sorry. I didn't know you were there.' She put the lid back on my pram and set me down very gently and thudded away at great speed. I waited a long time, but none of them returned. I've stayed far from the path since then."

Oberon smiled. "In that you have used wisdom," he said. "It is best to stay far from the paths of men, although, since we have been assured that this human is not dangerous, I see no reason to fear the creature with hair of rope. Go, now, Mompen, Lastborn of the Fernlord. I thank you for the telling of your tale."

Mompen blundered to his knees, attempted to kiss the King's extended fingers, lost his balance, and would have fallen on his face had not Oberon steadied him. Before he had a chance to rise, Titania reached over, seeking to relieve him of the shame of another clumsy obeisance, and extended to him her hand. He kissed it noisily, letting drop two pained tears, then rose too quickly and fled, tripping over a root and falling heavily before he gained the comfort of the shadows.

Oberon turned to his consort with a sigh.

"The Lastborn of the Firstborn," he murmured. "All of our hope and all of our despair."

"Well," Titania smiled, discreetly wiping her hand with a fine woven handkerchief, "he may not have power or beauty or grace, but he does have a good heart, and I judge a fair amount of intelligence. But under the circumstances we now have no choice but to resort to an exchange."

"An exchange?" the Vicar cried. "Is that what you are here for?"

Oberon looked at all the company for a moment in silence, his eyes grave. Then he spoke quietly and deliberately.

"We are diminishing, reverend sir. The way things are going now we shall soon be as extinct as so many other races of creatures who have had the misfortune to dwell in the same world with men. Those few of us who remain are all old, unbelievably old. Though age does not deprive us of beauty or wit as it does you humans, it does set aside in time our power to reproduce our kind. Has it not occurred to you that you have never seen or heard of a fairy child? At least not outside of your ridiculous pantomimes and insulting picture books. We have searched our realm for just one such child or a female capable of bearing one. There are none. The tribe of Garumpta, long forgotten, remained as a last hope that we might be able to bring new life into our dying race. You see, Robin, my insufferable Puck, has for some reason retained his youth (perhaps because he is so frequently protrayed on your stage by a child), and we hope he yet has the power to produce young, if we could but find him a mate. It is to this purpose that we have come. Our search ends here in failure. The Lord Garumpta's lastborn is young enough, but is, as Robin made such pains to point out, a male. Even we do not have the power to bring forth children from the union of males. So we must use the power that we do possess. We must take a human child in exchange for one of our own people. I realize that such an exchange is looked upon with great disfavor by men; therefore we must do what we must do in secret. The least I can ask of you is that you do not betray us; at the most we would welcome your help in this difficult enterprise."

"I cannot speak for my companions, who must make their own judgments," the Vicar said, his tone and his look exactly matching Oberon's in steadiness and gravity. "But for myself, I am wholly at your service."

He dropped to one knee before the King, who extended his left hand. Unlike its highly decorated mate, his hand had on it but one ring. In its center was a large, ornate *O* etched in the metal that seemed to catch and reflect the glow of the fire. Slowly and deliberately the Vicar pressed this ring against his forehead.

"I am grateful indeed for your offer of assistance," Oberon said, tactfully helping the old man to his feet, "for you have wisdom, I deem, rare in a man, especially a clergyman. But what do your companions say? Do you stand with us as well?"

The two women had been conversing in rapid whispers. It was Miss Crawley who now addressed the King.

"I suspect Your Majesty can understand somewhat our reluctance to enter into such an enterprise. But if there is no other way, then we are yours. We ask but one condition: that both members of the exchange go freely and willingly into an alien world, that no one will suffer because of it. There are harrowing legends among our people—libelous, I'm sure—that the changeling left by the fairies is in some way inadequate—deformed, perhaps—or grotesque or not even human in form."

"The stories are most definitely libelous," Oberon objected. "The people of the forest are not thieves, nor do they cheat. We have never taken anything from men without giving a true and proper exchange in goods or services. The same cannot be said for your people. Therefore I will make this agreement with you. On the part of the fairies the exchange will be willingly made, and the changeling a superior specimen of human child. We expect the same from you."

"Agreed. Then we are with you." The ladies knelt to receive the touch of Oberon's ring.

"I presume," the Vicar said, "that the burden of selecting the child to be exchanged will fall on us."

"Yes," said Oberon, "and the selection of a suitable and willing fairy volunteer falls to the Lord Garumpta. The volunteer need not be either young or female."

Garumpta turned to his people, who had been listening to all this in stunned silence. He allowed his eyes to drift slowly over the group, letting them rest briefly on each face. Not a bad lot, all in all, he thought, but old and tired; hardly the sort to welcome change or seek adventure. It crossed his mind that if pressed he might be forced to volunteer himself. The silence was growing long and uncomfortable. No one moved or made a sound.

"I am certain, Your Majesty, that we can come to a decision on this matter after some discussion," Garumpta began in an uncertain voice. But he was interrupted by a rustle and a murmur as out into the open stumbled Mompen.

"I'll go, Father," he cried a little shrilly. Garumpta raised his hand and opened his mouth to protest.

"No, please," said the bashful lastborn, who had never before dared to interrupt his sire. "Let me go. I'm of little use to my people as I am. This at least I can do." He smiled wistfully. "Who knows? Maybe I'll turn out to be a capital human."

Garumpta cleared his throat, looking around a little desperately. He wasn't sure whether to be relieved or appalled, and did not know what to do. At length he took Mompen by the arm and brought his son before Oberon.

"Your Majesty," he said, his voice a little unsteady, "Mompen our lastborn has offered to go into the world of men in exchange for a human child. Is he acceptable?"

"More than acceptable," Oberon answered. He placed his hand on the trembling volunteer's shoulder and guided him successfully to his knees. "May you prosper in the world of men, lastborn of Garumpta's tribe; you will be ever remembered in honor by your people for your great courage and willingness to sacrifice yourself for the common good." He offered his ring, and Mompen without hesitation and for once without mishap, laid his forehead against it. The tribe raised a cheer.

"I—I don't really deserve such praise, Your Majesty," Mompen said as he stumbled to his feet. "I'm not all that self-sacrificing. You see," he shot a quick smile in the direction of Mrs. Hubbard and Miss Crawley, "I rather like humans, at least the ones I know."

"You'll learn," the Puck muttered from the shadows where he had been taking in the whole proceedings unnoticed. He might scoff and feign indifference, but actually he was deeply concerned about all that had been going on, for the matter was of great importance to him personally, and he was more than a little anxious about its outcome. Well, it all seemed to have been decided, if in a manner not wholly pleasing to him. It could have been worse. That miserable little runt might have been born female. In any event, the business meeting seemed about to adjourn, and refreshments were no doubt next. He did not want to be left out of that part of the proceedings.

He turned on his heel quickly to rejoin the group around the fire. There was a slight movement, he thought, in the thicket near him. Some nocturnal animal lured by the odor of food, something succulent—a rabbit, perhaps, or a young hedgehog. He braced himself to spring. But it was probably only a trick of the eye brought on by the constant movement of leaves in the air and flickering shadows cast by the fire. No, there was another rustle and a sound like a quick-drawn breath. Robin held his body rigid only an instant; then he pounced. The prey was neither as large nor as strong as he had expected. It was not as large even as he was. But it put up a valiant fight, which did it little good in the end. The Puck was a skilled hunter and a master wrestler, and fairly easily brought his captive to the ground. He dragged it, still struggling, into the firelight.

"See here, Master," he crowed. "I have caught me a spy from the world of noble and honest men." He spat contemptuously.

"Ian James!" Miss Crawley gasped.

"Bring him before me," Oberon commanded.

Thus it was that Ian James, bachelor of Elvinwood, found himself in the presence of Oberon, King of Fairies. The Puck delivered him to the very feet of his master, throwing him face downward onto the ground. The two trumpet-wielding guards took up positions at once on either side of and slightly behind the captive. Oberon towered over him, his carved staff slightly upraised, as if prepared to strike at the least provocation. When he spoke his thin voice sounded powerful and menacing, like the angry hum of a wasp whose nest has been threatened.

"Who are you," he asked, "and why have you come to this place unbidden?"

Ian did not reply. He was incapable of speech. His mouth had gone completely dry and his facial muscles numb with terror. Oberon looked sharply at the three other humans who stood together at one side. They were all deeply disturbed, even frightened, for they knew their hosts well enough to appreciate the danger of their own situation. Yet they were Englishmen and behaved like Englishmen, witnessing the interrogation of their fellow man with a show, at least, of cool detachment.

"Do you know this man?" Oberon asked.

"Yes, Your Majesty," the Vicar replied in an even voice, picking each word carefully and examining it for hidden traps before releasing it to the critical air. "We all know him. He lives in the town below and is a person of good reputation. How he came here," he glanced at the two ladies, who shook their heads, "we do not know."

Desperately forcing saliva into his dry mouth, Ian strove to speak. He rose slightly, bracing himself with one arm, and spoke falteringly.

"I followed the Vicar and Mrs. Hubbard into the forest simply because I was curious as to where they were going on such a cold, rainy night. I was only curious. I meant and mean no harm to anyone."

"You entered the forest the normal size of a normal man. How did you diminish?"

"I—I saw them put chestnuts to their lips. Then they seemed to disappear. That frightened me, but my curiosity got the better of my good sense, and—I don't really know why, but I swear I meant no harm—I did as they had done, and became as you see me now."

Oberon nodded. "And yet how is it that you, being apparently a respectable Englishman, when you found yourself where you had no business, did not do the proper thing and return the way you had come as quickly and discreetly as possible?"

"I cannot in truth answer that question, Your Majesty, because I do not know. I was afraid and thought to go back at first, but the wonders that were before me quickly robbed me of that resolve. I was as if in a dream and would not force myself awake. I wish now with all my heart that I had returned at once and had not seen or heard what I have tonight. I can only beg your pardon and the Lord Garumpta's and that of all present for my trespass."

"Aye, and well you may, Ian James. But pardon, I fear, will not suffice. Nor will you now be able to return as you came. You have seen and heard what you ought not to have, and you are a danger to us. You do not approve, do you, of what we propose?"

Ian looked up at the creature standing over him. The eyes of the King of Fairies held his, searching his private soul.

"I know of such things, Your Majesty, only through what has been written in the books of men. It doesn't make very comfortable reading."

"If you were allowed to return, knowing what you do . . ."

"I would hold my tongue," Ian interrupted. "Though my actions tonight may indicate otherwise, I am really a discreet man and can keep a secret."

"When you saw strange things happening to a child you know?"

Ian opened his mouth to reply, then closed it, looking away in confusion and uncertainty.

"You would betray us, wouldn't you?" Oberon prodded.

"I—I don't know."

"So here you are, where you were neither invited nor wanted. You cannot be trusted to go back where you came from. So it is left to us to decide what is to be done with you."

"That shouldn't be too difficult," the Puck remarked with a low chuckle.

"Indeed, Robin," said Oberon, raising his pointed eyebrows in amusement. "And what would you in your wisdom do with this unfortunate fellow you have caught?"

"To begin with, dear Master, I would in my wisdom reject outright this man's feeble alibi. Curiosity, indeed. I'll warrant it was curiosity that brought him here tonight, and well has he satisfied it. He is a spy, no doubt of that, though he swear by his very blood that he is not. Men are not to be trusted." He glared at the Vicar and the two ladies, who stared back at him impassively.

"Having established his guilt," the Puck continued, "and perhaps confirmed it by forcing him to confess under torture (that's their way, is it not?), there would be nothing left to do save the selection of an appropriate punishment for his crime. And that would be more pleasure than duty."

He walked slowly around his victim, examining him. Ian watched him, keeping as aloof a mien as possible, hoping that his face did not reveal the terror he felt. The Puck rubbed his chin as if in thought. He had an attentive audience, something he always enjoyed, and he was giving it all the play it would tolerate.

"I think I should enjoy flogging him to death with stinging nettle; human skin is extremely sensitive to it. I unstand. Or perhaps I might try my hand at metamorphosis—some highly appropriate transformation into a creature preyed upon by men, a rabbit; a fox; a plump, tender pheasant."

Suddenly he snapped his fingers and began dancing with delight around and around his victim. "Now I have it. The true and just fate for a curious man. If he would be like us, let him. Let him remain as he now is, the size of an ill-fed insect. Let him face as we do daily the peril of our shrinking lives; to flee in terror at the footfall of a squirrel. Let's see how long he would last, and let mindless nature choose his doom. May he be snatched up for supper by a short-sighted robin, or crushed under the shoe of a hiking Girl Guide or—or accidentally drowned by a stray dog innocently passing water."

He concluded with a dancing school pirouette, lost his balance, and fell, rolling over and over on the ground, choking with laughter. As he began to calm he jumped to his feet and made a deep bow to his lord.

"What say you, Master?"

"That your malice exceeds your taste," Oberon snapped. "But there is some wisdom hidden in your folly." He addressed the man at his feet. "I do not bear you such hatred, Ian James. I do not wish you ill, but I do not trust you. I have had too many dealings with your kind. As I see it I have but two alternatives. The safest course would probably be to leave you as you are at least until the exchange has been safely accomplished, placing you in the Fernlord's custody. I certainly do not wish upon you the fates my Puck has suggested, but the life of my people is filled ever with danger. I could not in good faith guarantee your safety. Therefore I will make you another offer. Pledge to me your support and help in this most important venture, and I will release you to return for the present to your own world. On Mid-summer Night I shall return. If a human child has been acquired and all made ready for the exchange, and if you have made yourself useful in these matters, I will release you from my service, and unless you again concern yourself with them, the people of the forest will trouble you no more."

"If I should fail to make myself useful?"

"See that you do not fail. Things are at a bad point with us. Time is important. This is our last chance, let it be yours as well. Will you pledge?"

Ian looked up at the tangle of thorns above him, the thick logs surrounding him, which he realized were actually twigs, at the creatures around him: Oberon, stern and radiant; Garumpta, scowling and biting his underlip; the Puck, hunching his shoulders as if suppressing laughter; and Mompen, staring at him from the shelter of Aneelen's arms. He looked long and hard at little Mompen. Finally he closed his eyes in an attempt at prayer, then opened them and looked with the calm of despair at Oberon.

"Very well. If I must, I pledge—to do what is in my power to help in this—this awful enterprise. I am a man of my word, and I give my word."

The King of Fairies extended his left hand. The solitary ring glowed red, not, Ian realized with a shudder, in reflection of the great fire that glowed in the Fernlord's hall, but with a terrible fire of its own. He gave Oberon a single pleading look, but the King's eyes glinted stern command. Ian James set his teeth, closed his eyes, held his breath, braced himself, and quickly pressed the searing ring to his brow.

Chapter 4

Tea with Little Sympathy

It was well into February before they caught up with him, for he had been very careful, keeping out of public places as much as possible, refusing to answer either his telephone or his doorbell unless he was certain who the caller was, and always examining the street before leaving the shelter of a doorway. But he could not keep up this cinema-spy game indefinitely. Sooner or later he was bound to make a slip.

He had stopped in at the wine merchant's to purchase his customary bottle of Cockburn's ruby port and had been distracted by a conversation with the American children who were there with their mother placing an order for assorted table wines. He stepped glibly out into the street without making his usual reconnaissance and was caught by Mrs. Hubbard, who just happened to be passing at the time, stolidly trundling her grocery cart up the street behind her.

"Good afternoon, Mr. James."

"Good afternoon, Mrs. Hubbard."

She walked beside him as he turned off High Street and started up Station Street. Not that there was anything sinister in that. It was her way home.

"We haven't seen much of you recently," she said.

"I—I have been rather busy, the holidays and all. And I haven't been keeping too well. This beastly weather. It seems as if winter will never end." There, that was safe. The weather was always a safe topic.

"Oh it will end, all right, Mr. James. Sooner than you would believe possible. And as the poet says, 'When winter comes can spring be far behind?' Time is passing, and there is much to be done. It would hardly be to your benefit to be caught short."

Ian said nothing. He had not before realized what a dangerous topic the weather could be. They were approaching the auditorium now, and he quickened his pace in anticipation of escape from his persistent traveling companion.

"Are you free tomorrow afternoon, Mr. James?"

They stood before the auditorium steps. Ian glanced nervously up the street, where Miss Crawley's office was. He wondered if he were in danger of being surrounded.

"Yes, yes. I think so," he said absently. Anything to end this conversation with a minimum of rudeness and seek refuge from his fearfully vulnerable position.

"Come to my house around teatime. We could have a bit of something while we talk this thing out. Sweetens the dose a little, you know."

Ian tried to return her ingenuous smile, but it was all he could do to keep his voice steady.

"Thank you, Mrs. Hubbard. That's very thoughtful of you."

"Splendid. Then I shall expect you at half after five. Cheerio. I do hope you get to feeling better."

"Cheerio." Ian stood for a moment watching her respectable back round the corner by the police station; then he bounded up the steps, through the auditorium door, up the winding stairs to the little cubbyhole he used as a sort of private workroom, where he collapsed, trembling, into the nearest chair.

Well now, my silly friend, he berated himself, you've been caught out. Can't run and hide anymore; the thing won't go away just because you don't look at it.

He closed his eyes and leaned back wearily, recalling the scene he had for the past two months been trying to force himself to forget. And he remembered what followed, waking up in that grim December morning to find himself on the sofa in his lounge, fully clothed, with two empty bottles on the floor beside him and a bitter ache in his head. Now why, he had asked himself, did he drink so much when it made him ill and gave him madmen's dreams? Groaning, he stumbled to his feet and staggered into the bathroom to rinse his cotton-wool mouth. He had glanced in the mirror above the washbasin to ascertain how bloodshot his eyes were. This was a discipline he always performed when he drank too much, a sort of examination of conscience. But that morning he did not get as far as his eyes. The instant he looked at his reflection he saw it. There was a small oval red spot little bigger than the head of a pin in the middle of his forehead. He had to grip the edge of the basin to keep from collapsing. He had remained there for some time, his head bowed over the basin, uncertain whether he was going to faint or retch. Finally he had stumbled back to the sofa, and there he had stayed the better part of the day, moaning and shaking, even weeping at times. He had slept fitfully for periods. Each time he had wakened the shadows had been longer and his suffering somewhat less acute.

It was upon waking from one of these naps that the thought had struck him: maybe it was just a pimple. Of course that's what it was, nothing but a damned schoolboy hickey. He had laughed with relief and self-derision. That was all it was—a bad hangover and a pimple. The rest had come from his wine-fuddled imagination. Some men saw snakes and crawling insects, but when Ian James drank he saw cross-eyed fairies and panicked over a pimple. He ought to take another look at it, he had thought as he began to recover his composure, examine it in the shaving mirror, then he would be certain. He rose, still a bit unsteadily, but he did not approach the mirror. Instead he went into the kitchen and brewed a pot of strong tea, made himself a supper of toast and jam, and took two aspirin for his still-throbbing head. He had been unbelievably tired, but before going to bed, properly in his bedroom this time, he had carefully cleaned all the mud off his shoes, brushed his trousers, and mended the tear in his overcoat. He did not look again into the mirror. In fact, for the past two months he had avoided getting a good look at his forehead as carefully as he had dodged into doorways. But now there was no more need to do either. He was caught out and had to face up to it. He was committed to tea at Mrs. Hubbard's—and he had seen it, right where it should have been, directly in the center of her forehead, midway between her gray widow's peak and the bridge of her gold-rimmed spectacles, the exact same red mark.

Mrs. Hubbard's cottage on the knob of the hill at the corner of Churchill Lane and Buckingham Avenue was surrounded on three sides by an exquisite and carefully tended garden. The cottage itself sat at the rear of the lot almost directly against the low hedge that separated it from the American family's garden. Though quite small, it was a warm and gracious house, Ian observed, as he was ushered into the bright sitting room. It could have been a stage set for a Victorian melodrama. There was the upright piano overloaded with pastel tinted photographs of grandchildren, there were antimacassars on the arms and back of the horsehair sofa, and in the center was a makeshift table (probably a card table of some sort) hiding its true identity under an embossed white linen tablecloth set for tea.

The Vicar was seated comfortably in a large armchair by a window watching the American children playing next door. He rose as Ian entered and extended his hand.

"Good to see you, James. I trust you are in a somewhat better state than when we last met. Sybil tells me you haven't been well."

"Recovering from a bit of a shock, Vicar," Ian replied, taking the chair on the other side of the window. Now that he had been forced to accept the reality of his predicament, he had decided to go through with it in the best spirit he could muster. "I believe I'm on the mend now."

"Splendid." The Vicar placed an encouraging hand on Ian's knee. "Don't worry. Everything is going to work out beautifully."

Mrs. Hubbard bustled in carrying a tray that held four cups and a steaming china pot.

"Marian may be a little late, so we are to start without her." She seated herself before the table and commenced to pour.

"How do you like your new neighbors?" the Vicar asked, gesturing with a biscuit toward the running, shouting trio in the adjacent garden.

"They're quite nice people, really, Thomas. Friendly and pleasant enough, but a bit more lively than what I'm used to. The baby is a delight. Have you seen her?"

"Only from a distance," the Vicar answered. "Why?"

"She is quite intelligent and of about the best age, I should think."

"Aah," the Vicar's eyes widened with comprehension. "You may have come upon something, Sybil."

Ian stiffened as he began to realize what it was his hostess was proposing.

"It might be best for Mompen, too," the Vicar went on. "They'll be going back at the end of summer, won't they? He'll be able to forget much more quickly in strange surroundings. And they're not at all likely to become suspicious."

Ian laid his cup down on the table and rose abruptly.

"It's out of the question," he cried, his voice high and strained. "These people are guests in our country." He turned on Mrs. Hubbard. "You cannot be seriously thinking of playing such a trick on them."

"We are not playing tricks, Mr. James," she replied with quiet dignity. "They came to this country with a baby, and they will leave this country with a baby, possibly a bit better than the one they came with."

Ian paced the small sitting-room floor, from the piano to the window and then back again, rhythmically hitting his right fist against his left palm.

"It's no use," he said, more to himself than to the others. "I can't go through with it."

"If you see strange things happening to a child you know?" the Vicar quoted, following him with searching eyes.

Ian halted in front of the window, turning his back as much as he could on the proceedings. He was determined not to be intimidated.

"The whole thing's wicked. It's evil," he burst out. "And I will not have anything to do with it."

"You've no choice, James," the Vicar persisted. "You have sworn a pledge, and you will have to abide by it. Anyone who takes the mark of Oberon lightly is a very great fool, indeed."

Ian winced. "I should think so," he muttered. "It wasn't given exactly lightly."

The Vicar raised his eyebrows and looked at Ian with new interest. "So you did receive it with fire. Well, you certainly put a good face on it. You hear that, Sybil?" he called to Mrs. Hubbard, who was just coming in the doorway with a large frosted white cake. "This fellow's made of pretty tough goods, after all. You had me fooled, my lad. Though for the life of me I couldn't figure out why he had spared you. He obviously didn't trust you, and with good reason, it appears."

"I don't understand," Ian said. "Do you mean to say that the ring did not burn you? Why?"

"Because he was sure of us. He knew that he did not have to impress us with his power. We are well aware of it. He is not cruel, you know. He doesn't inflict pain when he doesn't need to. But he has had many dealings with men through the ages, and he knows that we are greatly impressed by pain; that if a little suffering accompanies the taking of a vow we will be bound to it more firmly. I'm sure he did no more to you than he deemed absolutely necessary."

Ian stared out the window. He knew that what the Vicar had said was true, for the ring had burned him only for an instant, and the mark it made had caused him no discomfort.

The garden next door was now empty, as the children had been called in to their evening meal. Only a large soccer football and a cricket bat remained beside the still creaking swing. The boys, it seemed, had been trying to combine Britain's two popular sports into a new ball game all their own. Ian felt like crying.

"What if it doesn't bind me?" he asked, struggling to keep his voice calm. "What if I simply resign from this hellish conspiracy?"

"Oh Mr. James," Mrs. Hubbard gasped, rising from her chair and going to him. "You cannot mean that. Why, you bear his mark. He could find you anywhere. You could never escape from him. His anger is dreadful." She pulled at his arm, almost weeping with anxiety. "Come now, sit down and eat your cake, and don't even think of such a thing." He allowed her to lead him back to his chair, she was so very agitated. "I'll get you some more tea."

As she was pouring the tea the doorbell rang. She handed him the cup and left to answer it, calling beseechingly over her shoulder, "Talk to him, Thomas."

"See here, James," the Vicar admonished, laying his hand rather firmly on Ian's knee. "None of us is exactly enjoying this business. But there's no other way, it seems. It would really be a shame just to let them die out, now, wouldn't it? It may go a bit against the grain at first, but I suspect that before it's all settled you'll be seeing things a little differently. In any event there's nothing to be gained by wild talk. It upsets the ladies, and you know perfectly well you're not going to do anything of the sort."

Before Ian could reply, Marian Crawley breezed into the room.

"Good afternoon, gentlemen. Please don't rise; I don't approve of that sort of thing. Well, I see I've got here in time for the sweet, anyhow." She accepted a piece of cake and a cup of tea, and seated herself on the horsehair sofa. "Now, what have I missed?"

"Sybil has suggested that we use the American baby," the Vicar said, wasting no time on preliminaries.

"Jolly good. An excellent choice. You've my vote right out."

"I think we can consider that settled, then," the Vicar said with a sidelong glance at Ian, who avoided his eyes.

"How's it to be done?" Miss Crawley asked.

"To tell you the truth, I'm not really sure," said the Vicar. "Garumpta seemed to take for granted that I would be familiar with the proceedings. I have combed my books, but I can't find more than a general outline. Certain spells and potions are mentioned, but nothing specific enough to work from. I'm going down to Cornwall Friday to see what the master can do for us." He turned suddenly to Ian as if struck with an idea. "I say, James, if you've nothing better to do, why don't you go down with me? It's just a pleasant day's drive, and I think you'll find the master interesting. He might be able to help you over some of your, er, difficulties."

"No thank you," Ian said shortly. "Spells and potions aren't my dish of tea."

The Vicar refused to be offended. "Please yourself," he replied. "But if you should change your mind, just give me a ring. I'd be glad to have you along."

Mrs. Hubbard began gathering up the dishes." Well," she said, "that seems to be about all we can settle at the present. Perhaps we could plan on another meeting after you get back from Cornwall, and we have a better idea of what's to be done. Is everyone free Monday at the same time?"

"One moment," Ian said suddenly. "Before this meeting adjourns, might I be permitted to ask one question?"

They all turned toward him expectantly. He cleared his throat.

"There was a lot of talk in the forest about, shall we say, mutual consent. I should humbly like to know how an infant not a year old can be expected to understand what is to become of her, much less consent to it?"

Mrs. Hubbard smiled. "Evidently, Mr. James, you've had little acquaintance with year-old infants. They are better capable of understanding such a proposal, I dare say, than you are, and quite up to making a wise decision about it. The problem is that we human adults cannot communicate very well with them. The little folk can, though. They converse quite easily with children of that age. An older baby who was starting to talk extensively would present more of a problem. When we are conquered by speech we lose the ability to converse silently, you know. Or perhaps you don't. In any event I'm glad you brought the matter up. See, you're proving useful already. This should certainly be the first order of business, since if she does not consent we'll have to look for another candidate. Perhaps we ought to consult Garumpta. He could select someone. . . ."

"Why not Mompen himself?" Miss Crawley interrupted eagerly. "It would get him a bit used to the family and the ways of men, so that the exchange, when it comes, would be something less of a shock."

"Do you really think Mompen could handle that touchy a mission?" the Vicar asked.

Miss Crawley exploded in unexpected anger. "I should think by now that people who don't know any better would have stopped belittling Mompen. He has the courage and the good sense to handle any situation he might find himself in, and he could persuade the feathers off birds."

The Vicar shrugged with a slight smile. "You know him better than any of the rest of us."

Miss Crawley's eyes were now glowing with excitement. "It will work perfectly." She drew from her valise-sized handbag a leather-covered datebook. "They're due for a routine inspection. Let's see. I could make an appointment for ten-thirty Wednesday morning. That's day after tomorrow. I could go out and fetch Mompen tomorrow night, keep him at my place. That would give me a little time to prepare and instruct him. The next day I could easily deposit him between the slats of the baby's cot while I'm looking over the bedding. Splendid." She closed the datebook with a firm, self-satisfied slap and rose to serve herself more tea.

"You seem to have everything quite well under control," Ian said, rising. "I do not really see where I can be of any use to you." He reached for his coat, anxious to escape from this mad tea party.

"Then we jolly well ought to find something for you to do," Marian Crawley exclaimed. "You're on probation, you know. If you don't make yourself useful, or at least give the appearance of doing so, you're likely to find yourself right back where you were Midwinter Night, only with old Garumpta over you this time." She shook her head. "Whatever I may think of you personally, Mr. James, I should not enjoy the sight of your disembodied head decorating a spike in the Fernlord's Throne Room."

Ian sat down again very hard. Miss Crawley's sharp eyes glowered at him from above the china teacup.

"I have known Garumpta the Fernlord for many years. He is good and kindly and wise. But where the safety of his little tribe is concerned, he is like a brooding hen and will not hesitate to attack anyone he thinks might be a threat to his people. He could not say anything in the presence of the King, but I could see that he was very disturbed at the discovery of an unknown man lurking in his halls. Had you been found earlier and brought before Garumpta instead of the King, you would not have escaped with your life. As it is, Garumpta is going to be eager to find some way to discredit you, so you'd best at least give the impression of being busy with the cause."

"What do you suggest?" Ian asked glumly.

"Well, for a start you could come out with me to fetch Mompen tomorrow night."

Ian threw back his head and laughed.

"You have to be joking," he cried. "As much as you prefer my head where it is, I like it there even better. I would not set foot in that forest again if I had all the Fairy King's power behind me."

"You have enough of that already to protect you," Mrs. Hubbard interposed. "Oberon's mark has its advantages, you know. If you are ever in danger while you bear his mark you have but to call on him. . . ."

"Then why, pray, is she filling me with stories about my head on a spike? Is this some sort of game you people are playing?"

"You should have let Mrs. Hubbard finish," Miss Crawley said. "What she told you was true, but you must realize that you would be protected only until the King could judge whether or not you deserved to be. If he found that you did not, he would immediately remove his mark and leave you to Garumpta's mercy."

Ian groaned and bowed his head in his hands. He spoke in the lifeless voice of a doomed man who has accepted his fate.

"And he could find me anywhere. I could never escape him. . . ."

"Precisely," Miss Crawley said. "Now you're getting it. You really oughtn't carry on so. After all, it's your own fault you're in this fix. Any man who walks in the forest uninvited on Midwinter Night is either a very brave man or a fool."

"I am not a very brave man, Miss Crawley."

"Evidently. So you'd best screw up whatever courage you do possess and come out with me tomorrow night."

There was a long pause. Then Ian's despairing voice came through his hands as from a great distance.

"I have choir practice tomorrow night."

"When does it end?"

"Ten o'clock."

"Where can you meet me discreetly?"

"Pass the churchyard at ten-thirty. Everyone will be gone by then. I'll be waiting under the gate roof. Walk past quietly, and I'll follow you. It's very discreet. I know. I've used it."

Chapter 5

The Estate Agent's Tale

At least the weather's improved, Ian thought as he threaded his way along the narrow path, striving to match Marian Crawley's rapid, self-assured pace. It was a clear night, brisk rather than cold. The moon was full and lit the dark forest with a silver radiance that made the feeble yellow glimmer of Miss Crawley's torch all but unnecessary.

He was somewhat surprised by the estate agent's familiarity with the place, for she found the spot she wanted without difficulty. Ian recognized the thicket at once, but observed that there were no chestnuts near the all but invisible entrance. Miss Crawley, who had not spoken through the entire trip, now began groping for something in her handbag.

"How do we get down there?" Ian asked.

"Since we are not expected, we shall have to present our calling cards," Miss Crawley replied crisply. "Here, hold this a minute, please." She handed him a leaf that she had plucked from a nearby holly bush. "No, not like that, straight out, like a plate."

Ian held the leaf, and then watched dumbfounded as Miss Crawley produced from her bag a small plastic case such as might contain nail clippers. She took from it a sewing needle, the tip of which was wrapped in cotton wool, saturated with what Ian's nose assured him was alcohol. Removing the cotton wad she coolly pressed the point of the needle into the ball of her middle finger, producing a perfectly formed drop of blood. This she transferred carefully onto the leaf and, steadying Ian's shaking hand with her own, breathed on it.

"Your turn." She took the leaf from his hand and, after wiping the needle, handed it to him. He was so nonplussed by the whole proceeding that he jabbed his own finger vehemently, making a nasty little gash. He managed to smear some of the overabundant blood on the leaf and blew at it somewhat inaccurately.

"Dear me," Miss Crawley said, handing him a tissue. "We needed only a drop. It hardly called for a major incision."

"Sorry," Ian murmured, dabbing at his smarting finger with the tissue. "I'm rather nervous."

"I can understand that." She placed the leaf carefully where the chestnuts had been before.

"What do we do now?" Ian asked.

"What any well-bred visitors would do after presenting their cards. We wait politely for a reply." She led the way to a fallen tree, which served as a comfortable bench.

"Well, I just hope they know my blood type," Ian grunted.

"You will be admitted, *if* you are admitted, only because you are with me. Hereafter, though, they will recognize your card, and you will be admitted or refused on your own merits."

They sat for a while in silence, listening to the night music of the forest: the constant flutter of leaves, the occasional rustle of something in the underbrush, the steady, mournful dirge of the wind punctuated by the hoots of a distant owl.

"You strike me as a thoroughly sensible, down-to-earth sort of person," Ian remarked. "How did you get involved with—all this?"

"Much the same way as you did, Mr. James. Through curiosity. Only I was considerably younger than you are, which perhaps somewhat excuses my folly."

Ian stared out into the silver mist and said nothing.

"You want to hear about it, I suppose," Miss Crawley prodded.

"Only if you want to tell about it."

"It would pass the time, and since we seem to have become associates, albeit reluctant ones, you might just as well find out what sort of people you've gotten yourself involved with, though I warn you the story is both sordid and sentimental."

She closed her eyes. "Now, how would Chaucer do it? And so the agent thus her tale began.

"I was, as I said, young, certainly no more than thirteen or fourteen the first time I came. I had been fed as a child all the usual nursery pap about fairies, some rather good, like Grimm and the Arthurian stuff, but most of it unpalatable treacle. As I grew older, I began to learn to discriminate between the good and the poor, but then I wanted to discriminate even further, between truth and make-believe. Despite very good training, the idea still persisted in my mind that somewhere in all this nonsense a great truth was hiding. I could get no satisfaction from books or teachers, and my mother was frankly appalled at my asking that sort of question at my age. I was annoyed and frustrated and stubbornly determined to find out the truth. I had always loved the forest beyond the town, and so I decided that it might be the best place to start my research. I told my parents that I was staying the night with a friend, and after sundown I came alone to the forest to see—I don't really know what I expected to see, but I came."

"Alone?" Ian marveled. "That must have taken a great deal of courage."

"More than I possessed, I'm afraid," Miss Crawley laughed. "I had not even brought a torch with me, and when it grew dark, I became frightened and decided that there were no fairies in that forest at least, and that I might as well go home. But everything looked different at night, and I couldn't find my way. I must have walked around confused for better than two hours before I admitted to myself that I was lost. I was exhausted and terrified, but it was summer and I could lie on the ground comfortably. I lay down just about where we are now and cried myself to sleep. I awoke after an hour or so and saw a very little man looking at me."

"Like Mompen," Ian said.

"Oh he was as handsome as dear Mompen is ugly. He looked, well, try to imagine how Garumpta looked in his youth, slender and fair, clear-eyed and graceful. He stood right by my ear so that I could hear him easily.

" 'Why are you crying?' he asked.

" 'Because I am lost,' I said.

" 'Where do you want to go?' he asked.

" 'Back to the town,' I said.

" 'Come,' he said. 'I will show you the path.' He bowed charmingly from the waist. 'I am Fremna, Lastborn of Garumpta the Fernlord.' "

"I thought Mompen was lastborn," Ian exclaimed.

"He is now," Miss Crawley replied in a flat tone and continued her narrative without further comment. " 'Do you live here?' I asked him. 'Are there many of you?'

" 'We live in the thorn thicket,' he said. 'It forms a protective fortress.' He pointed to a portion of the thicket near us. 'Our Great Hall is right under there.'

" 'Oh I wish I could see it,' I said.

" 'Do you really?' he said. 'I could take you there. I know where magic nuts are kept. It could be dangerous, though. My father hates most humans, and if he found you in his halls, he would most certainly cut off your head and mount it on a spike in his Throne Room.'

"That quashed my eagerness a little, but I felt that I couldn't very well back out without looking like a coward. So I waited while he went back to fetch a chestnut. I had kissed the blasted thing before I realized what it was for. It is something of a shock, isn't it, going down like that? But I was in for yet another shock when I arrived. He had brought Mompen back with him. I found it hard to believe they were brothers, but I liked Mompen from the first. He was so gentle and anxious to be helpful. He idolized Fremna, you see, and would do anything for him. He showed us a secret entrance and a chamber just off the Throne Room where I could see most of what went on without being seen. Fremna sat with me for a while, telling me in a low voice who the people were and what they were doing. Mompen stood watch to warn if anyone was coming and even brought us some food and drink. As it got near dawn Fremna showed me the way back to the main path and explained how I could return to my natural size. I told him I wanted to come again. He said that if I could let him know when, he would leave a nut near the secret entrance, and I could let myself in.

"I came regularly that way over the next three or four years, slipping out of the house at night and returning before dawn. But after a while it was not curiosity that brought me. Believe me, the daily life of Garumpta's tribe is not all that interesting. As I grew older it was Fremna I came to see. We supped together night after night in the cozy darkness of the little chamber, with Mompen patiently keeping watch outside. In time we became lovers."

Ian stared at her in silent astonishment. She laughed shortly.

"I warned you it was a little sordid. But there it is. When the sun was up I was a demure schoolgirl, proper and modest, but at night I was mistress to a fairy prince. Naturally, we got caught. It wasn't Mompen's fault; he was called away on some errand just when Aneelen decided to have a look about the lesser chambers. I suppose we were bound to be discovered eventually, so it was just as well that Aneelen was the one who found us. Once I had persuaded her that I truly loved her son she was ready to do anything she could to help us. She insisted, though, that Garumpta be told. She was afraid he might chance on us himself some time and slice us all up before he'd considered it. Mompen offered to take on the job of breaking it to him. I don't know what he said, but as you see I did not lose my head. I knew what I was doing, Mr. James, when I insisted on Mompen being used to get the American child's consent. He is an eloquent persuader when his heart is in it. I also know what you went through at Midwinter before the King, for I stood alone that night before Garumpta and endured a grueling interrogation. He was a crusty old fellow then, and the years have done little to mellow him. May I offer you some advice based on my own experience? If you find yourself questioned by him, be absolutely honest. If you try to evade him he will find you out. You didn't make too good a showing at Mrs. Hubbard's. That sort of thing won't do at all around Garumpta. If you are going to get to him at all you will have to grasp the nettle straight out. No more hiding in doorways."

Ian winced and strove to get her back onto a more comfortable subject.

"How did he react to you?"

"Not at all in the way I expected. He couldn't, of course, think I was spying; the affair had been going on too long for that. But he was shocked, would you believe it, by the love affair itself. I had no idea he would be so conventional. He was willing to let us all go unpunished, but he forbade me to see Fremna again. A regular Victorian patriarch he was. Well, neither of us was about to accept that; we really were in love. I swore that I would diminish permanently and become a member of the tribe rather than give Fremna up. And I meant to do it."

"In an exchange?" Ian asked.

"No," said Miss Crawley. "Only an infant can be exchanged. You must realize, if you think about it at all, that it would be impossible to teach even a fairy to exactly imitate an adult's personality and mannerisms so that his closest friends could be fooled. A baby is a stranger to even his parents and can be replaced fairly easily.

"In the case of an adult who is accepted into the other world there is no exchange. He simply disappears from the human world, covering his tracks as best he can, and he remains a human, only diminished. That is what I meant to do. Garumpta after considerable persuasion was willing to permit it, but Aneelen would not hear of it. She was concerned about my parents. I wasn't. I had never been that close to them and felt, probably rightly, that they would not miss me overmuch. She insisted that we wait, though, until I was old enough to leave home in some normal way and drop out of sight painlessly. I was allowed to visit the Great Hall on public occasions, but we were heavily chaperoned. Little Mompen, bless him, dug out a new secret entrance and another hidden chamber. I came to public gatherings often enough to allay suspicion, but much more frequently I was entertained in private. I lived in two worlds and had the best of them both."

"But you did not join them after all?"

"No, for I lost the only incentive I had for taking that step. Nearly two years later, while gathering herbs for the Midsummer feast, Fremna strayed to close to the bridle path and was stepped on by a skittish horse. There was no way of informing me of the tragedy, so I came as usual to the festival to find the Great Hall empty except for Mompen, looking even worse than usual because his ridiculous eyes were red and swollen. He had been elected to break the news to me that the climax of that season's celebration was to be my lover's funeral and Mompen's reluctant accession to the position of lastborn of the tribe."

Miss Crawley sat silent staring into the moonlight.

Ian spoke quietly, more to himself than to her.

"And so you have never married."

She laughed, assuming her customary defensive armor.

"You give me too much credit, Mr. James. I was quite young, and the young are blessedly callous. I got over my loss quickly enough, but I'm afraid the affair rather spoiled me for the company of men. They have always suffered by comparison. I don't know that they really are inferior; the memory of lost sweets can be deceiving. Be that as it may, I have been unable to get seriously interested in any man. That is how I have ended up on my own, not entirely out of choice. Rather like *La Belle Dame sans Merci*—in reverse:

> *O what can ail thee, businesswoman*
> *Alone and palely loitering?"*

She turned to him with a strange smile and said, "The estate agent ended thus her tale, and the company thought it none too soon. Shall we see if the door has been answered?"

She rose and Ian followed her in silence, being able to think of nothing appropriate to say.

"See?" she said, pointing to the spot where she had put the holly leaf. "The door is open."

Reaching down, she picked up two identical chestnuts and offered Ian his choice. Faced with it like that, he found himself drained of all resolve. He backed away a little, keeping his hands at his sides.

"The descent is a bit unsteadying until one gets used to it," Miss Crawley said, with an uncharacteristic show of sympathy. "Take my hand and we'll go down together. Come now; it would be rude to keep them waiting."

Ian James sighed, took a chestnut in one hand, Marian

Crawley in the other, and descended once more into Oberon's kingdom.

They were met by a grossly humpbacked old fellow who led them through the Great Hall to the Throne Room. The Hall was much as Ian remembered it, with its vast domed roof and central fire. The fire was much smaller than it had been the night of the feast, and the great board was all but empty. He noticed, in passing, narrow corridors leading off the main hall, connecting, no doubt, with chambers such as Miss Crawley had described. From some of these passages he could hear voices and sounds of activity. The Fernlord and his lady sat upon their double throne as they had before, but seemed older and more feeble than on the festival night. In place of their finery they wore the same tattered homespun that their subjects wore, and, like their subjects, they were working. Aneelen, who was spinning, set aside her distaff and rose to greet them. She embraced Miss Crawley affectionately and extended her wrinkled hand to Ian. He bowed low over it. They went together to the throne where Garumpta sat carving a long piece of wood. The old lord greeted Miss Crawley with a paternal kiss on the cheek, pointedly ignoring Ian's bow.

"We were not expecting company," Aneelen said. "And I fear we have no food to offer you."

"We haven't come on a social call," Miss Crawley replied, "but on a matter of pressing business. Otherwise we would have at least given you a little warning."

"No matter," the old woman assured her. "Business or no, you shall at least have something to drink." She bustled off toward the Great Hall and, much to Ian's discomfiture, Miss Crawley went with her. He was left alone, standing, awkward and uncomfortable, at the foot of the Fernlord's throne. The old humpback approached with a low stool, bowed, and departed. Garumpta gestured with his knife toward the stool.

"Be seated and tell me your business," he said gruffly. "Keep it simple and to the point. I'm too old and tired to tolerate a lot of nonsense." He returned to his carving.

"We have selected the human child we wish to use in the exchange," Ian began, making certain to emphasize his part in this decision. "She is the younger sister of the

American child who disturbed your Mompen awhile back."

"Now, isn't that nice?" Garumpta muttered. "You mean to say you have come all the way out here on a winter night just to tell me that?"

"No, my lord, not just that. We also decided that since we have difficulty communicating with our own infants, one of your people would be best able to gain her consent, and we have come to fetch someone for that purpose. Mompen was the one we chose."

Garumpta looked up sharply from his work, his bright old eyes glinting dangerously.

"And whose idea was that?" he asked.

"I believe it was Miss Crawley who suggested it. She seems to set a great deal of store in his powers of persuasion and feels it would be a good experience for him."

"I suppose she's right," Garumpta admitted, "but it will go hard with his mother. This has all been rather difficult for her, but she hoped to have him with her at least until summer. We had another son, you see, who . . ."

"I know," Ian interrupted before his sense of tact could intervene.

"You know?" Garumpta snarled. "And how is that?"

"Miss Crawley told me."

"You seem to get your curiosity satisfied easily."

Ian flushed. "I did not request the information, my lord."

Garumpta said nothing, but continued silently with his work, never hesitating in the short, swift strokes of his knife. Ian watched with delight the skill in the old fairy's withered hands. He had not before seen such fine work done with such ease. In the short time that they had been conversing the stick had become covered with an intricate relief of flowers, leaves, bees, nuts, and fruits. He wondered what it was to be: too thick for a wand, perhaps a walking stick.

"The women are taking quite a while just to fetch drinks," Garumpta observed at length. "So I think we can safely assume that Marian has delivered her message to my lady in private, which indicates more thoughtfulness than I usually give her credit for. So much then for her errand. You still have not told me what brings you so soon into my halls."

Ian fidgeted and swallowed air. The interview was becoming painful, as he had been warned it might. Out of the corner of his eye he could see a neat row of long, spikelike thorns standing point upward on the far side of the Throne Room. They were, at present, vacant.

"I—I was accompanying Miss Crawley."

Garumpta laughed, a thin, crackling, scornful laugh.

"For better than five-and-twenty years she has been coming out here alone, and now, at this late date, you tell me she needs an escort." He laid down his carving and leaned forward, fixing Ian with piercing eyes. "You will have to do better than that, Ian James. I am not to be taken for a fool. You would do well to tell me the truth. Keep it simple and to the point. Understand? Now, what brings you here? More curiosity?"

"No, my lord," Ian murmured. "I am quite healed of curiosity."

"What does bring you then?"

"Fear, my lord."

Garumpta sat back, evidently not having been prepared for an answer that simple and to the point. Then he chuckled. "So you're afraid of me, eh? And not without good reason. I'm a rough old fellow, for my life has made me so. My body may be getting feeble, but I have yet power enough to deal with your sort." He took up the knife and stick once more and continued carving without hesitation exactly where he had left off. "What's the matter? Couldn't they find anything more useful for you to do?"

Ian sighed. "They could not. I am worse than useless. I'm in the way. That is the truth, if you want it."

"That is not good. You are wise to be afraid."

Marian Crawley entered the Throne Room quickly, carrying a tray containing three carved wooden mugs. Ian rose, and accepted with some relief the cup offered him. His throat was painfully dry, and he remembered that the fairies' nectar, which he had drunk on his previous visit, was delicately sweet and refreshing.

"Well," said Miss Crawley with studied casualness as

she accepted the stool Ian offered her and sat down, sipping at her drink.

"We have discussed the business at hand, among other things," Garumpta said shortly, downing the contents of his mug in one noisy swallow. "How does my lady feel about your plans?"

"She's taking it all rather harder than I expected," Miss Crawley answered. "After all, it's only temporary this time."

"Midsummer seems to us to be approaching with fearsome rapidity," said Garumpta. "Be a little easy on us if we tend to cling to what we know we must give up."

Miss Crawley gently touched his withered hand. "I'm sorry. You have often told me I am a hardhearted wench."

"And you have often told me I am an ill-tempered old tyrant. I am old, that much I will admit to. Tonight I feel very old indeed."

He shook off her hand and continued with his carving.

"How long do you suppose this, er, diplomatic mission will last?" he asked at length.

"If I know Mompen," Miss Crawley replied, "he'll be back in a week; if I know the intransigence of children, it could take as long as a month."

Garumpta shook his head. "We have so little time."

Ian stood to one side feeling embarrassed and uncomfortable, as though witnessing the funeral of a stranger. They seemed to have forgotten he was there. Looking toward the doorway he saw Aneelen approaching, and with her—indeed, all but surrounded by her—walked little Mompen wrapped in a patched woolen cloak. He looked even more impossible than Ian had remembered. Small wonder he had mistaken him for a character in a boozy nightmare. His unspeakable eyes seemed magnified because of the pair of oversize tears that welled up in the corners. He walked as directly as he could to the throne and stood before his father.

"You have heard what is desired of you?" Garumpta asked quietly. Mompen nodded, rubbing his sleeve across his face. "You are under no obligation to make this extra journey. Do you wish to go on this mission, or shall I send someone else?"

"I will go, Father. I think it is best." He seemed close to breaking down, but kept a firm hold on his emotions. The effort to mount the two low steps at the foot of the throne was too much for him, though, and he tripped over his unruly feet. Without being quite aware of what he was doing, Ian reached forward and steadied him. For a moment his eyes met Garumpta's, and he felt the truth being wrung from him. Under the power of that look he made bold to ask the question that had been bothering him the last while.

"How will he live so long in an alien world? How will he get food?"

Garumpta rose slowly and painfully from his seat, supporting himself with the stick he had been carving. He placed his free arm around Mompen's shoulders. As they walked like a solemn procession through the Throne Room and the Great Hall, where the other members of the tribe stood around the walls silently watching, he answered Ian.

"He will live as his ancestors have lived in the halls of men for many ages: by honest stealth. He will take quietly and cleverly only what he needs to stay alive and will pay for what he takes in any way he can, in goods or services."

They stopped at the entrance to the Great Hall. Before them stood a green chestnut burr almost as high as Ian's shoulders. At a gesture from Garumpta, the top half was removed, revealing a soft, feltlike interior. It did look comfortable. The Fernlord laid his hands firmly on Mompen's shoulders.

"You are going into the world of men, my son. They are not always honorable, but you be so. Never forget that you are the Lastborn of the Firstborn and the hope of all your people. Farewell; go with my blessing, and return when you have fulfilled your duties worthily." He kissed Mompen ceremoniously on both cheeks and released him into the arms of his mother.

"Do take care, dear," Aneelen murmured into his shoulder. "Don't get trodden on; they are so big. And eat enough; they can afford it. Please, please come back quickly." She finally forced herself away, accepting Miss Crawley's comforting embrace and a clean linen handkerchief. Rather overwhelmed and completely miserable, Mompen turned and prepared to mount the side of the burr. Ian's heart went out to him. Poor little fellow, he looked as though he wouldn't survive the sendoff, much less the mission itself. Impulsively he touched the fairy's trembling hand.

"Have a good time, Mompen. Be careful and get the job done, but enjoy yourself, too. All right?"

Mompen looked at him, his eyes alight with astonishment and gratitude. "Thank you, sir. I'll try to."

He stepped a bit more steadily into his strange vehicle, and the upper half was fixed once more into place. It was then that Ian became aware that Garumpta was staring at him. He returned the gaze, questioning.

"You like my son, don't you?" Garumpta asked.

"Why yes, I do," he replied, a little astonished himself at the revelation. "I like him very much indeed."

Garumpta chuckled. "Don't despair, Ian James. You just may prove useful to us yet. You bear the King's mark as a memento of your first visit to my halls. Let the Fernlord's cane serve as a remembrance of your second." He extended the beautifully carved stick toward him.

"Here, take it," he urged impatiently when Ian protested. "I was under the impression that you admired it. I've rooms full of them. I make them just to keep occupied. I don't know what you can do with it once you're back to your usual size; use it for a toothpick or a collar pin. Or perhaps just keep it on hand as a reminder of the hazards of undue curiosity."

Chapter 6

The Lastborn of the Firstborn

The American mother glanced nervously at the grease-smudged face of the kitchen clock. It was half past eight already; and it was one of those mornings. Anything was likely to happen. She had to get breakfast on as soon as possible; this was her husband's day to go into London, and he wanted to catch the ten o'clock train. At ten-thirty the formidable Miss Crawley was coming over for inspection, an ordeal neither the house nor its tenants were prepared for. She hurriedly gulped at her coffee (which was, of course, too hot and burned her tongue), and peered into the oven. The toast was still soft to the touch, but she knew that by the time she checked it again, no matter how brief her absence was, it would be too hard and on the point of burning. The bacon, at least, was done, and she could lift it out of the broiler and set it aside, hoping as she did so that she could avoid brushing it with her arm and dumping it on the floor. It was the sort of day things like that happen. Any time now her husband would become excited because he was in a hurry and couldn't find something, the children would start fighting, or the porridge would boil over. A crisis was inevitable, the only question being which one would occur.

A bellow from upstairs indicated which crisis. On her way upstairs to help hunt for a missing alien identification card, the mother had to stop at the playroom to investigate a scream. Ned was beating Anne over the head with a plastic Crusader. The ID card, it turned out, was on the dresser where it should have been. As the mother fled back to the neglected breakfast, she could smell it, even before she got to the kitchen and saw it oozing and bubbling over the burners and seeping into the oven to contaminate the burned toast. The porridge had boiled over.

It was almost ten before she got the kitchen into any sort of reasonable condition, husband fed and sent breathless on his way, children fed and driven into the garden with threats of dire retribution if they tracked anything in. A valiant attempt had been made to feed the baby who, after ingesting two spoonfuls, had indicated her displeasure with the porridge by upending the loaded spoon over her mother's already stained housecoat. The cooker had been scrubbed and scraped until it appeared clean if one did not examine it too closely, but the odor of burned porridge still hovered in the air. The mother went quickly through the lounge, picking up remnants of the *Times* and scattered library books. Neatness counted high, she knew, in making a good impression on visiting landladies, and neatness was not one of her virtues or her family's.

One furtive glance into the playroom and she quickly closed the door and fled upstairs. She had no more than twenty minutes to make the beds and dress herself. If she managed to get through that in time, she would make a stab at the playroom. She wished she weren't so nervous, since her nerves slowed her down considerably. A little less coffee might have been desirable. No, she knew that coffee was not the real source of her jitters. The truth was that she was just a bit afraid of Miss Crawley. From the time of their first meeting the mother had been awed and intimidated by the brisk and businesslike estate agent with her pointed wit and perfectly organized handbag. From that remarkable portable filing cabinet she had produced a legal-looking black book that she called the inventory, but that became to the mother something similar to the Great Book of St. Peter, where all one's sins were balanced, ledgerlike, against one's good works. In tedious detail it listed everything—a black mark on a bedroom wall, a crack in a teacup, the exact number and style of every fork, every cake tin. All had to be checked, and every deviation from the listing carefully noted. ("Be very particular when you move in," Miss Crawley had quipped, "for we shall be very particular when you move out.") And now this fearsome creature was on her way over with her inventory book, her sharp tongue, and her unruffleable poise.

With no more than five minutes to spare the mother pulled on a pair of crimplene slacks. She had lost some weight since she had bought them, and they were now somewhat too large. Miss Crawley, she knew, would notice that, as well as the worn condition of her house slippers, and the spot on the hall carpet. A crash from downstairs sent her flying, pulling a sweater over her head as she ran. The baby in an investigative mood had pulled over an end table, dumping its burden of books, magazines, and a forgotten, fortunately empty, coffee cup onto the floor. The mother had scarcely gotten the mess straightened out when the doorbell raucously announced the approach of the enemy. Miss Crawley was, as the mother knew she would be, impeccably dressed. Every hair was in place; not a spot, nor a blemish, nor a blasphemously presumptuous speck of dust anywhere about her. Her greeting was cordial enough, if somewhat condescending. The baby helped ease tension with her natural friendliness, for she feared no living thing.

They walked through the house slowly, the mother with her baby in her arms, the agent with a shorthand notebook in her left hand, pencil poised in her right, occasionally writing notes that the mother, in spite of her best efforts, was unable to read. Were the drains working better now? Had the handyman mended the leaking chimney pipe? What about that table leg; had it been loose when they moved in? Was it noted in the inventory? The barrage of questions was broken by regularly dispersed comments of a more cordial nature. How were they surviving the winter? Had the baby been to clinic? Did they enjoy the pantomime? Miss Crawley observed that her tenant was nervous, but she felt sympathetic toward her today, rather than slightly scornful, as she ordinarily would, for she was more than a little nervous herself. The last hope of a dying people lay at the bottom of her handbag; and even more a friend, dearer to her than her own brother, a friend whom she had elected to place in danger.

As they neared the playroom door, the American

mother began talking rapidly. Miss Crawley, with an understanding smile, removed her hand from the doorknob and started up the stairs.

"Shall we have a look at those loose tiles in the bathroom?"

"Oh they're fixed now," the mother said, much relieved. "But the drain pull still slips. Not that it matters to us, you understand. We never use it. I just wanted you to know, for the inventory." She was a little breathless, trotting as best she could after the agent. The bedrooms, at least, were in pretty good shape.

The two women stood at the window of the girls' room admiring the charming view of the downhill march of chimneys smoking gently. Miss Crawley was standing beside the baby's cot. The mother hoped that she wouldn't notice the yellowish stain on the mattress and gestured toward the street below in an attempt to divert her attention.

"That's the young curate, our neighbor. He's a very personable young man."

"Yes," Miss Crawley agreed, reaching quickly and stealthily into her handbag. "They've a new baby too, you know. Have you seen her yet?"

The mother strained forward, trying to make out the distant face looking dolefully out from under a mountain of knit and satin robes in the great pram rolling down the street below. With the dexterity of a stage magician Miss Crawley palmed something round and, on the pretext of examining a worn spot on the drapes, slipped it between the slats of the cot and the mattress. The mother noticed nothing, she was much too involved in her own problems and apprehensions, but the child in her arms watched in wide-eyed fascination.

"I think that covers things well enough for the present." Miss Crawley closed her notebook and returned it to her bag. "I'll have the electrician look in on that faulty switch."

Miss Crawley's departure from the house was a relaxed and cheerful as her entrance had been stiff and uncomfortable. As she stepped into her automobile everyone, including the agent herself, exhaled a sigh; but before she closed the car door Miss Crawley glanced up once, quickly, at the bedroom window above. Not that she expected to see anything, but simply as a gesture of farewell.

With the flight of her personal recording angel, the mother could get her mind back to her normal duties. She loaded the baby on her back and, marching the older children ahead of her like prisoners of war, went down the long hill to the shops. This was an outing the baby always enjoyed. There was so much to be seen from her high perch: movement, excitement, the enigmatic interactions of adults circling about one another in an elaborate dance. The walk home was uphill, difficult, and wearying for all except the privileged infant, who delighted in it all, even the inevitable accident when an overloaded shopping bag broke, sending a jar of costly Oxford marmalade crashing into the pavement. It had looked so beautiful shining on the gray sidewalk like a golden reflection of the midday sun. The lunch that followed, though, had been a somewhat peremptory affair, as the mother was exhausted and the groceries still needed to be unpacked. But the baby hadn't minded that much since she was, as usual, not especially hungry. But she did feel that she had been dumped into her cot for her nap a bit more rapidly and enthusiastically than was called for. After such an exciting morning it was difficult to settle down to the monotony of rest.

As she lay pensively examining her toes, she remembered the strange thing she had seen the lady with the wide mouth do that morning. She had hidden something in the cot. By squirming up just a little she would be able to reach the very spot between the mattress and the slats. Yes, there was something there, something round and scratchy. She took it gingerly in her fist and studied it. Had the surface been less prickle she would have put it in her mouth, for she had found that to be the quickest and most accurate method of discovering the essence of unfamiliar things. This thing looked rather like a ball. She wondered if it were hollow, for it felt very light. She squeezed it a little to see if it would crumble.

"Oh don't do that. You'll break it."

Startled, she dropped the thing and turned her head,

trying to locate the source of the small voice that addressed her.

"Turn your head just a little, and you will see me. I'm quite small." There, now she saw him, sitting on the sheet next to her ear.

"I am Mompen," he said by way of introduction. "I live in the forest. What are you called?"

"Penny, I think. They call me a lot of different names, some of them very silly, but mostly they call me Penny."

She observed to her surprise that she could converse with him quite easily. It was such an effort to talk to or understand the people around her. Sounds were so hard to make, and there were so many complicated rules to remember—everything with a different name, and whole series of these strung together in just the right order if she hoped to get what she wanted. At this stage it was easier just to cry and let them figure out what she was after. But with this strange-looking little person it was different. He did not actually speak to her as the others did, yet she understood exactly what he was telling her. And she had only to wish to tell him something, and he instantly understood. He seemed very pleased for some reason about her name.

"That is good," he said. "Our names are quite similar, a coincidence that will probably help in the exchange. There is power in names, you know."

"What does that matter?"

"It matters a lot, because I want to change places with you."

Penny smiled. "You don't mean really? You couldn't do that. What would Mommy say?"

"She wouldn't know, because I would look just like you. And you? No, you wouldn't look like me, do not fear. You would look like my people, though, only beautiful, for you would be a princess."

"A princess?" Penny smiled. Anne had shown her pictures of princesses in story books. They were always quite pretty and wore lovely dresses. "Why would I be a princess?"

"Because my people need you. We have no children, you see. We want you to be our princess and mother our children. So that your parents will not grieve, I shall become their child in your place. Do you understand that?"

"Not really," Penny yawned. "You're not so different from the others, after all. Always saying long things that I don't understand."

"I'm sorry. I suppose I have been going a little fast. You're tired, aren't you? I tell you what I'll do. You just lie there the way you always do, and I shall tell you about the forest where I live. You will see it in dreams and won't have to try to understand."

She did as he told her and was soon fast asleep, with Mompen's gentle voice planting pictures in her dream mind of his home and family and the beauties and delights of his forest world. He was pleased by this first contact, for to his delight he found she was able to look at him directly without laughing or, worse yet, averting her eyes in embarrassed revulsion. To Mompen she was a princess already.

The day, that most dreadful of days, ended at last in blessed quietness. With the children finally asleep, the mother eased herself into a large chair before a warm coal fire in the lounge to read and sip sweet sherry until her husband's return on the late train from London.

Upstairs Mompen sat in the corner behind the bedroom door, his arms wrapped tightly around his bony knees, waiting. In spite of his excitement and unaccustomed activity, the nocturnal habits of his race still dominated him, and he could not sleep. Besides, he was becoming painfully hungry.

The house was quiet for a while; then the murmur of voices drifted up from downstairs. He wondered how long it would be before all the humans would at last sleep in the protective dark. Laying his head on his knees he wept a little, quietly. He was so awfully alone. It hadn't been too bad while the children were awake. For one thing, his mind had been thoroughly occupied with the tricky business of staying hidden from the inquisitive eyes that seemed to be constantly searching him out. At one point he had made the mistake of curling up in the rear corner of a drawer for a quick nap, only to have it thrown open abruptly by Anne in search of a lost hair ribbon. Terrified, he had frozen where he lay and had been mercifully passed over—mistaken perhaps, for a blob of dust or an old scrap of gray cloth.

But it had been a close call and had made him realize how carefully he was going to have to proceed. Under a bed had proved only a slightly safer hiding place, for there he had made the acquaintance of the dust mop, a fearsome human instrument that was capable of crushing, smothering, and strangling a hapless fairy all at the same time. Finally he had made himself a fairly comfortable nest out of the dust and bedspread lint and balanced it on the wide edge of the baby's cot springs. There he precariously slept, when he was able to sleep.

But now sleep would have no part of him, and he sat, homesick and hungry, waiting for the humans to go to bed. He knew he ought to be pleased with the way things were going. The child was responding well to his descriptions of forest life and was obviously intrigued with the prospect of becoming a princess; why, Mompen could not figure. He was a prince, after all, and it hadn't done him any good. It was hard on him describing as favorably as possible the land and life that he missed and grieved to lose. An outburst of irrepressible emotion had brought from the child an astonished query. If he loved the forest life so much, why did he want to change places with her? That part he did not seem to be able to make her understand. He could see now that it was going to take a while to gain that unqualified acceptance and agreement from her that it was his duty to acquire. It had been easier for him in a way: a sudden decision in the heat of excitement, with leisure afterward to regret it in vain.

The humans were coming upstairs at last. Lights clicked on and off; water flowed on and off; bedsprings creaked over and back; there were a few whispered words, a few grunts, a sigh, silence. Cautiously Mompen crept from behind the door and slipped into the hall. From the top the stairs appeared steep and treacherous. Mompen squirmed uneasily to the edge and, lying on his belly, attempted to lower himself onto the first step. He slid down until only his hands clung to the ledge. Looking down nervously he saw that his feet were still a formidable distance from the step. With difficulty and no little fear he scrambled back up the ledge. No, that would not do at all. He would be of no use to his people if he broke his foolish back. He sat discouraged on the ledge, his bowed legs dangling over the side. He had inferred from what he had been able to overhear and from the information the baby had given him that all food was downstairs, so downstairs he had to go if he were not to starve. He recalled bitterly something Marian Crawley had told him a long time ago. According to the stories told human children, his people were possessed of wings and fluttered amongst the flowers like butterflies. He almost wished now that the silly stories were true. Wings would have been very helpful in his present predicament. Out of the corner of his eye he observed something in the hallway that caught and delicately reflected the moonlight coming through the window. As much as anything to divert his attention from his painfully empty belly, Mompen scrambled over to have a look at it. It was a sphere of beautifully marked opaque glass, deep blue for the most part, interspersed with irregular veins of yellow and white. Well, his father was wrong after all when he declared, as he so often did, that men produced nothing of beauty. This thing he had to admit was beautiful, though he had no idea of its name or function. Then he remembered. There had been a commotion in the hall earlier that evening. The boys had been rolling things they called marbles down the stairs. The mother had become quite upset about it and had made the boys pick up all of them and put them away. This one must have been overlooked. Mompen gave it an experimental push. Though heavy it rolled easily; he caught it just before it started to bounce down the stairs. An idea was developing in the back of his mind—an idea that made him shudder. He was a fairy of little physical courage, and he feared rapid locomotion almost as much as he feared heights. Just looking down the cavernous stairwell made him lightheaded. No, he could never bring himself to do such a thing. His stomach growled threateningly and twisted itself up into a warning cramp. Mompen sighed. He could see no other way to get past the stairs, and he must get food soon or he would become ill. Reluctantly he returned to the bedroom to fetch his pram, which he had carefully stashed in the dusty corner where the leg of the cot met the wall. Padding it as thoroughly as he could with a soft bedding of coagulated dust (grateful that his hostess was so imperfect a housekeeper), he dragged it into the hall. As he was unable to lift the marble he had to place the open burr on its side and with great care and effort roll the marble into it. Then he pulled himself in and closed the lid over his head. For a few moments he lay wrapped in dust, his heart thumping, trying to work up the courage to give the push that would propel his strange vehicle forward.

"I am the Lastborn of the Firstborn and the hope of all my people," he muttered through clenched teeth. "May Oberon protect me."

Wrapping himself around the sphere, he pushed it forward and began his journey down.

It was a dreadful journey; the worst experience he had ever had—rolling, then flying through invisible space, only to land with a bone-jarring bump on the next level. It was the burr's nature to cling rather than to roll, and at every stop he was forced to dismount and push his carriage by hand to the edge of the next precipice.

Bruised and weary he stepped out at length on the lower floor only to realize that he had no idea where or how to get the food he sought. He had no trouble locating the kitchen in the threads of moonlight that managed to filter through the drawn drapes, for his night vision was as keen as a cat's. But he found the human kitchen a distressing place, so unlike the open kitchens of his father's halls. Everything was closed and put away. He was confronted on all sides by tightly fastened doors and unreachable shelves. A few bread crumbs carelessly spilled under the table did little to assuage his furious stomach. His ancestors, he mused, must have had something more to work with than he had.

He decided to have a further look around the place. He wandered into the lounge, which he found quite pleasant, as the floor was covered with a soft carpet that reminded him of the forest floor. Most of the furniture was upholstered, and he discovered he could climb it, as he had the drapes upstairs. He tried his luck with the large sofa in the center of the room. The upholstery was rough and loose, giving him something to grasp as he worked his way up to the cushioned seat. Here he discovered that he must indeed be under the Fairy King's protection. In a corner of the cushion lay a hunk of pale yellowcheese as big as the hungry fairy's head. Blessing the careless human who had dropped it there, Mompen consumed every crumb. Further investigation revealed a delicate-looking glass vessel sitting on the table next to the sofa. With a degree of skill that would have surprised those who had long lived with his shy clumsiness, Mompen turned the vessel carefully on its side, greedily drank the few drops of rich amber liquid that spilled out, and proclaimed it very good. It warmed his entrails like a gentle fire and gave him a feeling of elation. It must be a potion of some sort, he thought, but he felt no fear. His loneliness was somewhat relieved, and he became almost cheerful.

Suddenly he remembered he had a duty to perform and scampered off to seek a way to pay for his supper. The playroom curtains were not drawn, and the moonlight poured in unhampered, revealing a formidable clutter of dolls, blocks, books, and assorted toys. Mompen clapped his hands in delight. Here was an opportunity to earn his stolen bread and fulfill his promise that he would enjoy himself. But before settling down to his delightful task, he selected an especially jumbled corner in which to hide his pram, where he might rest in safety when work and play were done. You know, Mompen, my lad, he cheerily remarked to himself, giving a spin to the glass sphere that he had used for his dreadful journey downward, I think you are going to do quite well in the world of men.

Chapter 7

The Sorcerer

On either side of the highway as it rose to cross the bright new bridge stood a stately beast (a horse, a unicorn, perhaps even a griffin; it was hard to be sure passing at high speed) erect upon its hind legs, and bearing in its forepaws a coat of arms with the caption "Duchy of Cornwall."

"Ostentatious, isn't it?" the Vicar remarked dryly. Ian James grunted a noncommittal acknowledgment. He felt obliged to make some sort of comment, as these were the first words to pass between them since the normal brief salutations with which they had greeted each other early that morning when the Vicar had called for him at his flat. Ian had been concentrating on the scenery, for he contended even to himself that it was only for the pleasure of the ride that he had decided to come at all. The Vicar seemed lost in thoughts of his own, or perhaps he found it necessary to give his full attention to the problem of safely propelling his somewhat disreputable automobile to its destination. But now the atmosphere inside he car was becoming somewhat oppressive. Ian felt that he really ought to make a further contribution. The conversational ball had been served to him; good breeding required that he return it as best he could.

"The Cornish are a rather proud people, I understand."

"I really wouldn't know," the Vicar replied. "I've had very few dealings with them myself."

"But isn't this master of yours a Cornishman?"

The Vicar laughed. "Not on your life, he isn't. And he'd be wild if he heard you suggest such a thing. He despises them, you see, all Celts. Had some rather disheartening experiences with them. He continues to live down here, I think, mainly for the climate and the solitude."

Ian did not speak for a moment, for a peculiar thought had come into his mind. He realized that he had come on this trip to visit someone he didn't know. He had not the slightest idea who or what "the master" was, other than that he was located in Cornwall and was a reliable source of spells and potions. Why, Ian wondered, did he keep getting himself into these absurd situations? Perhaps he was not healed of curiosity, after all. While staring studiously at the bare, almost treeless hills that passed his window—made to look even more desolate by the intrusion of an occasional cheerful-looking cottage—he struggled to pose a simple, direct, complete, and tactful question. Before he had a chance to arrange the best possible words in the best possible order, the Vicar pulled up in front of a pleasant-looking roadside inn.

"What would you say to a spot of lunch, James? This place has good beer and excellent pastries—the real thing."

They ate hot and savory Cornish pastries and drank good beer in silence, for the bar was crowded with workingmen of the area, young and old, all friends and all talking to everyone at once about local matters. Ian sat back contentedly nursing his pint. After his recent experiences it was a relief to be in the company of commonplace men in an ordinary public house drinking beer from a familiar knobbed mug, to forget for a few luxurious moments that any other world existed. Unfortunately the Vicar was not of a similar mind and urged his companion to finish so that they could get on with their journey.

"Sorry to rush you, James," he explained when they were once more on the road, fleeing through winter-bare moors, showing little more for the territory they took up than thorny skeletons of gorse and the brackish shadows of withered heather. "I had forgotten how long the trip took, it's been such a while since I was last here. I'm afraid we may not be able to get back tonight."

"Don't be concerned on my account," Ian assured him. "I'm free until tomorrow evening. That's the first rehearsal for the spring show."

"Oh what are you doing this year, *Pinafore* again?"

"This year we're really going out on a limb," Ian laughed. "We're reviving *The Sorcerer!*"

The Vicar swerved the car a bit recklessly around a snaking curve. When he once more had the wheels under control, he turned his head sharply to stare at Ian for a searching half second before returning his attention to the road. "Are you serious?"

"Quite," Ian replied. Then he chuckled. "It is a trifle ironic under the circumstances, I suppose. . . ."

The Vicar exploded in great gusts of laughter.

"You've no idea how ironic it is. And you, I presume, have been assigned the name part?"

"It was offered me, but I haven't definitely committed myself."

"Then do so, man. Do so, by all means. You'd do an excellent job, it goes without saying. And it would be a rather delightful inside joke. Keep your eyes open this afternoon; you may pick up a few pointers." This idea seemed to amuse him greatly, for he continued to laugh softly to himself. Suddenly he raised his voice and began to sing in a surprisingly full and firm baritone.

> *My name is John Wellington Wells,*
> *I'm a dealer in magic and spells,*
> *In blessings and curses,*
> *And ever-fill'd purses,*
> *In prophecies, witches, and knells.*

Startled and rather delighted, Ian picked up the verse. When they reached the quick and complex patter section, he was forced to retire in defeat, for he had been in possession of the music only a few days. But the Vicar picked up his cue and carried on with a precision and flair that would have done Martyn Green himself proud. Ian joined in heartily on the final chorus, and they ended together with a flourish, like a pair of exuberant schoolboys on an outing.

"You do a passing patter, Vicar," Ian said with admiration when their laughter had subsided sufficiently to allow speech. "Perhaps I should abdicate in your favor."

"Don't you think that would be carrying irony a bit too far? I indulged in the theater when I was younger, but now I'd probably trip over my boots or take a stroke and ruin the final curtain. I am grateful, though, that I have kept a remnant of my voice, enough at least to amuse myself in the bath."

"What do you mean?" Ian prodded, seeing a perfect opening for the introduction of the difficult question that had been bothering him before lunch. "That I might get some pointers this afternoon? Is this master of yours 'a dealer in magic and spells'? I hate to appear ignorant, but I'm not quite sure whom I am supposed to be visiting."

"Why, bless me, I suppose you don't know. I'm really sorry. You've fitted in with us so well that I tend to forget that you are rather new to all this." Ian didn't like the implications of this remark but made no rejoinder. The Vicar continued. "He is not a sorcerer, you see, but the Master Sorcerer, whom our friends in the forest call the Old One, because he was here even before they were. As an educated Englishman you are probably most familiar with him under the name Merlin."

Ian stared very hard at the scenery, seeing nothing. He felt again that now almost familiar sensation that opening before him was a vast nightmare world from which he could not escape. Desperately he tried to collect his thoughts and arrange them in a suitable formation to launch an attack on this latest challenge to his sanity. He was aware that the Vicar was watching him keenly.

"You astonish me, James," he commented. "After all your experiences you can still be so easily and so thoroughly shocked."

"It—it isn't exactly that, Vicar," Ian interposed, having decided to apply the directness of a Roman phalanx. "He just strikes me as a rather unusual master for a clergyman to take up. He is, if I remember my Malory correctly, supposed to be the son of the devil."

It was the Vicar's turn to retreat into studious silence. Aha, Ian thought. I have him.

"No," the old man shook his head slowly after a half minute's silence. "No, I don't think that's in Malory. He was too much preoccupied with the cleaving of helms and the rape of maidens to bother with any matter that abstruse. Sounds more like Geoffrey of Monmouth to me. He was cleric, too, you know, and we all suffer from a propensity for sticking our noses where they've no business to be."

But Ian would not be easily put off. "Well, is he?"

"I really wouldn't know," the Vicar said coolly. "I've never asked him. I was brought up to consider such delicate matters as the details of a fellow's paternity his own private affair."

"All the same, don't you think it might have been wise to inquire into the matter? After all, a man cannot serve two masters."

"Nonsense," the Vicar laughed. "I've been doing it for nearly half a century, and neither has raised any objection yet. Besides, like most laymen, you're quoting out of context." He reached into his pocket, produced a handful of coins, and jangled them under Ian's nose. "There's the second master that a man cannot serve—Mammon, a minor demon in the diabolical hierarchy, but one that has caused the Church considerable woe. Don't quote Scripture to me, son, unless you want it thrown back at you in second-century Aramaic. My commentary on the Synoptic Gospels is still standard textbook in most seminaries."

Ian stared straight ahead in sullen silence. He was annoyed with himself and more than a little embarrassed. But unable to hold his peace, he finally asked a question far enough removed from the subjects of the Vicar's necromancy and his biblical scholarship to seem reasonably placating.

"Why did you want me to come down here with you?"

"Because I like you, primarily, in spite of your somewhat disconcerting tendency to make an ass of yourself. I wanted an opportunity to get better acquainted with you, and I thought you might learn something valuable from the experience. I suspect you've done that already. Now I have a question for you: Why did you come?"

"I don't really know. For the same reason I went into the forest, I suppose."

"A good answer. Well, you will have at least some of your curiosity satisfied shortly. Before we arrive we've time for one more question, if it doesn't require a three-volume exegesis. Anything particularly bothering you?"

"I've no desire to make a further ass of myself," Ian muttered.

The Vicar patted his knee. "Oh come now, don't be touchy. I didn't mean quite that. Just don't quote Scripture inaccurately in my presence. It does nasty things to my professional vanity."

Ian grinned. He found it impossible to stay angry with the old man. "All right. Now I know this is in Malory. He, your master, Merlin, if you will, became after a while something of a dirty old man and ended up trapped in a cave somewhere down here by a nymph, or whatever, that he wouldn't stop pestering."

"Ah yes," the Vicar chuckled. "Nimue. A naïve ruse, but one that worked. It was at the end of what he calls his political phase. He thought that if he could gain control of and influence over a powerful ruler he could do a valuable service to the men who had settled on his land. But Arthur turned out to be a bitter disappointment, more interested in holding bloody tournaments than in planting gardens, and unnaturally preoccupied with his wife's activities. Arthur is one of the main reasons he's so down on the Celts. The master could see that things were going to end badly, and since Arthur didn't any longer heed his councils anyway, he decided to retire. Arthur refused to let him go, so he paid Nimue to invent the cave story and slipped off to live in peaceful solitude, taking on an occasional student to keep his work going. I am at present the only student he has."

They entered a small, pretty village. The Vicar turned his car with the ease of familiarity off the single business street onto a narrow uphill lane lined on either side by attractive, unpretentious houses and gardens filled with early spring flowers in full bloom.

"I do have one other question," Ian stammered hesitantly, "a quick one, though I don't know that I ought to ask it."

"Carry on," the Vicar replied, turning up another street past a small park built along the banks of a narrow river, and turning again onto a sparcely settled country road. "I give my word. I won't laugh."

Ian gulped and stared at his knees. "Have—have you sold your soul?"

"No, James." The Vicar controlled his laughter with considerable difficulty, almost swerving into a parked car. "I have not sold my soul; nor, as you may have observed, have I been given back my youth. He is my tutor; I am his student. He has possession of knowledge and power that I desire, so he teaches me as much as he thinks good for me to know. He does it as a favor and because he enjoys teaching. He charges no tuition of any nature."

He parked the car in front of a small stone cottage sitting almost hidden among trees and bushes and got out.

"If you're worried about your soul you can wait for me here."

It was a challenge that Ian could not let pass, no matter how uncertain he felt. He got out of the car and followed his companion up the neatly trimmed path to the cottage.

Spring came much earlier in Cornwall than it did in Surrey, as Ian had observed from the car. Along the path he now followed ran a border overflowing with crocuses in full bloom—white, yellow, purple, clump after cheerful clump of them from the street to the open front door. Near the center of the flawless green lawn was a large, circular flowerbed crowded with daffodils and narcissi planted in neat circles of graduating shades, from intense sunny yellow bells of daffodils in the center to orange-centered white narcissi at the edge. Over this bed an old man in a frayed sweater the color of diluted oxtail soup was crouched, adjusting the curve of the border with a trowel. He was so intent on his labors that he was not aware of the approach of the two men until the Vicar spoke practically in his ear.

"Good afternoon, Master."

The old man looked up quickly. His face was pale and surprisingly smooth, and the features of it were small and pinched as though shrunk from overwashing, except for his eyes. Ian long remembered those eyes; they were blue, yet so pale a blue that they seemed almost colorless, as wide and guileless as a baby's. They now shone with genuine pleasure. He rose with surprising vigor and embraced the Vicar.

"Tom Heaton, what a delight. So you've finally come to see the old man."

Releasing the Vicar, he cast an inquiring look at Ian. The Vicar urged him forward.

"This is Mr. Ian James, Master."

The old man extended his hand. Ian was surprised at the power of his grip.

"You're more than welcome, Mr. James. Do come inside and have a sip while you tell me how things fare in the Stockbroker Belt. You do drink beer, don't you, Mr. James? I brew my own, and its the best in the British Isles, eh, Tom?"

"The very best, Master."

He led them into the small parlor and fluttered off to the cellar. Ian sat down and looked about him. It was as conventional a sitting room as Mrs. Hubbard's, complete with overstuffed horsehair sofa. Leaning toward his companion, he asked in a stage whisper, "Where does he stash his pitchfork?"

"In there," the Vicar replied, jerking his thumb in the direction of a closed door that Ian had assumed to have led to a closet. Before the conversation could be carried any further their host reappeared bringing three handsome pewter tankards on a tray of the same metal. Brimming over the top of each was a round hillock of fine white bubbles. If it was not, as claimed, the best beer in the British Isles, it was certainly the best beer that Ian James had ever tasted.

"Now, Tom." Merlin seated himself on a hassock that he had placed between and slightly in front of his callers, his arms on his knees, his tankard tenderly nursed in his hands. The expression in his eyes, Ian noticed, had changed to one of guarded shrewdness. "What do you want this time? No, don't protest, please. I know very well that you never come to see the old gaffer anymore unless you've got your hat in your hand. You don't need to tell me you've gotten involved with the little people again. I can see that you've both been decorated by royalty. What are they up to this time?"

"Not very much, I'm afraid," the Vicar said. "They're hardly capable of being up to much of anything. They are diminishing rapidly now, and without help they will eventually die out entirely."

"That would be no great loss," the other grunted.

"Some of us feel differently about it." The Vicar remained polite and apparently undisturbed by the blunt remark. "We have pledged to help in the performance of an exchange for a child-bearing human female."

"An exchange?" Merlin said. "Now, is that the sort of activity for a man of the cloth to get involved in?"

"It isn't entirely to my liking, but there seems to be no other way to preserve the race."

"Very well, then why preserve it at all? They're of no earthly use to anyone." He turned to Ian. "You strike me as an upright and sensible man, Mr. James. How did you get mixed up in this mad scheme?"

"You might say I was drafted," Ian replied.

Merlin laughed loudly.

"Well, he has wit, at least," he said to the Vicar. "That is always a good sign." Turning again to Ian he continued, "You must tell me the whole story. But first I want to hear your opinion of this business and of the creatures who have conscripted your services."

"I don't like the whole idea of the exchange at all, but I am committed to it, so I intend to try to do my part honorably. As for the fairies themselves, I think well of them and would be pleased to see them prosper."

Merlin snorted. "You've strange tastes for a well-bred gentleman. I'd call them a rather disreputable lot myself, especially the clan that infests the forest up your way: gory old Garumpta, with his spikes and his grotesque caricature of a son. At least you've been spared the acquaintance of darling Fremna, the late heir to the Fernwood. A regular rustic rake he was. Slept with half the schoolgirls in southwestern Surrey. He came to an untimely end, the victim, they say, of a jealous playmate."

Ian, who had been growing increasingly angry during this speech, now shot a startled glance in the Vicar's direction. The latter responded with a warning gesture indicating that Ian should say nothing. But Ian could not let these remarks go unanswered. He spoke slowly, trying to keep his voice under control.

"If I have no love for Garumpta, I do have respect for him; I am frankly quite fond of Mompen, who more than makes up in goodness and courage for any physical defects he has. The other I know only through hearsay, but from a source whose judgment I would sooner accept than that of the present company."

The old wizard's eyes flashed in sudden anger, and it seemed to Ian that the iris changed color like shifting kaleidoscope, from blue to a glinting pale green flecked with red.

"Master." The Vicar made a placating gesture toward him, sending at the same time a warning scowl in Ian's direction. A tense few seconds passed, then Merlin spoke in a low voice that held in it an undeniable threat.

"That's a Celtic name—Ian. Are you a Celt?"

Ian recalled the Vicar's remarks about his master's aversion to Celts, but here he was on safe ground.

"Not to my knowledge," he said. "According to family tradition my mother got the name from a romance she had been reading at the time of my birth. The hero's name was St. John, but she felt that was awkward with the surname James, and my father would not let her change that even for the sake of meter and assonance. So I ended up bearing the Christian name of the (doubtlessly Celtic) villain. It must have been an omen, for I have been taking the villain's part ever since."

The angry light slowly faded from Merlin's eyes, and he chuckled, muttering in the same low voice, now free from menace, yet still disquieting.

"Stick with us, Ian James, and we'll make a hero of you yet."

"No, thank you," Ian laughed, so relieved to see that his host was no longer angry that he forgot his own pique. "The role little suits me."

"We shall see," Merlin said and turned to the Vicar. "So what do you want from me, Tom, a baby?"

"We have already selected both subjects, Master; but our knowledge of the mechanisms of the exchange, the precise formulas and procedures, is sadly limited."

"And you decided to beard the old lion in his den to see if you could inveigle the information out of him. What if I refuse to give it to you?"

"It had not occurred to me that you might," the Vicar cried, obviously taken aback. "If you do refuse, I don't see how we can make a successful exchange. And if we fail, James here will more than likely forfeit his head."

"Oh I see." Merlin regarded Ian with new interest and not a little amusement. "You have gotten yourself in deep, haven't you? Very well, tell me what all this is about, but don't take too long at it; tea is running late now."

The Vicar, when he had been active in his calling, had acquired quite a reputation as a preacher. It was not difficult to understand his popularity, for he told a tale well. Ian listened fascinated as he related the events of that Midwinter feast. It was strange hearing it told from another's viewpoint, and a little disquieting. Merlin also listened attentively, occasionally interrupting with a comment or question. The nasty little scene between Mompen and the scornful Puck caught his attention. Ian saw that there was at least one ground on which he and the wizard could agree. They both detested the Puck. Mompen's offer of himself as changeling did surprise Merlin, but it also caused him to smile.

"I suppose he's right," Merlin chuckled. "Any change would be an improvement for that poor little monstrosity. But you'd best make jolly sure you . . ." He paused in midsentence, quickly lowering his head as though in private meditation. When he looked up again his eyes were bright with silent glee. "Hmm. Well, go on, Tom," he prodded impatiently, leaving the admonition unfinished and quickly forgotten by both Ian and the Vicar. As his own part in the story began to unfold, Ian found himself becoming increasingly embarrassed and uncomfortable, not least because Merlin was getting so much amusement out of his predicament. Merlin did grow a bit serious when the Vicar described the taking of the pledge and the painful infliction of Oberon's mark.

"He gave it to you hot, did he?" the old man commented with a low whistle. "How did you respond to that?

"I went home and got drunk."

The old wizard laughed long and vigorously. "That," he gasped, "is the most sensible thing you did all evening. So that's how things stand with you. No wonder you are so quick in the fairies' defense. You owe them your head. Let me give you one bit of advice, my quick-tempered young friend. You would do well to speak softly when you come begging with your head in your hand."

Ian reddened. "I did not come begging," he retorted, with rapidly rising indignation. "I came only for the ride. And as far as the exchange is concerned, help us if you will; if you choose not to we will just have to bumble through as best we can. Though I am not anxious to decorate Garumpta's Throne Room, I should prefer not to have my head used as a bargaining point."

"You wish to withdraw your head? Very well, consider it withdrawn." Merlin laughed appreciatively at his own witticism. "I ought to thrash you for your impudence, but instead I'm going to give you what you want. Not tonight, though. It's way past my teatime and I'll be half the night looking up all those formulas. Come back in the morning, not too late, or you'll ruin my lunch. Let yourselves out. Good evening."

He got up heavily and lumbered off in the direction of the kitchen, leaving his callers staring at each other in stupefied silence at the unexpected ease of their triumph.

The Vicar knew his way about the little town and was evidently known to it. He had no trouble securing a room for the night above the local pub, which in better days had been a hotel and still took in the occasional traveler.

After a hearty dinner of fish and chips at a small side-street cafe, he led the way in the rapidly advancing darkness up the hill to the little riverside park. The air was soft with the early approach of southern spring, but still slightly cool with the memory of winter, and they appreciated their jackets. It was wonderfully peaceful walking together through the dew-damp grass along the river, alone except for an occasional late bicyclist. As if by unspoken rule, it was the Vicar who broke the companionable silence.

"I don't know if you're aware of it, but you were in something of a tight spot this afternoon."

"Yes, I suppose I was," Ian admitted. "But I didn't realize it at the time. I could swear his eyes changed color. Is that possible?"

"Yes it is, but I wasn't aware it had happened today. How did they change? To what color?" The Vicar's voice was edged with anxiety.

"Green," Ian said. "A queer light green, like the sky before a storm, with bits of dark red."

"My God, James, that ridiculous story about your name is probably all that saved you. He can't resist a good story. What on earth provoked you to speak to him like that? Don't you realize he has the power of metamorphosis? He could do anything he pleased with you."

"I—I suppose I rather forgot who he was. He didn't exactly look the part. I know I ought to have kept my mouth shut, but he annoyed me. He reminded me of Oberon's Puck with his arrogance and his glib scorn." He laughed. "A few days ago I would not have believed that I'd be risking my skin in defense of the fairies."

"Perhaps I ought to have warned you," the Vicar said. "There is considerable bad feeling between him and the little people. He gave them what magic they possess, but according to their claim he betrayed them. They hold him responsible for both their diminution and their dependence on us. All that talk about Tinkerbell is not idle, you see. I don't know where the truth lies, but they at least are convinced that it is our ambivalent and condescending belief in their existence that keeps them from diminishing into nothingness. The master claims that the fairies are greedy and ungrateful, and that if they have diminished it is their own fault." He sighed. "I have lived in peace and friendship with both sides these many years. It hasn't been easy. I think I am qualified by now to hold a sensitive post in Her Majesty's Foreign Service."

They stood for some time leaning against the trunk of an ancient oak watching the river flow quietly past them. A few lights were extinguished in the village below. Ian took courage to ask the one question that had been bothering him all evening.

"Was it just vindictiveness, what he said about the other son—what's his name, Fremna? Or was he really, well, that sort?"

"He was a handsome, charming fellow, and there was a lot of gossip among Garumpta's people about his supposed escapades with young girls of the community. I know for certain of only one such affair, and that was not casual. However, it is a fact that the riding party that trampled him consisted of senior girls from the Oak Haven School. There were eyewitnesses to the tragedy, reliable and honest fellows taking part in the herb-gathering who swear to this day that the girl saw him and deliberately turned her horse." The Vicar shrugged. "Draw your own conclusions. You understand, of course, that Marian knows nothing of this."

"You can trust to my discretion, Vicar, though my outbursts this afternoon might cause you doubt."

The Vicar smiled. "Oh I trust you, all right, probably more than you deserve. I say," he added, glancing at the luminous dial of his wristwatch, "if we shoot right back we may have time for a leisurely pint or two before closing."

Their first act on later entering their room was to pool their shillings, for even in Cornwall winter nights are chill. A cold, damp wind crept in through a crack in a window, and the only source of heat was a small, coin-operated gas fire. To this contraption they gratefully sacrificed all their change. The Vicar undressed, but Ian chose to sleep in his shirt and trousers as a precaution against incipient chilblains.

"You know, Vicar," he said drowsily, relishing the ease brought on by four pints of strong beer rapidly consumed, "I really don't like your master very much, no matter who he is, and I'm quite afraid I shall have as much trouble suppressing my feelings tomorrow as I did today. So what do you say I take up your offer to let me wait in the car? It might be the safest place for my soul and my body."

"Suit yourself." The old man sounded just a bit miffed. "You're under no obligation to me; you only came for the ride. But you might miss some things well worth the seeing."

"Then suppose I sleep on it, all right? Good night."

"Good night, James. Sleep well."

Filled with fresh air and good beer, Ian dropped off to sleep almost at once. The Vicar sat for a while in thought, staring out the mist-frosted window into almost total darkness. Even the streetlamps were extinguished by midnight.

The Vicar sighed; time was running short, and he had to come to a decision. After about a half hour he rose and dressed quietly. Pausing beside the other bed he studied his companion's face for a moment. Ian was sleeping heavily, sprawled over the large old bed like an exhausted child, his arms wrapped around his pillow. Though there seemed little danger of his waking for at least seven hours, the Vicar raised his hands over the bed and whispered a few potent words before slipping out the door, creeping down the back stairs and out into the street.

The little cottage on the hill was as dark as any of the other dwellings in the village, but that gave the Vicar no pause. He rapped three times sharply on the door, paused for a count of three, then knocked twice lightly and entered without waiting to be bidden. The parlor was empty and dark except for a coal fire glowing gently in the grate. The Vicar stretched himself out comfortably in a large chair before the fire and waited, as he had so often in the past. Finally the rear door opened, and Merlin entered clad in an ancient brocade dressing gown that had once been quite grand, carrying the same pewter tray with two pewter tankards. He seated himself on the opposite chair and launched at once into the business at hand.

"Are you getting senile, Tom, or did you really bring that young fellow down here just for the ride? You surely cannot be seriously presenting him as a candidate."

"On the contrary, Master, that is exactly what I am doing, though, as you have no doubt gathered, he is quite unaware of it. I hope you will not do as he has done and judge rashly from first appearances. Whatever I led him to expect today, it was certainly not an irascible old gaffer weeding daffodils."

"Ah, I would have provided a few parlor tricks if I had known that was what he wanted. He is fortunate, you know, that he is still dressed in man's flesh after the scene he pulled here this afternoon. No, Tom, I'm sorry, he will not do at all."

The Vicar sighed. He had not expected an easy conquest, but he was determined not to be put off. As a student of long standing he was free to take liberties that would have brought disaster to most men. And this was one argument he had not the least intention of losing.

"As you have often taken pleasure in reminding me, Master," he continued in a quiet firm voice, "I am getting . I am your only student. For the past ten years I have been looking in vain for a successor. I am convinced now that I have found the one I want. You cannot deny that he has spirit; he has courage as well. I have observed him under fire. Though he does not know it, Ian James is an extraordinary man."

"He came wondrously close this afternoon to becoming an extraordinary toad," Merlin retorted.

"He accepted and endured the touch of Oberon's ring without flinching."

Merlin sniffed. "Public school training. A few years of that and they'll put up with anything. Excellent for the development of stiff upper lips and thick heads."

"Oh he's well endowed in those departments," the Vicar chuckled. "But he can be handled. I've seen it done; had a hand in it myself, as a matter of fact. He is an actor, you see, a man of the theater. If he is placed in the proper setting, given the proper cast, and fed the right cues, he will respond. But he cannot be given time to think, to reconsider. Like all his sort he is an expert at rationalizing—anything. It happened before, what with Christmas and all we left him on his own too long after the Midwinter feast. We got him back, though. The problem is it doesn't seem to have taken too well. Only three days have passed, and he's already getting his bloody British back up again. What he needs is another good scare."

"It sounds to me as if he's a great deal more trouble than he could possibly be worth," Merlin remarked. "My advice to you is to let Garumpta have his head and look elsewhere for a disciple. What do you want with an actor, anyway? They're rather unstable, aren't they? What's wrong with a nice studious seminarian? I've always had such success with the clergy."

"They're a different sort these days, Master. They're all very serious and earnest and sure they can save the world through the Youth League. They don't believe in anything unless it's been stamped by the bishop and approved by the Student Union. They just haven't the imagination for this sort of work. I do wish you would give James a chance. He needs a little shaking up, that's all."

"Oh very well, Tom, if you have your heart set on it. Bring him around in the morning, and we'll play some games with the globe. You say he can rise to the occasion, and I can judge for myself how well he rises."

"I think he may surprise you."

Laughing, Merlin drained his tankard. "I, at any rate, shall certainly surprise him. Oh no, Tom," he added, seeing a sudden shadow cross his student's face, "no transformations; nothing permanent. You can trust me. But if you don't get out of here and let me get back to work, I won't be ready for you by morning. So be off with you."

The old wizard rose quickly, gathered up the crockery, and swept through the door he had entered from, closing it behind him with a thump. The Vicar sat for a moment looking into the dying fire. Why, indeed, he wondered, was he taking so much trouble for such an unco-operative subject? Instinct, probably. Years of experience had taught him always to trust his instinct above all other senses. He rose wearily, for now that his mission was completed, he became once more conscious of his age and that of the night.

The mist of the evening had developed into a heavy fog through which he walked like a disembodied spirit, unseeing and unseen, passing down the hill and through the moon-silent park. He felt lighthearted in spite of his weariness, for he was pleased with the evening's events and looked forward to the morning.

The village was wrapped in deep sleep, tucked in by the fog as by a soft, thick eiderdown, and did not hear the voice raised in cheerful solitary song floating down from the park above them.

My name is John Wellington Wells,
I'm a dealer in magic and spells,
In blessings and curses,
And ever-fill'd purses,
In prophecies, witches, and knells.

Chapter 8

Magic and Spells

Ian James slept as he had rarely slept since childhood. He found waking difficult, a bit like struggling through a thick fog. Yet he knew he must struggle through to the distant daylight. He was being summoned irresistibly in words he could not understand but that his will comprehended. With considerable effort he forced aside the warm haze and sat up. The Vicar, standing smiling beside his bed, handed him a steaming cup of tea.

"Breakfast in fifteen minutes."

"Thanks." Ian gulped the tea and swung his feet over the side of the bed. "I don't remember when I've slept so hard."

"Good country air," the Vicar replied. "There was enough of it blowing through this room last night to freeze your whiskers."

Ian gingerly set his bare feet on the floor, winced agreement, and made a dive for his socks.

Breakfast was served them in the public bar, and a memorable breakfast it was, rich and hearty, a classic country breakfast of eggs and lean back bacon and thick slices of bread fried crisp in the dropping. And great pots of strong, dark tea. By the time they had done justice to this feast and finally started up the hill the fog had lifted, and the sun was shining cheerily.

"Now that you're fully awake and properly fed, have you made up your mind whether to come in with me or not?" the Vicar asked.

Ian gazed out of the car window at the neat houses and sun-brightened gardens gliding past. "I don't know. It hardly seems worth the risk."

"Oh if he didn't translate you yesterday, you're probably in no danger now. He'll be in a good mood after a night's work. He's always mellow when he's been at his books."

"You said I would see something interesting. Just what will be going on?"

"Only formulas and that sort of thing for our business. But if you ask him politely he might do a little conjuring for you. No, James, not devils, just visions and such. It's quite an opportunity, really; he wouldn't do it for everyone."

"What makes you think he'll do it for me? He obviously dislikes me."

"He might do it anyway, as a favor to me." The Vicar stopped the car and opened his door. "Well?"

"My good English common sense is telling me to stay clear of it, but it is being shouted down by the part of me that walks in the forest on Midwinter Night."

The front door was closed but not locked. For when the Vicar had knocked (three times sharply, a pause for a count of three, then twice lightly), he opened it and led the way into the parlor.

The door to the room that Ian had taken for a closet on his previous visit flew open suddenly and Merlin stood before them. He wore a long, flowing dark blue robe decorated with signs of the zodiac and other mystic symbols in some luminous white material. On his head was a conical hat covered with the same stuff. He seemed taller than he had on the previous evening and inspired in Ian an awe he had not before felt. His eyes, Ian noticed, were the very color of his robe and shone with a similar eerie light. Merlin smiled almost cordially.

"You'll excuse my work clothes. I've been rather busy. Why don't you come in and have a look about while I finish this formula?"

They followed him into the room, which wasn't really much bigger than a closet, and was most unbelievably cluttered. Three of the walls were covered by bookshelves bursting with large and for the most part ancient-looking volumes. One corner of the floor contained an untidy pile of scrolls. In the opposite corner against the fourth wall stood a small two-burner gas cooker of venerable age upon which something in a saucepan was bubbling. Beside the cooker sat a complex apparatus that Ian assumed to be used for distilling. Large, glass-enclosed cabinets filled to overflowing with all sorts and shapes of vials, jars, and bottles occupied the rest of the wall. The center of the room was taken up by what hinted at being a very beautiful large antique table, but its beauties were now hidden under a jumble of books, half-unrolled scrolls, and great sheets of age-yellowed paper covered with recently made illegible scrawls. Some of these looked like chemical formulas, but most of them resembled something taken off the Rosetta Stone. In the center of the table—indeed, dominating the entire room—there sat on a pedestal a large ball the size of a soccer football. It was a beautiful thing, iridescent dark blue interspersed with cloudy portions and veins of yellow and pale green. It looked like nothing so much as a giant agate marble.

"That is my globe," Merlin said, noticing Ian staring at it with admiration. "Tom brought it to me from Egypt. How he got hold of it I don't know. It is a treasure beyond price." He ran his hand affectionately over the surface of the ball.

"What does it do?" Ian asked a little uncertainly.

"Practically anything I ask it to. Mostly I use it as a sort of private secretary. I don't need it, of course. I've conjured successfully for centuries without it. But it does save time and effort, struggling through all this." He indicated the muddle of books and scrolls. "I use it that way, but it also has power of its own. After we get this business out of the way, I shall be glad to give you a demonstration."

Ian did not respond. He wasn't at all sure he wanted a demonstration of the mysterious globe. There was something strange about it; he could sense its power, and that made him nervous. He tried to look away from it, but his eyes strayed back to it against his will. Then he stared incredulously. The pattern in the marble had shifted and, even as he looked, moved again. The principal color changed from blue to dark green. Ian jerked his head away quickly. The damned thing was trying to hypnotize him. The Vicar and his master, engrossed in the papers strewn over the table, were unaware of Ian's discomfiture.

"I believe I have everything you need here," Merlin was explaining. "I've written the spells out in careful detail. I don't need to remind you how important the precise wording is."

Trying to get his mind off the globe, Ian walked over to the cooker to see what was going on in the saucepan. The simmering liquid looked like a dense beef broth. Absent-mindedly Ian picked up a large spoon resting on a dish next to the pan, stirred the mess, and lifted the spoon as if to take a taste.

"Hold on, young fellow!" Merlin crossed quickly to him and took the spoon from his hand. "It's dangerous business sampling my cooking. That one's not meant for you."

"What is it?"

"A releasing potion. You'll need to use that as soon as possible, Tom, and I had all the ingredients on hand, so I made it up for you while I was puttering about this morning. The rest of these you'll have to do yourselves. It's a good thing you have until summer to get these things together. You're going to need quite a few spring-blooming plants, and they're always better fresh."

He took Ian by the shoulders and propelled him away from the cooker to the other side of the table.

"Now come over here like a good lad and try to stay out of mischief until Tom and I get our business out of the way. No, no, don't sit there," he cried sharply as Ian started to seat himself in the only chair the room contained, a massive, black-leather-covered morris chair that had made him think on first entering of a picture he had seen of the electric chair used in American executions. He stared at it now, looking perhaps for restraining straps or electrical connections.

"What's wrong with it?" he asked.

"Everything in this room has a purpose and a use, Mr. James. It is not merely unwise, it is downright dangerous for an untrained person to touch anything here without strict supervision. You surely wouldn't go into a scientist's laboratory and start pulling switches or mixing chemicals.

Now Tom, let's see if we can get back to the process of setting this spell."

Ian turned his back on the table with its offending centerpiece and stood with arms folded staring at the dictionary-size volumes in the bookcase in front of him. None of the titles appeared to be in English or, for that matter, in any language written in an alphabet he knew.

"The first thing, then," Merlin was saying, "is to give this releasing potion to both subjects, Mompen and this foreign child."

Ian spun around, suddenly alarmed. "What will it do to them?"

"Make all their hair fall out," the wizard retorted. He sighed. "Has it occurred to you, Mr. James, what it might feel like to change your identity? To become wholly and completely someone else, in a new and unfamiliar world? We are all embarrassingly fond of ourselves. Even a creature like Mompen thinks more highly of himself than he realizes now. He will understand well enough when the time comes to leave that self behind. This potion will simply make the break easier for both of them. It works very gradually, you see, so gradually that the subjects themselves are hardly aware of what is happening to them. By Midsummer they will have reached that enviable state of detachment achieved by a few of your mystics only after decades of rigid study and painful self-denial; and the shock of parting from the once irreplaceable self will be much softened. Hardly an evil potion, eh? They should partake of it together, if that is possible, with some sort of pledge; the form is unimportant so long as they mention each other's names and their resolve to change identity. I say, do you really think Mompen can handle this?"

"Certainly he can," Ian snapped. "He's not a fool."

"Ah," the wizard snorted. "I had forgot we had the champion of the small and underestimated in our midst. Well, we shall see. I have included in the potion an ingredient that will make them highly sensitive to the will of others who have partaken of the same stuff. If you take some of that stuff yourself, Tom, you will be able to communicate with them after a fashion. That could be helpful. Here, we'd better take care of that now, before we forget."

Ian watched as Merlin took from the glass-enclosed cabinet a small crystal bottle and a decorated gold cup the size of an egg cup. Carefully he measured out three drops of clear liquid from the bottle into the cup, which he then filled with something from the pitcher that stood on a shelf above the cooker. He lifted the cup to his lips and drank. He then held it before his eyes with his two thumbs and forefingers, muttering some guttural sounds into it, and handed it to the Vicar, who took it in the same manner and drank. He did not, Ian noticed, drain the cup but handed it back to his master still about a third full. Merlin placed it on the shelf beside the pitcher and turned back to the table. He had thrown his robe back over his shoulders. Ian saw with some amusement that he wore underneath a modern rubber laboratory apron.

"The actual exchange spell," he continued, groping about among the cluttered papers on the table, "is a beastly complicated business. It will be centered, of course, on a chestnut. . . ."

"Why always a chestnut?" Ian asked.

"Because it is the seed of your forest," Merlin exclaimed in some exasperation. "If I'm going to have to explain every detail to you, we're never going to get through this."

Ian shrugged. "Sorry. I just wondered."

"The nut is the seed—the egg, if you will—of the tree, the life symbol of the forest. Every forest in England has its own characteristic seed, and all magic worked in that forest is worked through that seed. Now, do you think you understand sufficiently that we can proceed?"

"Yes, sir." Ian felt like a reprimanded schoolboy. Turning his back once more on the proceedings, he resolved to interfere no further.

"Old Garumpta will no doubt want to select the seed to be used, as it should be as nearly perfect as possible. This is the formula for an ointment that must be rubbed over the nut before it is wrapped in items that have been in frequent contact with the subjects, one from each. This should be done fairly soon, too, so that the characters of the subjects clinging to these articles will have time to invade and permeate the nut. Here, and this is most crucial, is the full text of the spell to be recited at the exchange itself. I have taken great care that the wording is clear and precise, so don't tamper with it in any way. When the final words of it are uttered the nut is to be crushed by a single blow from a mallet made entirely of chestnut wood (Garumpta can probably provide that as well). If everything has been properly prepared, the speaker will have no difficulty crushing it to powder with a reasonably well-aimed stroke. Who, by the way, is to be speaker?"

"Why, we hadn't really gotten far enough to consider that," the Vicar began; then his voice trailed off. There were a few moments of silence, a lively silence filled with unspoken dialogue that Ian James did not like in the least. He could feel two pairs of eyes staring into the back of his head.

"No, thank you," he said, speaking slowly and distinctly, keeping his back turned toward them. "If you are about to suggest what I think you are about to suggest, the answer is 'No, thank you.' I am no conjurer."

"But you are a damned good speaker," the Vicar said. "I cannot think of anyone more perfectly suited to the task."

"Besides," Merlin added, "it would be excellent, shall we say, head insurance."

"I withdrew my head yesterday." Ian struggled to control the resentment rising in him. "I'll make myself useful in other ways—collecting herbs, or whatever. Why don't you say this spell, Vicar? It's more in your line of work."

"I'm getting old. I can't trust my memory well enough, and it cannot be read, but must be spoken, declaimed. Style is all-important in the proper execution of a major spell. And accuracy. I would feel much safer for the entire affair if I knew you were doing the spell. You don't need to understand what you are saying, but it has to be said exactly as written. I've heard it said, by those who ought to know, that you've never dropped a line."

Ian ground his teeth. The old fox; he knew what he was doing, appealing to his vanity like that. He was proud of his justly earned reputation for adherence to the script as written. With sudden vehemence he turned on his tempters.

"I'm not going to be forced into doing one more thing I don't want to do. If I had started saying 'No' to the whole lot of you a bit sooner, I wouldn't be so deep in this miserable business now. I will not do it and that is final."

The Vicar smiled at him paternally. "Oh very well. We'll manage as best we can without you. I must say I admire your fortitude. It's not easy to turn down such a rich part, a regular one-man show. But never mind, if you won't, you won't, and there's no help for it." He turned to the table and began gathering up papers. "Is that the whole of it, then, Master?"

"Yes, that should do it, but it's a tricky business, so don't blame me if it doesn't go well. I've done my best." Merlin bustled over to the cooker like a nervous housewife. "You'll have to wait just a bit while I let this mess cool enough to be safely bottled. Perhaps we could pass the time by giving our temperamental guest a demonstration of the globe."

"No!" Ian cried, backing toward the door. "I—I would prefer not to fool with that thing if you don't mind." It was attracting him again; he could feel it even when he avoided looking at it.

"What's the matter?" Merlin asked, looking at him sharply. "What are you afraid of?"

"I'm not afraid." Ian found himself reluctant to admit the real source of his fear and lamely sought other excuses for his reluctance. "It's just that I don't care to take part in anything of that sort. It isn't the kind of entertainment I go in for, that's all."

The two old men said nothing, but continued to regard him with persistently questioning expressions on their faces. He was starting to feel desperate. No matter how hard he tried to avoid looking at it, the ball kept catching the corner of his eye.

"Look here, Vicar," he started talking rapidly, "I've seen the ball and I'm quite impressed. Now I would consider it a favor to a friend if you would not insist that I have any further dealings with it." He tried to work himself both away from the table and near enough to the door to make an escape if the opportunity arose, but the Vicar always managed to maneuver himself into a position between Ian and the door. Ian was becoming really frightened, beginning to suspect that a trap was being laid for him.

"I don't like the way it keeps attracting me," he stammered. "It's probably nothing to you, but I'm not used to seeing inanimate objects move and change of their own power."

He stopped, for he became aware that the Vicar was staring at him in amazement.

"What are you saying, James? Have you actually seen the globe change? When?"

"Why, it's been doing it ever since we came in here. Haven't you seen it?"

With a sweeping gesture Merlin dropped the robe once more around him and walked slowly toward Ian.

"This requires some looking into," he said.

The deep black pupils of his eyes widened until they completely obliterated the iris, and they stared ominously through Ian as he gestured toward the black morris chair, which Ian found himself standing almost in front of.

"Have a seat."

Before Ian had a chance to realize his peril, much less brace himself for a defense, he was abruptly pushed into the seat. There was no need for restraining straps; the chair itself held him fast. He could move his arms, legs, and head freely, but no matter how he struggled, he was unable to rise.

"He's right, Tom," Merlin cried excitedly, picking up the globe and spinning it skillfully on the tips of his fingers. "It's alive, fairly boiling with life. Perhaps you've struck the right stone after all."

He approached the chair holding the spinning ball aloft. Ian grabbed wildly at his erstwhile drinking partner's sleeve.

"Vicar, get me out of this!"

"It's no use, James," the other replied. "If the power in the globe will communicate with you, you have no choice but to heed. Don't be afraid. You can't come to any harm. The master will guide you and keep constant control over the globe. I'll stay here by you if you wish and keep my hand on your shoulder. The globe may have something to reveal to you. Trust me, please, this once. Afterward if you wish to terminate our friendship, I'll make no further demands on you."

The wizard stood directly in front of him holding the rapidly spinning globe before his face. Ian closed his eyes, clutching the arms of the chair with all his strength. His chest was tight, and he found breathing difficult. He began to sweat heavily.

"Take the globe in your hands," Merlin commanded in a calm compelling voice.

"No!" Ian shook his head, struggling to control his slowly rising hands. He fought hard, but to no purpose. In time he held it in his hands and stared into the depths of his fear.

"Tell us what you see," the quiet voice insisted.

Oh he knew well enough what it was he saw. It had been a rare night recently that he had not dreamed of this very image. The whirling circles of the globe had changed motion and were now moving inward on themselves. He spoke haltingly.

"I am looking into the maelstrom—a great whirlpool of light and color drawing everything into its center. I've seen it before in dreams, but never like this. If I were not so frightened I should find it beautiful—spiraling streams of color, blending and separating, whirling in ever faster and smaller circles toward a bottomless center. There are people in the whirlpool, but they are floating freely, not drawn into the center. I see you, Vicar, and Miss Crawley, and Mompen, and even that bloody Puck. It's coming closer to me now. It's drawing me in! No! Stop it! Get me out of this! Get me out of this!"

His voice had risen to a terrified shriek. The whirlpool before him had rapidly increased in size and speed. It was close to him now and was starting to surround him, powerfully sucking him into its center. The Vicar's hand tightened on his shoulder.

"Take it easy, son. You're safe. Everything's under control. Go with it; don't try to resist it."

Ian sobbed. He had no power to resist the force of the spinning pool. It surrounded him, drawing him in with overwhelming power. As from a great distance he heard the command, "Tell us what you see."

But what he now saw he could not bring himself to tell. He was staring into the center of the cone, and his own face was staring back at him. It was not a reflection he saw, for when he moved his mouth, the face in the well remained still. The expression on that face was grim, but there was no sign of fear.

"What is it?" Ian begged the silent face. "What do you want? Answer me." The face's persistent silent stare angered him. "Answer me, damn you," he shouted. "Answer me."

In answer came only the Vicar's now urgent questions: "What is it, James? What do you see?"

A thin, bitter, mocking smile slowly emerged on the face in the well. Ian lunged toward it, gasping the insistent command that had hounded him into this nightmare, "Tell me what you see!"

Far behind him he heard the Vicar's sudden anxious cry, "Master, something's happened."

The last thing Ian heard was his own wild scream as he fell headlong into the Pit.

Ian was calm when he awoke and filled with a peace that was beyond despair. He felt empty, a not unpleasant sensation. He certainly felt no uncertainty, nor any fear. He knew now that something was required of him and accepted it freely, no matter what it turned out to be. He had no idea where he had been or what he had experienced, but he had none of the confusion usually associated with coming out of a faint. He remembered everything clearly up until his fall but had no recall of what had happened afterward until he had come to himself, still sitting in the old morris chair with his face covered by what seemed to be a wet cloth smelling of incense and lavender. He sat for a while without moving or thinking, enjoying the relief of acceptance. Gradually he became aware of voices near him, excited, disturbed voices.

"I don't know, Tom. It never happened before. I lost control of the globe. It was all I could do to gain it back. I have no idea where he went or what he saw. I lost control when he demanded the globe to answer him. It's almost as if it obeyed him. I don't like it at all. I want you to give him up, do you understand? He's just a bit too extraordinary for our purposes, perhaps."

"But will he be all right?" the other voice queried anxiously.

"We won't know that until he comes to, if he does. I've done what I could for him. Now we'll just have to wait and see."

"Oh dear."

Ian was moved to pity by the Vicar's concern, but he was nonetheless cautious about revealing himself. Along with his newly gained peace and blessed emptiness, he had brought back from the depths of the Pit a sense of caution that now warned him not to reveal that he had heard any of this strange conversation. He moved his arm slowly as though he were just rousing and pushed the cloth from his face. The room was as it had been before, except that the globe had been returned to its pedestal and covered with a square of black cloth. The Vicar and his master stood together at the table watching him. The former rushed over to him at the first sign of life and pumped his hand anxiously.

"My dear James, are you all right?"

"Yes, I think so. A bit shaken up, but all in one piece, I trust."

He rose from the chair with no difficulty and walked over to the cooker.

"Your potion seems to have cooled sufficiently for bottling, Master. I have a rehearsal to make this evening, so perhaps we ought to get going."

Tucking his robe once more over his shoulders, Merlin took from his cabinet a very small bottle and a funnel.

"Do you wish to talk about your experience?" he asked, favoring Ian with a searching look.

"Not especially, thank you." Ian returned his stare. "It was a rather private experience."

"I'm awfully sorry about that," the Vicar murmured. "Nothing of the sort was supposed to happen."

"I know." Ian laid an affectionate hand on the old man's shoulder. "Don't let it bother you. I think on the whole the trip has done me good. But I am sorry for the scare I must have given you. Would it cheer you a bit if I told you I've decided to take the part after all?"

"The spell, you mean? Will you cast the spell?"

"As a personal favor to you."

Merlin corked the small bottle with an emphatic grunt and laid it on the table beside the pile of papers.

"What made you change your mind?" he asked.

Ian smiled. "Perhaps I am gaining a little more confidence in my own powers."

Merlin gave him another questioning look.

"Be careful how you use those powers. They can be treacherous."

He took the small cup down from the shelf above the cooker where he had placed it earlier, handing it to Ian, who took it on the tips of his fingers, as he had seen the others do. The liquid inside the cup had neither color nor odor.

"This was intended for me from the first, wasn't it? What, may I ask, will it bind me to?"

"Nothing more than you are already bound to by other means. It will heighten your perception, though, and make you capable of being more useful to your colleagues in various ways. It would be foolhardy to attempt an important spell without its aid."

"In that case, down it goes."

The stuff tasted remarkably like Cockburn's ruby port.

The four conspirators met at Mrs. Hubbard's Monday afternoon to discuss over tea the information from Cornwall. The ladies were delighted with the sheaf of enticing formulas. There was a great deal of work to be done, but there were four pairs of ready hands waiting to get to it. The Vicar had been busy over the weekend sorting things out and had worked up a schedule and division of labor that was immediately acceptable to everyone.

"Here," he said, removing a packet of papers from his bulging briefcase and laying it on the already crowded tea table. "This is a list of the ingredients needed for the various potions. Look it over and see what you already have on hand. There are a lot of wild herbs and the like that we men can gather off the moor the first chance we get. And these are actual instructions for preparing the stuff. I think we shall leave that part of it up to you ladies, if you don't mind. I'm not an especially good cook, and we'll be busy enough getting the spell down perfect."

"Who's going to cast it?" Miss Crawley asked absently, scrawling marks and notations on the list.

"I am," said Ian.

The estate agent's eyes widened. "Really?"

"Upon my honor. I was elected in Cornwall and after careful consideration accepted."

"Isn't that grand?" Mrs. Hubbard cried. "Now you really are one of us."

"Yes, I suppose I am."

While the Vicar and the two ladies studied over and discussed the contents of the lists, Ian sat back in his chair watching the two boys in the garden next door attempting to kick their unruly football. Most of the time their feet rose far wide of the mark, causing them to lose their balance and fall over in the damp grass. Occasionally one of them did succeed in making contact, with nearly disastrous results. The first kick struck the kitchen window, but fortunately lacked the force to break it; the second one landed the ball deep in the branches of a large juniper tree that stood against the wall below a bedroom window, and it took considerable shaking and poking to dislodge it; the third kick sent the wayward ball sailing neatly over the low back hedge into Mrs. Hubbard's kitchen garden.

"I beg your pardon," Ian said, rising and executing a theatrical bow in Mrs. Hubbard's direction. "But your garden has been visited by a runaway football. With your permission I shall endeavor to return it to its owners."

"Thank you, Mr. James. That's very thoughful of you."

Marian Crawley stared after his gracefully retreating back.

"I must congratulate you on your protégé, Dr. Heaton," she commented. "I don't know what you and your master did to him, but it certainly has produced results."

The Vicar frowned. "I don't know that it was anything we did at all. Something happened to him that I don't myself understand. And he cannot or will not talk about it. But whatever the cause, I must say I'm glad he's come around at last. It makes everything less complicated."

"It's nice to see him so much at ease," Mrs. Hubbard murmured benevolently.

The door swung open with violent suddenness, and Ian ran into the room holding something tenderly in his cupped hands. The look of distress on his face brought the others at once to their feet. On the palm of his hand lay Mompen, looking pale and ill, his eyes closed.

"I can't find his heart," Ian panted.

"Wouldn't be of much help if you could," Miss Crawley snapped, reaching into her handbag. "It's too small for you to hear." She opened a small vanity case she had removed from her bag and laid the mirror against the fairy's mouth. A spot of gray film slowly developed. "Well, he's alive at least. Do you have any spirits, Mrs. Hubbard?"

The widow shook her head. "Would tea do?"

"Wait, I've something here," Ian exclaimed. He laid the unconscious fairy gently on the table and hurried out to the entrance hall, where he had deposited a package. In it were two bottles, for, tempted by the exhilaration that had possessed him since his experience in Cornwall, he had bought a scandalously expensive bottle of Madeira to have on hand for some special occasion. But for his present purposes he took out the other bottle, the inevitable Cockburn's port, and brought it into the room. The others were kneeling on the floor in front of the table. Miss Crawley raised Mompen into a partially sitting position, supporting his back with the index finger of her left hand. In her right she held a small coffee spoon she had taken from the table. Ian poured out a few drops of the wine into the spoon and watched as the estate agent gently but persistently forced the liquid into Mompen's mouth.

"Come now, dear," she urged, "you're going to be all right. Drink a bit for Marian. There's a good lad."

Mompen swallowed and spluttered. His head turned a little and his eyelids moved. Ian refilled the spoon. The second dose went down more easily. Mompen opened his eyes and smiled dreamily.

"Man's potion," he murmured. "Very good."

Before he could drop back again Miss Crawley gave him a slight shake.

"Here, wake up, now," she said sharply. "Shame on you giving us all such a fright."

Mompen blinked and sat up, staring in confusion at the circle of faces surrounding him.

Ian broke a small piece off his slice of bread and handed it to him. He seized it greedily and swallowed it in one convulsive gulp.

"My God, he's starved," the Vicar whispered.

"Don't do that, Mompen," Miss Crawley scolded. "You'll get a bellyache if you eat like that."

"I have one already, Marian," he answered meekly. "I am so awfully hungry."

Ian broke off another piece and held it tantalizingly just out of his reach.

"Slowly, this time," he remonstrated.

"Yes, sir."

Ian gave him the piece and watched closely as he took a careful bite and dutifully chewed it.

"You are at Mrs. Hubbard's," Ian explained, forestalling the onslaught of questions that the little fairy was obviously preparing to launch. "I found your pram attached to a ball the children accidentally kicked over the hedge. How you got that far I don't know."

"I think I fell out of the window. I was in a tree the last I remember. You see, I couldn't get food, and I felt I was dying. It seemed too bad, because things were going nicely, and with a little time I think I could get her consent. I didn't have the strength left to look for food. I placed myself under the King's protection and went to rest on the window ledge where the passing wind might be able to do his bidding. And I think it must have. Could I have some more potion, please?"

Ian made a quick mathematical calculation based on the estimated safe level of alcohol concentration in the bloodstream by weight and shook his head.

"I think you've had enough in your present condition. It is a strong potion, and an overdose can cause grievous reactions. Take the advice of one who has suffered the consequences rather too frequently."

Miss Crawley clapped a discreet hand over her mouth.

"Perhaps you ought to have a spot of Mrs. Hubbard's tea instead. It is a potent draught, but not so treacherous as this gentleman's brew."

Mompen was now recovering rapidly, for he took advantage of the diversion caused by the search for a suitable container for his tea to investigate unsupervised the bounty of the table. He was discovered a minute later, struggling to free himself from the sticky center of a treacle tart into which he had in his eagerness fallen face forward. When Miss Crawley pried him loose, he came up grinning and licking as much of his treacle-coated face as he could reach.

"Don't bother about me," he said. "I'm fine."

"You are an incorrigible imp," Miss Crawley growled, applying a damp towel to his face with punishing roughness.

"Gently, Miss Crawley," Ian interposed. "That is hardly the way to treat the Lastborn of the Firstborn." He firmly removed the grateful fairy from the estate agent's clutches. "Now that you are feeling better, perhaps you would like to tell us how things are going for you in the world of men."

Mompen sat on the edge of Ian's upturned palm while the others drew their chairs around in a very tight circle, leaning close so that they could hear his small voice. He told them in detail about his successes and his difficulties. After the dreadful journey downstairs the first night, he had discovered that if he were clever he could usually get where he wanted by dropping into one of the deep pockets of the mother's housecoat, which generally contained at least one handkerchief under which he could hide. Had it not been for the scarcity of food, everything would have been proceeding splendidly. The child was pleasant and amenable. He had little chance to talk to her, since there were always other members of the family about, except when she was put in for her afternoon nap. She was tired then, though, and was willing to listen for only a short while. But Mompen was far from discouraged.

"If I could be sure of getting enough to eat," he insisted, "I would just hold out until I had her, if it takes all spring. I know I could persuade her in the end."

"We should be able to work out some method of smuggling food in to you," Ian said. "You have a passkey, don't you, Miss Crawley?"

The estate agent fixed him with an indignant stare.

"I do, Mr. James," she said. "But I would consider it unethical to use it to gain illegal entry."

"Unethical? At this late date are you going to start quibbling over ethics? My dear lady, it is neither ethical nor legal to steal other people's children, and yet that is what we're all about to do, isn't it? Is there any time, Mompen, when we can be sure no one will be at home?"

"Yes, sir; on Friday afternoons they always go to the library and have dinner out. I have heard the children speak of it frequently."

"Splendid. Now a tin like this" (he took a small tin from the table) "should hold enough bread and cheese to keep you for a week. What about water?"

"The bathroom tap drips. I have a toothpaste lid I found in the dustbin that I can fill there."

"You are a resourceful little rascal, aren't you?" Ian laughed. "Where can food be hidden safely that you'll have no trouble getting at it?"

"In the cot springs. That's where I sleep. The lady never cleans there."

Ian gave Miss Crawley a questioning look. "If my scheme is too much for your delicate scruples, you can have another key made, and I'll take care of things myself."

"That will not be necessary, Mr. James. I can handle it."

"Good girl." He patted her arm condescendingly. "So, Mompen, I think that takes care of business; now what about pleasure? Are you having a good time, as I told you to? Do you like the family? Do you like the baby's life?"

"Yes, sir," Mompen replied smartly. "Yes to everything. It's a very different sort of life from what I'm used to, of course, and I'm often homesick. But there are many things that I like very much. Like Ah-yo. That's just wonderful."

The humans looked at one another in puzzlement.

"We don't understand what you mean by that, Mompen," Miss Crawley explained.

"That's what the baby calls it. I think the others say it a little differently."

"Could you perhaps describe it for us?"

"It's, well it's as though the birds called in our language. I'll try to do a little of it, though it's difficult for me." He wrinkled his low forehead in a frown of concentration that made the pupils of his eyes almost meet. Then he sang in a shrill voice, strained by the effort to reproduce unfamiliar sounds, but surprisingly accurate in pitch.

The King of France had forty thousand men.
He marched them up the hill, and then back down again.

"Ah-yo?" Mrs. Hubbard murmured. "Music? Song? Radio! That's it, radio!"

"I wonder why all our nursery songs have to be so damned political," growled the Vicar.

Ian turned astonished to Miss Crawley. "Don't they have music?"

"They may have had knowledge of it in the past; the King's heralds played a sort of primitive music, if you remember. But for as long as I have been associated with Garumpta's people, I have heard them make no music nor speak of it. They are experts, though, at the imitation of the natural music of the forest around them: bird, animal, and insect calls, and the songs of the wind."

"Oh that's not the same as Ah-yo," Mompen cried excitedly. "My people have no art that comes close to it. I wish I could teach it to them, but I'm not very good at it. You should hear Penny; when she does it it is a delight, it is beautiful."

"If she takes your place, perhaps she would be willing to teach your people this art," Mrs. Hubbard suggested. "It is not difficult to learn."

Mompen clasped his hands in joy at this prospect.

"Yes, she could, and I'm sure she'd be willing." He became so excited that he nearly fell from Ian's hand. "Oh dear, I must get right back so I can talk to her about it. I feel strong now that I have eaten. Could you take me back, please, Marian?"

"Now?" Miss Crawley glanced at her watch. "It's late, but I suppose I could make an unscheduled call to check on that faulty electrical switch."

"I'll pack you a lunch," said Mrs. Hubbard, briskly cutting a slice of bread into cubes of convenient size.

"Bless me, I nearly forgot," the Vicar cried, taking from his breast pocket a small crystalline bottle. "You ought to have this handy. It's a releasing potion. When you have gained the child's unqualified consent, you should both partake of it, making some sort of pledge to the exchange. Be sure you speak both your names. Do you have that, now?"

"Yes, sir," Mompen replied solemnly. "I understand. I won't forget."

"Oh I say," Ian exclaimed, jumping up. "I have got to run. We've an early rehearsal tonight, and I ought to go over my first act lines." He set Mompen down on the tea table a safe distance from the plate of treacle tarts and, removing a chestnut burr from his pocket, laid it beside Mompen.

"Good luck, Mompen, my lad. You are a credit to your people."

"Thank you, sir," Mompen murmured, blushing.

"Thank you for your tea, Mrs. Hubbard," Ian continued, gathering up his hat and coat. "It was, as always, splendid. Call me, Vicar, when you're ready to go herb hunting. I'm free most days. Cheer up, Miss Crawley; your life of crime won't bother you so much when you get used to it. Cheerio!"

The Vicar could not help thinking it was a splendid exit, if a bit overdone. But before the other actors in the scene could recover, Ian was back again.

"Now, do I strike you as the sort of chap who'd run off without his potion?" He whisked the bottle of port off the tea table and swung out once more, whistling Mompen's song about the King of France.

Chapter 9

The Sorcerer's Apprentice

Spring came to Elvinwood, and with it green leaves, crocuses, tulips, almost constant rain, and the spring production of *The Sorcerer.* There was general agreement among the townspeople and the local critics that it was the best production the group had mounted in many years, and that Ian James in the name part had really outdone himself.

It ran for two weeks to filled houses. It was the Friday of that second week that the American baby came at last to a decision concerning Mompen's strange proposal. She had wakened that morning unusually alert, and this feeling of exhilaration and expectancy had not diminished as the day passed. She had sat most of the morning on the playroom floor joggling her stuffed rabbit absent-mindedly, watching the others racing small cars, coloring pictures, squabbling, crying. They tried in vain to include her in their rites, but all she wanted to do was talk to Mompen. At last naptime came, the bedroom door closed behind her retreating mother, and they were alone. She stretched out comfortably on her back, holding her bare toes in her hands, while her companion took up his customary position next to her left ear (on the side away from the door, so he could hide quickly in the springs if someone came in).

"Talk to me, Mompen," she said.

"What about?"

"About everything. Tell me everything."

For once she did not fall asleep, but lay listening in wide-eyed comprehension. Mompen talked rapidly, eagerly, concentrating all his powers of persuasion on this effort. He told her about life in the forest, its delights and its hardships; he spoke at length and with passion of the fate of his people and of the important part she could play in their salvation, if she were willing. He described vividly the great Midsummer feast that she might be taking part in, though he found it difficult to control his own tears at the realization that he would not be there. The King, though, would be there, and the beautiful Queen Titania. Oh the King, he told her, was grand and fearsome.

"And the other lord, your father, is he fearsome?" Penny asked somewhat timorously.

"He is chief of our tribe, and that is a terrible responsibility. So he is often stern and even harsh. But he will not be so with you. He will be gentle and very kind to you. And my mother, the Lady Aneelen, is the most kindly creature that ever dwelled in the Fernwood."

"What about my fairy prince? Is he kind?"

Mompen frowned. He had avoided as much as possible any discussion of the Puck's personality. Indeed, he had not allowed himself to think too frequently or too closely about just who he was preparing this child to be bound to. Now he was faced with the need to give a direct answer to a painfully direct question. He was Garumpta's son and shared his sire's passion for honesty. He could not lie, but he would choose his words with great care. After some thought he answered.

"I do not know your prince well. I saw him only once and that in rather hard circumstances. He was not very kind to me because I am ugly, and my ugliness seemed to frighten him. But you will not be ugly; you will be beautiful, for so the spell is to be set. He was not kind to the man he caught either. I'm not sure why; I suspect he was afraid of him as well. But he will not be afraid of you. You will be his love, and one is always kind to those he loves, eh?"

Penny wasn't sure about that. Her family all claimed to love one another, but they were not always kind. She sighed.

"If he is at all like you, Mompen, I'm sure to love him."

"Will you be his princess, then?" Mompen could scarcely control his eagerness. "Will you exchange with me Midsummer Night?"

The baby hesitated a moment, examining her toes with scholarly intensity. "All right," she said at last. "I'll do it. For you."

Mompen squirmed down into his nest in the dust-clogged cot springs, and with great effort dragged up a crystalline bottle that, small as it was, was nearly twice as large as the fairy who struggled with it.

"What's that?" Penny cried, her relief at finally having made the decision changing rapidly to fear.

"It's a releasing potion. It won't hurt you. It just makes going easier. Don't take it unless you're sure you want to make the exchange."

"I'm sure, Mompen, but I'm scared, too. Will the exchange hurt?"

"You won't know it's happening. One night you'll go to sleep as usual, but when you wake up you'll be a fairy princess. Here, can you help me with this cork?"

Still a bit clumsy with her hands, Penny applied her newly acquired little sharp teeth to the cork with good results.

"You can't change your mind once you take this," Mompen reminded her. She nodded. "Will you teach my people Ah-yo?"

"I'll do my best. I promise."

"All right. Now we have to say something. I'll say it first, then you say it, changing the names to fit."

He stood stiffly erect beside her, his hands on the bottle.

"I, Mompen, lastborn son of Garumpta the Fernlord, pledge to exchange myself for the human child, Penny, lastborn daughter of Mr. Pierce of Pennsylvania, and I drink to the binding of that pledge."

Penny sat up and helped tip the bottle until a few drops of the liquid fell into his mouth.

"Does it taste bad?"

"No, it tastes all right. Nothing near so good as man's potion, though. Now you say the pledge in your own way, and then drink the rest."

"All right. I'll try. You help me. I, Penny Pierce, want to change places with my friend, Mompen, and become a fairy princess."

At a nod from Mompen she drained the little bottle.

"Mmm. Rose hips syrup. Oh dear, someone's coming."

Mompen quickly corked the bottle and slid it down under the mattress. Then he kissed the baby's cheek. "Good-bye, Penny. I'm going home now. Good luck to you."

"Good-bye, Mompen. I'm going to miss you."

After a moment the door opened, and her mother came into the room, carrying her sweater and cap.

"Are you awake already, sweetheart? Come get your wraps on. It's such a nice day, we're going to take a little walk by the pond before we go to the library. Want to go for a walk, love?"

She was surprised to find the baby not only awake, but also in tears.

About fifteen miles north of Elvinwood in the midst of wild moorland, kept open and free by the National Trust, stood Great Pond, a large expanse of water beloved of naturalists, yachters, and small children with sand pails. Even when the weather forbade bathing, as it often did on the windy moor, the environs of the pond were invaded regularly by armies of bird watchers and troops of horsemen, as well as the unashamed walker who had no more to gain from his visit than the pleasure he had in it.

On this particular Friday afternoon in the latter part of March, there were few who would dare to venture into this wild area for any purpose. Though the weather had been improving, the wind over the moor was still brisk and chill. Two men, however, had braved the damp: an elderly man and another of middle age. They might have been a professor of botany and his student assistant on a search for specimens as they crawled about the marshy head of the pond, occasionally picking up a bit of creeping vine or the newly arrived green shoot of some wild herb, studying and discussing it before either casting it aside or placing it in the sack the older man carried. But their conversation was hardly the sort one would be likely to hear from such an academic pair. The younger man was muttering words in singsong fashion, like a Bible lesson learned by rote, while the other one commented and corrected, consulting now and then a much-folded sheet of yellowed paper that he had in his pocket.

" 'Bone and flesh, blood and sinew, touch and tasting, smell and hearing, seeing feel not . . .' "

" 'Touch not'! 'Touch not'!"

"Oh sorry. 'Seeing touch not . . .' I say, would that really matter? They mean about the same thing."

"I have no idea whether it would matter or not. I'm only a minor student of the art. But of this much I'm certain: if they were vital words, and most of them are, a mistake like that could bring disaster. You'd best take it from 'Upon this stroke . . .' "

"Right-o. 'Upon this stroke let us be changed. . . .' "

" 'Them,' James, 'them'; not 'us'! Unless you're planing to go along for the ride. With no one to exchange for you, you might end up hovering in some half world, neither existing nor at rest, like one of those gory apparitions that show up at manorial houseparties."

Ian sat down on a rock jutting out into the stream, pounding his head with his muddy fists.

"Maybe you picked the wrong man for the job, Vicar. I just don't seem to be getting it."

"Oh come now, don't be discouraged. We licked old J. W. Wells between Truro and Winchester, didn't we?"

Ian laughed. "He's stopped every show. They made me repeat the whole bloody thing last night."

"There, you see? We work well together. Between my tutoring and your voice, we are going to produce the most magnificent spell cast in the forests of Britain since Morgan le Fay."

The Vicar leaned forward, staring intently at the ground near his feet. Then he reached down and picked up a clump of sorrel-like grasses.

"Aha, this is what I've been looking for. Very important to get the right one. A similar species is deadly poison."

"What's it for?" Ian asked a little anxiously.

"Why, for you, my dear, along with a few other ingredients it would probably be best for you not to inquire into more closely. . . ."

"Eye of newt and toe of frog?"

"Practically. The end result will set the spell."

"What does that mean?"

"Well, you're saying the right words in the right order

now, aren't you? Yet nothing's happened. Just before you are to speak it in earnest, I'll give you this potion. Whatever next you say will have the power of a spell."

"Oh I see." Ian tried to sound casual. "How are things progressing these days with all those potions?"

"Fairly well," the Vicar replied. "The ladies have run into some difficulty on the ointment that is to be rubbed into the nut. They have not been able to locate an essential oil that is rather rare these days. I do hope they locate it soon, as the preparation of the seed should be taken care of before another month is out."

Ian suddenly felt a strange sensation, a feeling of instant alertness, as if he had heard a sound that startled him. He sat upright and looked inquiringly about him. The Vicar touched his arm.

"Do you feel it, too?"

Ian nodded. "What does it mean?"

"One of us is near, someone who has shared the master's cup."

Ian pointed silently to a barren hillock some two hundred yards from the pond. A group was walking along the footpath, hunching over against the onslaught of the wind: a man, three children, and a woman with a young child strapped to her back. The child was looking directly at them, though they were hidden from view.

"Jolly good," the Vicar whispered. "He's got her. Bully for Mompen."

"I don't understand."

"The potion, man. He's given her the potion. She is sensitive to us now, and we to her. She must have given her consent."

They watched furtively as the family approached the pond.

"What an opportunity," the Vicar whispered. "We ought to get something for the nut while we have her. Her cap, that would do nicely. Do you still have her, James?"

Ian nodded.

"Fine. Let's see how your powers are developing. Get her to drop her cap. That's it. Concentrate now. Make her drop her cap."

The family passed within a few feet of the two men. The baby looked listlessly over the rather monotonous terrain. She usually enjoyed these weekly excursions, but today nothing seemed to give her pleasure. She knew that when she was put to bed that night she would be alone. Mompen would no longer sit by her ear telling her about the great Midsummer feast. She sighed. Midsummer seemed years away. Then she heard it, a voice in her head, talking to her the way Mompen did. It told her to take off her pink knitted cap and let it fall on the ground. Now, that was silly. The wind whistled fiercely around her ears; she had no desire to dispense with what little protection the cap offered. But the voice in her head insisted. She must give up her cap. Mompen would want her to. Reluctantly she loosened the string under her chin and let the cap drop over the side of the back-pack. The voice thanked her and added something that sounded like "Have a good time." It was the sort of thing Mompen might say. And it wasn't bad advice. Nothing could be gained by brooding. She might as well enjoy what babyhood she had left. Somehow this contact with a friendly force had lifted her spirits. She felt less alone.

The family was getting into their automobile, having decided upon investigation that it was still too cold for walking on the moor, before the mother noticed the absence of the pink cap. With much grumbling, they all returned to the pond in search of it. When they passed over the spot where she knew she had dropped it, Penny observed that it was already gone. Whoever had wanted it had taken it and left, for she no longer felt the strange sensation she had had before, and she heard no more voices.

When Ian James returned to his flat, tired, hungry, and coated with mud, he was surprised and a little disconcerted to be met in the reception hall by his landlady, a bustling prototype of the cinema comedy landlady.

"Oh my dear," she cried. "I thought you'd never come in. Wherever have you been all day? You had a caller this morning. You could never guess who it was: Miss Crawley, the estate agent. She was quite put out when she found you were not at home. She left a message for you. It feels as if there's a key in it." She produced an envelope from her apron pocket, favoring Ian the while with a questioning look. "She's not bad-looking, if a bit angular."

"I hadn't noticed, Mrs. Parker," Ian replied shortly. "I am acquainted with the lady only through business connections."

He read the note, which had been written on a sheet of business stationery with Miss Crawley's name, qualifications, and telephone number printed at the top.

Mr. James: [she had written in impeccable script]

Mrs. H. has located the stuff we need, and I am driving her up to Oxford to fetch it. It is an urgent matter that cannot be put off. Would you please take care of my usual Friday duties for me? Have a good time!

With thanks,
M. Crawley

Ian glanced quickly at his watch. It was after five. He had no idea how long the Americans would be about their dinner. Pocketing the note and the key, he hurried out. As he turned the corner to the Americans' house, he understood a little better Miss Crawley's reluctance to take on this task. It was rather unnerving to play burglar in broad daylight. He had no idea what sort of excuse he could give for his prowling if he were caught.

The house was empty, brooding under the influence of twilight shadow. Ian paused in the hallway, wondering what he should do. He felt something tug lightly at his trouser cuff.

"Here I am, sir."

Dropping to his knees, Ian lifted Mompen from the doormat where he stood patiently waiting to be called for, with his pram and the empty crystalline bottle beside him.

"So you've gone and done it."

"Yes sir, I've completed my mission, and now I should very much like to go home."

"And you will, as soon as possible. But first things first, and the first thing on my mind is getting out of here before I get arrested for housebreaking."

He tucked Mompen into his pram, placing it and the

bottle in his breast pocket, and slipped quietly out the door and through the gate.

He stopped briefly at the greengrocer's shop down the street. His original plan for the evening meal, a quick sandwich of some sort, seemed inappropriate for company, so he purchased a package of frozen rissoles and a tin of beans and a pint of cider.

When he had returned to his own place, he went at once to the kitchen, a cluttered, untidy little room. He set his package on the table and removed Mompen from his pocket. The fairy sat cross-legged on the table looking about him with great interest.

"Depressing, isn't it?" Ian chuckled, laying the rissoles on the grill and pouring the beans into a saucepan. "You've had an experience of human family life. Well, this is how it is for those of us who travel alone. What would you say to a hearty bachelor's tea?"

"I'd be pleased with anything that isn't bread and cheese."

"Yes, I imagine that could get very tiring as a steady diet."

"Please, sir," Mompen asked shyly, "do you have any of that excellent potion? I should really like some if it's allowed."

"In moderation it's allowed." Ian removed the cap from a small bottle of HP sauce, rinsed it out, filled it about a quarter full of port, and presented it to Mompen. "I hope you will excuse me if I do not join you. I have a performance to give tonight, you see, and the potion slows the tongue."

Mompen took a sip of his port and sighed happily. "Very good indeed. Pray, what is a performance?"

"Why, a theatrical performance, you know. Or do you? Well, it's like, let's see, it's something like Ah-yo with action, movement. Like this." He did a music-hall strut over to the cooker and turned the rissoles. Mompen watched him in blank puzzlement.

"You don't understand," Ian said.

"No, sir, I'm afraid not. My people have nothing like that."

"Don't your people have any rituals? Like spells, only acted out." He thought of the spell they would be acting out in only three months' time. "No, that's not it. It isn't serious, like a spell. It's done just for the pleasure of doing it or watching it being done."

"But is there magic in it?"

"Not all those who practice the art agree on that, Mompen. I suspect from my own experience that there is some sort of magic involved. I have practiced this magic and have experienced it practiced by others. It consists of becoming someone else for a while and yet never really stopping being oneself. That's a form of magic, I suppose."

"Oh I should surely like to see you do that."

"You have your chance tonight, Mompen. Since Mrs. Hubbard and Miss Crawley are off potion hunting, there is no one but me to take you back to the forest. I'll be done by eleven and can take you home then. As you're going to have to hang around here anyway, you might just as well come to the show. I can attach your pram to the top of one of the flats. If you stay inside you can't fall, and by looking over the side you can watch the magic from a most unusual point of view."

Mompen was excited by the prospect, but also somewhat apprehensive.

"Oh I don't know what Father would say. If it's anything like pantomime he'd be wild."

"I'll take responsibility for the decision." Ian prepared an acceptable serving of crumbled rissole and mashed beans on a coaster, filled his own plate, and sat at the table near his guest. "If it worries you, he doesn't really have to know about it."

"Nothing is hidden from Garumpta the Fernlord," Mompen pronounced as solemnly as he could with his mouth full of beans. He ate with his fingers, sucking them clean noisily after each mouthful.

Ian smiled. "I admire and respect your lord, Mompen. But I'm afraid I would not enjoy having him for a father."

"Oh he is tough, sir. He needs to be, for it is not easy leading a dying people. But don't think you have seen him as he really is. He does not reveal himself to strangers."

Ian recalled his last interview with the Fernlord. Then

he rose and went to the desk in his lounge. Taking from the penholder something that looked like an intricately carved toothpick, he brought it into the kitchen and laid it in front of Mompen.

"Perhaps I know him better than you think."

Mompen examined the stick with delight.

"He gave you this, sir? I do not know of any other human he has so honored. I wonder what moved him to make such a gesture toward you. He was rather down on you at first, sneaking into the hall like that."

"The Lord Garumpta and I came to an understanding, Mompen, on the basis of my evaluation of his lastborn son."

Mompen blushed and smiled shyly. "Oh you ought to have known my brother, sir. He was a worthy heir to the Fernlord's throne."

Ian had turned back to the cooker, preparing to brew a pot of tea. But now he was being presented with a splendid oppportunity to get a bit closer to a truth that had been tantalizing him for some time. Taking up the bottle of port, he refilled the sauce cap and resumed his seat, hunching over the table and resting his chin on his folded arms in such a way that his face was only a few inches from that of his guest.

"Tell me about your brother, Mompen."

"Oh he was a splendid fellow, handsome as a jay, though you may find that hard to believe, looking at me. He was very kind as well. He was one of the few of our people who never made me miserable. I would have descended into the Pit for him." He took a great gulp of his drink and rubbed awkwardly at his eyes. "I still miss him awfully."

"I have heard it said that he was something of a rascal," Ian persisted.

Mompen favored him with a quizzical, crooked grin. "Oh he was that to be sure. There's a bit of the Puck in all of us, you know."

"He liked the girls, didn't he?"

"Yes, sir, he had many women. Humans, of course, for there were no females in our tribe of suitable age for him. He took his pleasure where he could. Do you think ill of him for that?"

"He was Garumpta's son and your brother; I should find it difficult to think ill of anyone with such a kinship."

"The only one he really cared for was Marian. He loved her very much. You might find that hard to understand, but she was a fine-looking girl." Mompen shook his head. "Your people do not age well."

"She has had a difficult life," Ian commented.

"Yes, sir. I know. I believe she must have loved him as well. She was going to join the tribe so they could marry. Fremna gave up his other girls for her sake. That is why they killed him." He stared morosely into his once more empty cup. "Humans behave very strangely sometimes."

"There is a bit of the demon in all of us, Mompen. Here, have some tea to clear your head while I change my clothes."

In the bedroom Ian quickly discarded his knitted shirt and mud-stained trousers. He took from his closet a pair of close-fitting black trousers made of some artificial material that shone like silk under the stage lights. The shirt he put on was one he had purchased from a Chelsea boutique specifically for this role and with an eye toward the role he would be playing in the forest that summer. Not only did it have a silky texture and a gracefully flowing cut, but it was thin and cool as well, a considerable asset under the heavy black cloak he wore.

Returning to the kitchen he found Mompen dozing in boozy content, his head halfway into his tea.

"You were right about that potion, sir. It has fearsome power. I suspect it has quite done me in."

"The effect is fortunately temporary. Finish your tea and climb into your pram. You can sleep it off on the way to the auditorium."

Chapter 10

The Fernlord's Tale

It rained that night, not gently and warmly, as it should rain in spring, but in a heavy, chill downpour. Elvinwood Auditorium was sold out in spite of the weather, and the show proved well worth going out in the rain to see. Far from being dampened by the rain, Ian James put on a performance that astonished even himself. The Vicar's training had paid off, but there was more to it than that. He could feel the same power he had turned on the baby on the moor that afternoon working in him while he was on stage. And it was never far from his mind that in the auditorium was a representative of an alien race to whom his native magic was unknown.

It was nearly eleven-thirty before the guard finally locked up, and Ian, who was hiding among the side curtains, was able to dislodge his waiting guest from the top edge of a flat.

A clock somewhere was striking midnight as Ian reached the forest, wet through from his run through the darkened town. Here it was warmer, and the rain filtering through the trees fell with less force. Slowing to a walk, Ian removed the companion he had smuggled into the play from the shelter of his pocket and put him on his shoulder.

The forest was silent and heavy with moisture; footsteps sloshed rather than crunched. Mompen sat on Ian's shoulder looking about him in delight. His head was so full of wonders that he was not quite able to make sense of anything, especially the man whose ear he now clung to for support. Even the familiar forest looked strange from up here; perhaps this was how humans saw it. Be that as it may, he was terribly glad to be back in it. The evening had been a bit much for him. In spite of all that had been said to prepare him for his first experience of theater, he had been frightened more than once and had longed for the curtain to close and break the spell. Yet it had been wonderful. Never had he heard such Ah-yo coming not from a box, but from the mouths of creatures making the most incredible sounds. But nothing any of them did could equal the marvelous Ah-yo that the strange man who now carried him could produce. Turning his head, Mompen looked at the huge profile next to him. It was hard for him to study human faces, especially at close range; they were so vast. He could tell them apart, of course. One human didn't look like another any more than one fairy looked like another. But careful analysis, feature by feature, was a considerable task, rather like surveying a mountain. The mountain he now surveyed was a craggy one, like those jutting out from the southern coast of Cornwall. Mompen sighed. In such a study he could find no answers to his questions.

"How are you doing there?" The great mouth opened and words roared out. It was unnerving being so close to the creature's mouth; the sound of his voice was so loud.

"I'm fine, thank you, sir. C-could I ask you a question?"

"By all means."

"After what I saw you do tonight, I cannot understand how it is that you were caught like that at the feast and, well, forced to do the King's will. Why didn't you show your power then?"

The man laughed. Mompen did not like human laughter, though he understood that it was not usually malicious.

"Have I said something foolish?" he asked sheepishly, for it seemed to be his question that inspired this disconcerting sound.

"No, not really. I wasn't laughing at you, just at the whole situation. You see, the magic I worked onstage tonight depends not on me alone, but upon all the others as well—the people onstage, the people working behind the stage and, perhaps most of all, the people watching. Without their aid I cannot perform a spell of that sort. Any other powers I may possess I wasn't aware of at the time of my captuure. Besides, I think I should find it beastly difficult to conjure when I am frightened half out of my senses."

"Oh I can understand that, sir. I am often frightened. Do you go up in flames like that every night?"

"Every night and twice on Saturday. But after tomorrow night I'll be finished with it, and I must say it will be something of a relief. I don't usually like seeing a show end, but this one has been rather a strain. One spell in the afternoon and another at night. Sometimes I'm not sure which is real and which illusion. After tomorrow I'll be able to devote all my attention to launching you successfully into the world of men." Ian aimed his torch downward and began studying the underbrush. "Let me see," he said, as though to himself. "It's somewhere around here, isn't it? I haven't been out here by myself before. Oh yes, here's the fallen tree Miss Crawley and I sat on, and that's your thicket."

Crouching down he removed Mompen from his shoulder, setting him on the damp ground. "There you are, delivered to the door. Run along now and give my best regards to your sire and his kind lady. Cheerio!"

Mompen seized his trouser cuff, clinging determinedly. "Don't go, please, sir. You must come in that Father may thank you."

"Oh no. I think I had best go on. You'll want to be alone with your people after being gone so long. I would only be in the way."

"You must come in, I beg you. Father would be furious if I didn't bring you. Wait here, just for a minute, please."

Seeing his anxiety, Ian relented. "Very well, if it's expected. I certainly wouldn't want to get you into trouble."

Before he had finished speaking, the fairy had disappeared. Ian had never before been alone in the woods at night. He was thankful for his newfound courage and confidence, for it was an awesome place, strangely, unnaturally quiet, oppressed by the rain-soaked air that surrounded it. There was no wind; nothing moved; no creature raised its voice in pain or lust or challenge. A leaf fluttered soggily to the ground beside him, causing him to start in alarm. Then something struck his ankle smartly. It was a chestnut, powerfully and accurately thrown from the thicket.

Garumpta himself met him at the entrance, a flaming torch held aloft in one hand, a carved wooden walking stick in the other. Without speaking he turned and led the way down the length of the Great Hall, turning off abruptly into a narrow corridor near the Throne Room. Ian was aware for the first time of the complexity and size of the Fernlord's castle. Their journey ended in a small, attractive chamber carpeted in moss. A fire glowed in the center of the room, filling it with welcome warmth and dryness. Against the wall farthest from the doorway lay a long bench also cushioned in moss. The old hunchback was carefully arranging on a round table in front of the bench two mugs and a platter of dried fungi of some sort. Depositing his torch in a bracket in the wall of skillfully woven vine, Garumpta seated himself on the bench and gestured to Ian to do likewise. The servant filled the two mugs from a pitcher and at a motion from his master departed, leaving the pitcher on the table. Garumpta raised his glass, and Ian followed suit.

"You will pardon the Lady Aneelen if she fails to join us," the old lord grunted. "She is at present overcome by a bad case of motherhood."

He invited Ian with a gesture to partake of the strange stuff on the platter. It was roasted to crispness and tasted vaguely of meat.

"I should not have intruded at all, my lord, if Mompen hadn't insisted."

"It is well that you heeded him," Garumpta muttered. "It would have been unfortunate, wouldn't it, if I had been obliged to greet him after such an absence with a strong lesson in manners?"

Ian had call again to reflect on the difficulty of being the Fernlord's son.

"He needs no lessons at all, my lord, as far as I can judge. He has performed his task well and with no little courage. I am certain that life must have been easier for your ancestors, but we live no longer as our ancestors lived. A less hardy soul than Mompen would have given it up."

Garumpta nodded. "I should not have let him go if I hadn't thought he could do the job. And what of you?" The old lord was regarding him with keenly inquisitive eyes. "You have been keeping busy, I take it. I detect, if I am not mistaken, a change in you."

"You are observant, my lord," Ian smiled. "Yes, I have undergone a change of some sort—exactly what, I find it difficult to say for certain. I may have gained something; I don't know yet. But what I have lost I'm glad to be rid of."

Garumpta smiled. "It is your fear you have lost, isn't it?"

"Precisely. And I must say I find my visits to these halls much more comfortable without it."

"And how has this come about?"

Ian stared into his mug. He had spoken to no one, not even the Vicar, about his experience in Cornwall. He found himself reluctant now to expose it to the scrutiny of any other feeling creature. Garumpta's eyes he could feel searching him out. He would have to answer, and he would have to answer with nothing less than the truth.

"I have taken a long journey, my lord. I cannot say for sure where I was or what befell me; I think I have seen the depth of the Pit, experienced what we men call hell, and survived the ordeal. I am now free, as I have never before been, of any sense of guilt or fear. That is an unnatural state for a man, and a blessed one. You will find me in a much better condition now to be of use to your people."

Ian drank deeply of the bracing nectar and sat back, satisfied that he had handled the situation with wisdom, discretion, and undeniable honesty. It came as a surprise, therefore, when he realized that his words had had a most unexpected effect on his companion. The eyes that met his were hot with anger; the voice that addressed him was hard and bitter.

"You have been messing with the Old One. That is unwise and unfortunate. He is not to be trusted."

Ian looked at the old lord in surprise. Though he knew there were hard feelings between the wizard and the little people, he had not been prepared for such vehemence.

"Let it at least be said to my credit that I did not like him," he said.

"How is it that you let him play his diabolical games with you?"

"To tell you the truth, I did rather get tricked into that. But what happened to me was beyond his control, that I know for certain."

"Do not trust him, Ian James." Garumpta's long hand grasped his arm in violent solicitude. "He will seduce you to your doom, as he had done us."

"What ill has he done you, my lord?" Ian's curiosity once more got the better of his discretion. The Fernlord regarded him with a slow, bitter smile as he refilled their cups.

"We, the small folk, are mentioned, are we not, in the old tales of your people? Are there stories as well of large people tall as mountains, strong as thunder?"

"Giants?"

"Oh yes, that is the name you gave them, giants. They were my most distant ancestors." Garumpta laughed harshly. "What do you think of that? You drink with the descendant of giants. They would not have approved of me, my ancestors. They were a gentle people. Big people can afford to be gentle. Their whisper bent the trees, whereas my shout will not carry as far as my own Great Hall. They dwelt in the mountains to the north mostly, herding and farming and minding their own business. He, the Old One, lived alone in the South. What he is and where he came from, I cannot say. Perhaps your legend of his having been the offspring of a demon has some truth in it. I don't pretend to know. We call ourselves the First Folk, because it is our belief that our gigantic ancestors were the first people to live on this island. Yet they called him the Old One. Perhaps the name referred only to his looks. I don't know. In any event they had nothing to do with him, which was fortunate; that is, until your people came and tried to take over.

"Your people greatly feared mine because of their size, and at first kept clear of the places where giants dwelt. In time they discovered, as I suppose they were bound to, that the huge people of the mountains had no knowledge of war or conquest. They were not only peaceful but also wholly naïve. Men were of a different sort, but I don't need to tell you that. You're one of them, Ian James. You know what sort you are, don't you?"

Garumpta began muttering into his beard in a rumbling voice that gradually rose as his agitation increased.

"They couldn't leave things alone, those men. It was not enough for them to have the valleys; they must possess the peaks as well. What they could not seize by direct conquest they took by stealth and treachery. They taught my people to hate. They called themselves Jack, the really vicious ones, as if they were one person. But there were thousands of them, these giant-killing Jacks, tricking, robbing, murdering when they could. My people were defenseless against their villainy. They could not hide, for there was nothing large enough to shelter them. Your forefathers butchered my forefathers like so many oversized bullocks." The old fairy's voice rose to a near-hysterical pitch. He banged his staff furiously on the ground. Ian sat in stunned silence, wishing with all his being that Aneelen would come. She would know how to calm him. But only the old servant came to the doorway, summoned apparently by the banging of the staff.

"Refill the pitcher, Brulo," Garumpta snarled. The old fellow came forward quickly, cringing as if in fear of a blow, grabbed the pitcher, and fled. Garumpta sat staring at the floor in hostile silence. Ian felt compelled to make some sort of gesture.

"I apologize for my forebears," he said. "They were a barbarous lot, I'm sure; but I think we have become somewhat more civilized with the passage of time."

"That's debatable. You still exploit your own kind, I believe, and wage war over the ownership of land. My forebears were no match, at any rate, for yours. They saw that the Old One still dwelt in peace. Him the men left alone, for they feared his power. The simplest conjuring trick sent most of them fleeing in terror. Desperate, the leader of the giants sought his help. He advised them that, as they were well aware themselves, their size was a disadvantage. He gave to them the power of diminution and told them to take refuge in the forest, a place that men for some reason feared. To the King of my people, of whom the Lord Oberon is the descendant, he gave certain other powers as defense against men. My ancestors accepted his help gratefully, diminished, and fled to the forests, where they learned to hide by day and live by night as we do now."

"Don't you think, perhaps, my lord, that your ancestors diminished more than was judicious?" Ian ventured.

Garumpta smiled. "Oh no, they were not as you see us now. We have diminished steadily and at times rapidly since then. My first small ancestors were the size of half-grown human children and had no intention of diminishing further. What they did not realize until later was that by accepting the Old One's help and partaking of his fiendish potions they had placed themselves under his dominance. They trusted him, and that was their undoing. He had already made a pact of some sort with the humans, giving the land to them, as if it were his to give, and granting them the power to destroy my ancestors if they chose. They politely declined that option but accepted the condition that they might control the size of my people by their thoughts and concepts of them, and if it should prove convenient diminish us out of existence by simply forgetting us. You men are a cowardly lot; you don't like to look your deeds in the face. You are willing to turn your back on a creature, allowing it to die in pain, when you would scruple to openly strike the blow that would mercifully dispatch it. You played so with us.

"Not at first. You were satisfied at first to leave us alone so long as we stayed in the woods and underground and mined our own business. Dwarves you called us at that stage of our diminution. But in time your fears got the better of you. We gave you no cause to fear us; we had the woods and the caves and were content. We wanted no part of you. It was your own fear-haunted imaginations that invented for us crimes we could never have conceived of, much less committed. So you willed us to diminish until we were the size of toys; then you gave us to your children to play with. Later you tried to will us out of existence, but your children could not bear to be deprived of their playmates. You kept us on, for their sake, in the nursery, at least. You've always been soft about children, haven't you? You could have been rid of us centuries ago if it hadn't been for them and for those occasional adult humans who persisted in keeping us alive with their silly stories and insulting pantomimes. Every generation of children that claps for Tinkerbell and goes its way gives us the strength to survive until such a time as Tinkerbell is permanently retired from your stage. And so we continue, too small and weak to better our lot and too stubborn to give up and die out as we should."

The servant entered cautiously and filled their cups.

"There you have it, Ian James, a brief history of the decline of the first people of this land through the treachery of the Old One. I have told you all this, a wearisomely long tale for one as old and tired as I am, for your own good. Heed my warning and have no truck with the Old One, for he will deceive and destroy you. Do not play his games or drink his potions. Do not consult him or ask his help in any matter."

"Your advice is somewhat belated, I'm afraid," Ian said, feeling just a little uneasy. "For I have done these things already, and am committed, as indeed we all are, to such an extent that there is no way of turning back, even if we wanted to."

"What do you mean?" Garumpta asked sharply.

"Why, the exchange, my lord. All the spells involved are in his possession. The thing could not be done without his aid."

"Then it ought not to be done at all!" Garumpta cried. "Do you really think that he would help us after he has plotted so long for our destruction?"

"Yet he had done just that," Ian said. "We have the spells and formulas needed in our possession now."

"There is treachery here, you may be sure." Garumpta rose and began pacing the floor in jerky strides punctuated by vigorous assistance from his stick. "There will be no exchange. I will not allow my son to be sent. Far better to diminish to nothingness than to submit again to that one's treachery."

"I believe, my lord," Ian said quietly, "that it is too late to turn back now."

"Not so long as no one has drunk a potion."

"It is then most certainly too late. For Mompen has taken the releasing potion. And I have drunk, too."

Garumpta turned away from him abruptly, standing stiffly facing the fire, head bowed, fists clenched. He stood thus for many minutes before he turned and resumed his seat. He appeared calm now, at least outwardly, but his green eyes were glinting.

"You have shared the Old One's cup?"

Ian nodded.

"Why?"

"I was told it would be necessary if I am to recite the spell effectively."

Garumpta stared at him with sudden comprehension.

"You are to what?"

"To cast the spell, my lord. I ought to have mentioned it to you before. It was decided that I could best be used in this way, as I am accustomed to performing before an audience and would be the person least likely to make a dangerous error."

Garumpta nodded his head slowly, but the expression on his face was grim.

"Tell me, Ian James," he said after a long pause, "have you always been like this?"

"I beg your pardon?"

"Putting your head into the mouth of every lion you chance upon."

"To tell you the truth, my lord, up until Midwinter last I led a singularly quiet and uneventful life."

"At the rate you are going, by Midsummer next you'll be leading no sort of life at all!"

He banged his staff fiercely, and the old servant shuffled trembling to the door.

"See this man on his may, Brulo," the Fernlord commanded, "and be certain for the sake of your head that he does not show himself here again until he is summoned by the King's command at Midsummer."

Chapter 11

Midsummer Night

June in Surrey is generally a rather pleasant month, sunny and mild, the evenings often downright cool. But this particular June southwestern Surrey was visited with an almost tropical heat wave. It reached its climax on the twentieth day of that month, the eve of the summer solstice—Midsummer Night. At nine-thirty in the evening even the weather could damage his spirits. He admired his reflection in the glass as he attempted to brush back his unruly hair. He was aging, there was no denying that; but on the whole, age sat well on him. He had decided to wear his sorcerer costume, but those plans had been altered slightly by the weather. He certainly could not tolerate the cloak in this heat. The thin, sleek trousers and the shirt with the dramatic cut would go along, though, to represent the purveyors of the more earthly magic of the theater. Ian completed his costume with a light-weight tan sports jacket and started for the door. Then he turned back quickly to his desk, taking from the top drawer a well-chewed sheet of yellowed paper, which he crammed into his trouser pocket. Although he would probably have no chance to look at his script before he was on, he always felt better if he knew he had it with him.

The sun had only just set; in the heavy twilight air the odors of recently cooked dinners floated about, blending strangely with the delicate perfume of roses and the exotic spice of carnations that filled the gardens of Southdown Road. Ian had not walked far when he felt rather than heard footsteps approaching from behind, carefully matching his own but echoing more sharply on the pavement.

He slowed his own stride slightly and was soon joined by Marian Crawley, looking somewhat more feminine than usual in a soft blue shirtwaist dress and high-heeled pumps. They walked together in silence for some time, just another couple out for an evening stroll.

"Nervous?" Miss Crawley asked softly.

"A little," Ian grinned. "That's considered a good sign by students of theater, you know. The actor who isn't just a bit nervous before going on is likely to put on a bad performance. It's not a wholly unpleasant sensation; rather exhilarating, really."

"I'm afraid I would be more than a little nervous if I had a critic like Garumpta waiting in the wings."

"I can always count on you to say something encouraging, Miss Crawley."

"Oh I didn't mean it that way, Mr. James. I wish you all imaginable good luck; you know that. Just the same, I must admit I'd as soon not be in your boots tonight."

"That is one good reason why you aren't, my dear."

The Vicar had joined them so quietly that they had not been aware of his approach.

"It is considered bad form amongst theatrical people to wish an actor good luck before a performance, Marian. One is supposed to propose that he suffer a broken leg or some equally grave catastrophe. Eh, James?"

Ian laughed. "I don't subscribe to that particular tradition myself, Vicar. I'm ready to take any good wishes I'm offered."

They crossed Churchill Lane and started up Buckingham Avenue. Here they were joined by Mrs. Hubbard, looking charmingly delicate in a beige lace blouse.

"Good evening, Mrs. Hubbard," Ian greeted her warmly. "Will you wish me luck?"

"With all my heart, dear. But I don't really think you need our good wishes. You will do splendidly on your own."

Ian glanced up at the bedroom window as they passed the Americans' house.

"It's all right," Mrs. Hubbard assured him. "I've been keeping an eye on things over there all day. The baby was put to bed promptly at eight. She's no doubt fast asleep."

Ian scowled and shook his head. "I'm getting some sort of reaction. She must be at least partially awake. Ought I to give her some warning, do you think?"

"No," said the Vicar. "Let her sleep peacefully while she has time. She at least can be spared the anxiety of waiting."

They moved on quickly now through the warm dusk toward the housing estate.

"I do have my own private superstitions," Ian commented, producing the ragged paper from his pocket. "I always carry my script with me, you see. It gives me a feeling of confidence."

"Is that the spell?" Miss Crawley inquired eagerly. "Could I see it?"

Ian handed the paper to her.

"Be careful of it now. It's all but disintegrated. And be sure to give it back."

One side of the long sheet was covered with Merlin's difficult script. The Vicar had rewritten the text of the spell on the other side in a neat clerical hand. Miss Crawley glanced over the paper and handed it to Ian.

"It doesn't look too difficult. All the same, I'm glad I'm not in your boots."

The fire in the Great Hall was low, only large enough to allow for cooking. Light was provided by torches flickering merrily from brackets along the walls. Otherwise the hall was much as Ian remembered it from his first terrifying visit six months before.

Near the banquet table, very close to the spot where Oberon had descended on the last feast, lay a single polished chestnut, frayed threads of pink and the remains of a crumbling burr clinging in places to its surface, for as Penny had sacrificed her cap so Mompen had sacrificed his beloved pram to the preparation of the seed. A short distance from it a low stool had been placed; a finely made wooden mallet had been propped against the wall. Ian stiffened a little. So the stage was set, the props in place. He felt a slight twinge of fear, the first he had experienced in quite a while. It was not fear of his own failure, though, nor was it that momentary panic that always possessed him while awaiting his first entrance cue, the terrible, unavoidable instant of blankness when he could in no way remember his opening line. (It was against this awful moment that he had developed the habit of always carrying a script on his person.)

The little tribe of fairies was gathered in an uneven half circle near the waiting chestnut, a respectful foot or so behind their lord and lady. Garumpta and his mate were dressed in finery of lighter weight than what they had worn at the winter feast, and their cloaks, like Ian's, had been sacrificed to the heat. Mompen stood between them, white-faced, the only time in his life placed in equal rank with his sire. Ian's heart went out to him, standing shakily on his thin, wobbly legs, an incredibly ugly, deformed creature, whose eyeballs stared ludicrously at each other across the bridge of his nose. Ian longed to do something to help him through these last, terrible few minutes. Perhaps he could; he still had the power to speak to Mompen's mind. Quickly he sent a message of command. The miserable fairy turned to look at him. He was obviously close to either breaking down in hysterics or simply passing out.

"All right, my dear," Ian's will exhorted him, "you have been cast in the role of hero. You may not feel up to the part right now, but you are on. You don't need to feel courage to show it. That's it. Raise your head and straighten your back; that always helps, for some reason. There, now you've got it. Splendid."

Mompen sent back unspoken thanks for the capsule acting lesson and one last request. "Please, sir, will you visit me when I am on the other side?"

"Of course I will," Ian replied in the same fashion. "We all will. But you mustn't let on you know us."

Above them the strange trumpet call resounded through the hot night air. Ian did not witness the descent of the Fairy King and his court this time, for, like the others assembled in that hall, at the first blast of the fanfare, he dropped face down on the ground in homage. He rose only on hearing the thin-voiced command: "All rise." The King and his coterie were as he remembered them, bright, ethereal, thin, and sharp-looking, and even now vaguely menacing. The Puck's motley was brighter and cleaner than what was worn at Midwinter, mimicking the gay yellows, reds, violets, and greens of summer gardens. His behavior hadn't improved any, Ian observed, watching him strut and smirk amongst the lesser creatures of Garumpta's unkempt little tribe. Ian realized that this was the one living creature he would really enjoy thrashing.

Oberon spoke. "Let Garumpta the Fernlord come before me."

Garumpta stepped forward and knelt at the King's feet.

"Rise, Garumpta." He reached out a kindly hand to assist the old lord to rise on his stiff legs. "Are preparations completed for the exchange of your lastborn for a human child?"

"Yes, Your Majesty. All is ready."

"And what of the man you captured last winter? Is he present?"

Ian sprang forward, dropping gracefully to one knee with a bow of his head and a flourish of his arm.

"Ian James, at Your Majesty's service!"

"Well, his manners have improved, at any rate," Oberon growled in an aside to his consort.

"I am sure it is easier to show courtesy when one is not under guard and in fear of Your Lordship's wrath," Titania replied with a gracious smile for Ian. For the first time he came to see that she was in her own way strangely beautiful. He returned her smile, blushing slightly.

"What have you to report of this man, Garumpta?" Oberon inquired. "Has he fulfilled his pledge to your satisfaction?"

There was a pause.

"I cannot deny, Your Majesty, that he has fulfilled his pledge, perhaps more diligently than might be wished. But in any event I here relinquish all claims to his head."

"If the Lord Garumpta is satisfied, I am satisfied," Oberon declared. "Rise, Ian James, that you may be released with thanks from my service."

He raised his staff above Ian's head. Ian rose as he was bidden, but when the staff was lowered toward his forehead, he held up his hand.

"Wait. If it please Your Majesty, I should prefer not to be released from my pledge until I have fulfilled all my duties. I have yet one service to perform for your people."

"And what is that?"

"It is my privilege and fearsome duty to pronounce the spell that will bring about the exchange."

"You are to cast the spell?"

There was a general murmur of surprise and not a little indignation amongst Garumpta's people as well as the King's. The Puck burst out laughing.

"Now, this is quite a man. First he lurks around the halls like a heavy-footed burglar; then he comes right up and offers to cast major spells. We're in trouble again, I fear, Master. This fellow couldn't cast a leek in a stew-pot!"

Oberon silenced him with a look. The others hushed themselves rapidly. The Fairy King, his pointed brows tangled in a frown, turned to Garumpta.

"Do you have an explanation for this, Lord Garumpta?"

"The matter was settled and potions drunk before I was given any knowledge of such a plan. I deny all responsibility for it."

"I accepted this assignment freely," Ian said. "And I take full responsibility for the decision."

Oberon favored him with a scornful smile. "What makes you think you are qualified to cast spells? If you omit or alter one word, or make one incorrect gesture, you could do unthinkable injury to the subjects, to those witnessing the spell, or to yourself. Are you that certain of your ability and your powers of memory?"

"I am an actor, Your Majesty. I never drop my lines."

The pointed eyebrows rose until they almost disappeared under the curls that crowned the King's forehead. His thin voice acquired a distinctly threatening tone.

"So you are an actor now. I was not aware of that. Tell me: do you perform in the pantomime?"

"Yes, Your Majesty. Frequently. I am usually assigned the devil's part."

Oberon looked long and hard at Ian's face. He did not flinch, but returned the King's stare with a steady, questioning look of his own.

"You are qualified," Oberon acknowledged after a pause of tormenting length. "You will cast the spell."

Ian bowed low and stepped aside. The King spoke again.

"Let Mompen, lastborn of the Fernlord, come before me."

Mompen stumbled forward struggling at least to appear heroic. Under Ian's determined guidance he succeeded in achieving a kneeling position without falling completely on his face. The Puck turned away violently. He could not, it seemed, bear to see even for an instant that unfortunate visage.

"Are you prepared, Mompen, to give yourself in exchange for a human child?"

"Yes, Your Majesty." His voice was choked and barely audible.

"Your name shall be spoken with honor and gratitude throughout my kingdom. I wish you a good life in the world of men. Do you have any request to make of me?"

"P-please, Your Majesty. I'd like to get it over with." Tears filled his eyes and overflowed, running down his face and dropping in a steady drizzle from his beard. Mompen the hero was replaced at once by Mompen the heartbroken and terrified. Covering his face with his hands, he sobbed loudly without inhibition or control.

Oberon stepped aside for his Queen, who gently took Mompen's wet, trembling hands in hers, raised him to his feet and, holding him to her breast, soothed and comforted him, stroking his thin hair and speaking to him in a low, private voice.

"Are you ready, Ian James?" Oberon asked.

"I am ready."

Ian removed his coat because, he told himself, it might interfere with the free movement of his arms. He knew in his heart, though, that he did it to reveal the graceful flow of the shirt's well-cut sleeves, which would respond nicely to the movements of his arms and shoulders as he struck the nut. Style, the Vicar had often reminded him, was half the trick in the casting of an effective spell. This, however, was a bit of vanity he later had much cause to regret.

Mompen was quiet and apparently calm as Titania led him to the stool and seated him on it facing the chestnut. He stared at it fixedly, his eyes locked in an expression of almost mad terror. Ian went to him, anxious to offer a little comfort or encouragement. The Queen halted him with an upraised hand.

"Do not disturb him. I have sent him for a time to a different place where he will not be aware of what is happening to him. When he returns to himself, the deed will have been accomplished."

Ian nodded. Looking again at the forlorn figure on the stool, he understood. The Fairy Queen was wiser and more compassionate than he had realized.

The King's guards had cleared the company away so that Mompen and the chestnut sat alone in the center of a large open circle. There was no sound in the Great Hall. Even the fire had died down. They were waiting, all of them, waiting, tense with anxious expectation. Ian James started. They were waiting for him. He experienced that instant of panic, like a sudden surge of adrenalin, that he always felt when he knew his entrance was imminent. But this time there was no entrance cue. The show was all his, and he had to go on alone. He rubbed his sweating hands against his trousers, but before he stepped inside the circle he felt an insistent compulsion to look behind him. Turning half around, he saw the Vicar holding out to him a small bottle. Oh yes, that final setting potion; he had all but forgotten it. Quickly he grasped the bottle, receiving in the change of hands a surreptitious encouraging squeeze of his fingers. Ian raised the bottle to his lips and downed the contents without hesitation. The draught was, to his surprise, exceedingly bitter. He managed to swallow it with an effort, struggling to control the grimace brought on by the potion's dreadful aftertaste. There. It was done. He had taken the final, irreversible step. The words he spoke now would bear the weight of a powerful spell.

Resolutely grasping the handle of the mallet, he entered the center of the circle and took his position at striking distance from the waiting chestnut. His eyes played for an instant over the ring of spectators. The King and Queen stood erect and impassive flanked by their dragonfly guards, watching him. On their right stood Garumpta, leaning on his stick, glowering. Aneelen, overcome with emotion, clung to her lord's arm, weeping silently into a linen handkerchief Miss Crawley had fetched from her hand-bag. Then came his three fellow humans, all trying to look confident and encouraging, and all succeeding only in looking nervous. The Puck stood at his master's left hand, staring hard at the back of Mompen's head and vehemently chewing his fingernails. The rest of the ring was composed of Garumpta's people, a disreputable-looking group quiet and uncomfortable in the presence of the King's followers, who remained somewhat aloof. It was certainly a peculiar audience, but an audience it was, and Ian James knew what to do with an audience.

Standing erect with his eyes closed, as the Vicar had taught him, Ian intoned the invocation in a clear, firm voice, emphasizing the rhythm, as in a chant.

Powers of earth, of air, of sea,
Powers above, beneath, around,
Powers beyond all creature fear
Hear and heed my voice!

Powers of mine that dwell within,
Powers of arm and will and voice,
Possess me now that power I be—
I will speak with the voice of Power!

He stood then in silence waiting, as he had been instructed, for these Powers to possess him. He really did not know what to expect at this point. The Vicar had been of little help. The Powers, he had assured Ian, would come in the way they chose, and when they possessed him he would know it. The manner of their coming, Ian was sure, could in no way be more terrible than this waiting. The temptation to open his eyes was almost unbearable, but he held on firmly, willing with all his strength to be possessed at any cost. There was no sudden jolt, as he half expected, but only a gradual, ever-mounting sense of fear. He recognized the feeling; he had known it before. It was the same unbearable terror that had possessed him when he was forced to look into Merlin's globe. This time he did not resist. He knew now what it was that produced this feeling, the presence of the Powers. The other time they had drawn him unwillingly into the Pit; now he would take them and use them to his own purposes. He was not bound, as he had been then, and the urge to flee from the approaching terror was difficult to resist. It took all the will and determination he possessed just to stand fast and allow the Powers to surround and engulf him. Gradually the terror diminished, to be replaced by the same confident serenity that he had first known on returning from the Pit. He opened his eyes, then blinked and rubbed them. There seemed to be a mist or a veil of some sort impending his vision. The fire, the circle of spectators, even Mompen, sitting in a motionless daze on his stool, seemed distant and fuzzy, like a picture out of focus. Only the chestnut on the ground before him and the mallet in his hands appeared real and sharp. The time had come. He must do the thing now.

Leaning his weight on the mallet, he lowered his voice to address the Powers that now possessed him.

"I will to change the two persons whose characters now dwell in this seed, the being of each to enter the body of the other, with the differences to be declared in the spell. Let the Powers within me guide me to this deed."

It was rather prosaic, really, a bit like the wording of a rental contract. But it set down the matter legally, so to speak, so that there could be no mistaking what was intended. Ian paused a moment before continuing with the final, critical portion of the spell. Slowly he raised the mallet to his shoulder. The loose-flowing sleeves of his shirt added grace to the movement, as he knew they would. The mallet was heavier than he had expected it to be. Spreading his legs apart for better balance, he threw back his head and pronounced the words he had learned clearly and distinctly, searching constantly for the suggestion of error.

"Upon this stroke let them be changed" (there, he'd gotten by that), "being for being, essence for essence. Let the human form be left unaltered; the other let be raised to beauty: blood and flesh, touch and tasting, scent and hearing, seeing touch not" (good, he'd gotten it right at last), "speech and moment, man to maiden, rude to fair, thorn to blossom. Just so I will it."

He paused again. The thing was set now, the arrangements made. The outward appearance of the human child would remain the same, but Mompen's unfortunate body would be transformed not only in sex but also in all outward appearances—thorn to blossom. Ian felt an instant of profound regret. He had come to love the thorn that was Mompen; the blossom that would replace him was a stranger. He raised the mallet high above his head and took careful aim.

"By the death of this seed," he cried in a ringing voice, "let the deed be done!"

The nut exploded when he struck it with a thunderous blast and a great foundation of brilliant white sparks. Dropping the mallet, Ian staggered back, shielding his eyes with his arm against the shower of blinding light that continued to burst from the ground in front of him. It seemed an unbearably long time before it died down, leaving the chamber in shadow.

When Ian's eyes had finally caught up with these rapid and violent fluctuations of light, he could at first see nothing but the little pile of fine white powder at his feet. Slowly the veil was lifted from his sight and everything was once more clear. It took all his courage to force himself to look at the stool where Mompen had sat. But when he did raise his eyes to it, he was delighted beyond all hoping by what he saw. On the stool sat a fairy maiden, young, fresh, dainty of form, and exquisitely beautiful. She was dressed in a short-skirted gown of finely woven weblike material that reflected rather than held the yellows and pale lavenders of spring flowers. Her feet were bare and ought always to be, for they were so round and smooth and pink that it would have been a crime to hide them in the finest shoes. Her face was delicate and fragile, rather round in shape; her slightly upturned nose was decorated with a tantalizing sprinkle of light freckles. Her long hair, as pale and soft as corn silk, was held back from her face by a garland of tiny English daisies. A tight-fitting bodice, rather low-cut, emphasized a slender waist and firm, youthful breasts, while it revealed enticingly round, smooth, judiciously dimpled shoulders and arms. Her small, white hands lay folded in her lap; her eyes were cast modestly down, a becoming blush lighting her cheeks. A blossom indeed. Exultation rose in Ian as he gazed at the outcome of his labors. He had cast a perfect spell. He felt justified in forgiving himself for being most improperly proud.

There was a considerable murmur about the hall as the witnesses to his triumph recovered one by one from the shock of the explosion and responded to the result of his spell with wonder and admiration. The Vicar was beaming as proudly as if he had done the deed himself. Mrs. Hubbard and Miss Crawley embraced each other in their joy. Even Aneelen dried her tears and came around on her lord's arm to have a closer look at the little changeling. But the Puck, kicking up his heels in uninhibited delight, pushed ahead of them, placing himself in front of the girl directly across the pile of white dust from where Ian stood still lost in the contemplation of his handiwork.

"Lovely, lovely," murmured Robin in a gentler tone than he might have been thought capable of. Smiling, he extended a hand to her. "Come, my pretty little one come to me. I am your prince."

A soft smile passed over her lips as she turned and looked up at her prince. The Puck let out a horrible hoarse cry and turned away from her, doubling over as if he had been dealt a severe blow.

"No!" he wailed. "No! No!"

Startled, Ian made a motion toward the girl, who looked then at him in fear and confusion. Ian James did not recoil or cry out, but stood paralyzed with horror. For the eyes that nearly met his stared ludicrously at each other across the bridge of her nose.

Chapter 12

The Script as Written

The changeling rose slowly and turned to face the company looking anxiously from one face to another. But for the response she got she might have been a Gorgon of old, for she seemed to turn all who saw her to stone.

"Oh my God," the Vicar whispered at last.

The girl stared at him for an instant, raised her delicate hands to her face, broke out in tears, and ran stumbling past the company, through the Great Hall, and out into the forest beyond.

Garumpta gave a sharp order and hurried off in pursuit, followed by his servants and two or three of the heartier members of the tribe. There was now much running about and confusion of voices throughout the hall, the royal coterie alone remaining silent and aloof. Ian James roused himself with effort, still too stunned to fully grasp what had happened. His first thought was for the child of his handiwork, and he ran forward to join the search party.

As he ran past one of the dark corridors leading off into the depths of the thicket, he thought he heard a sound, like a child sobbing. He turned into the passage, groping his way through the blinding darkness, guided only by the sobs, which seemed now distant, then near at hand. He sensed rather than saw someone in front of him blocking the passage, but it was no child, being taller than Ian himself and fearsomely strong. He made a lunge for Ian, seizing him about the shoulders.

"Here, let me go!" Ian struggled to break his adversary's hold.

"You ruined her!" the Puck snarled. "You bungling

child of the devil, you ruined my changeling. And now you will pay for it—in flesh!"

With a sudden powerful turn of his body he threw the man violently against the wall of tangled briar. And Ian discovered to his woe another of the weapons in the Fernlord's fortress. Long thorns grasped him like manacles, holding him fast. Any movement he tried to make drove the points deeper into his skin. The Puck, hissing with rage, pulled from inside his jerkin a freshly cut twig of nettle, which he had brought with him in the secret hope that he might at last have his way with his captive of Midwinter. And so he did, for a time, as he whipped his helpless victim with all the strength of his fury, forgetful that the man yet held the most potent possible defense, the Fairy King's mark.

"Oberon!"

The cry was feeble, more a moan than a shout, but the power of the name invoked carried it through the thicket walls to the Great Hall, where the three other humans were not aware yet that their comrade was missing, much less in peril.

The Vicar groaned, "Oh my God!" And the hall fell into silence at once as Oberon raised his staff in answer to the call. From the depths of the thicket came the Puck's shrill yelp. Oberon's protection was swift and effective.

The guards flew off humming in the direction of the cry and returned almost at once, the first dragging the Puck while his companion more gently supported Ian, dazed, bleeding, and in great pain.

"Oh my God!" The Vicar would have rushed forward had not Mrs. Hubbard held him back. It would not do to interfere now; Oberon was in command, and all must wait on his judgment.

"What mischief is this?" the King demanded sternly of his Puck. "Have you dared to attack one who bears my mark?"

"He ruined my changeling," the Puck said in a low voice still hard with suppressed anger. "And I would have his lifeblood for it."

"It is not your place to pass judgment. If your complaint is just you shall have restitution, but if this deed has been ill done, know that we may yet see the color of your blood. Stand aside."

The Fairy King turned his unpitying green eyes upon Ian.

"You cry to Oberon for justice, man, and justice you shall have. You have presumed to cast a great spell, but your work, it seems, has gone amiss. What have you to say of your performance this night?"

There was a long, difficult pause. Then Ian spoke in a weak, faltering voice. "That—the error—was not—mine."

Having stated his defense, simply and to the point, Ian James fainted.

He fell back into the fleshless arms of his guard, who eased him onto the stool that had been Mompen's and left him to the care of Aneelen and her women. Mrs. Hubbard hurried to join in the effort to revive him and look after his wounds, while the Vicar assumed his place before the King.

Marian Crawley found herself standing alone on the edge of the circle. She was often left in this position when labor was so predictably divided, not sure if she ought to go forth with the men or stay back with the women. A call from Aneelen for a cup of nectar decided her position. She would go, as usual, where she was needed. But even as she fetched the nectar from the banquet table she was aware of what was going on before Oberon.

The Vicar was having his problems, for he could offer no proof beyond an old man's memory that the spell had been given word correct.

"The paper!" Marian Crawley cried, dropping the cup in her hand. She pushed through the circle of women surrounding the unconscious man and seized his shoulders roughly. He roused with a sharp cry.

"That paper!" Miss Crawley urged, ignoring Mrs. Hubbard's remonstrance. "Where is it? Oh here!" She groped impatiently in his trouser pocket, coming out with a key case and a rumpled yellowed sheet.

"Your Majesty's pardon." She dropped to one knee, panting slightly before the King. "The text of the spell is written here in the master's own hand."

She left it to them to study and find if they could the error, knowing better than to wait to be thanked. Taking another mug of nectar, she brought it to Ian with an apology for having hurt him. He seemed a bit better, at least more aware of what was going on. In a strained whisper he assured her that he was all right.

"That's it!" the Vicar cried suddenly: " 'seeing touch not.' There it is, Your Majesty. The error is indeed written into the spell."

"So it is," Oberon said quietly.

Ian groaned and clutched his head. He was fully conscious now and longed to return to the oblivion where there was no pain and no realization of disaster. He had known in his heart all along that something was wrong with the wording. It hadn't sounded right to his actor's instinct. He had gone over and over it searching for motivation and meaning. Well, the meaning was clear enough now. All had been changed by order of the spell, all but the organs of sight.

"Damned obedient, these Powers," Ian muttered.

"That is one of the dangers of calling on them."

Ian looked up to see Oberon himself standing before him. Ian stumbled to his feet, gratefully accepting Mrs. Hubbard's tactful assistance.

"You are excused from ceremony. Remain seated," the Fairy King said.

"I thank Your Majesty," Ian replied. "But I am somewhat recovered now and should prefer to stand in Your Majesty's presence."

"As you will."

Oberon handed him the paper.

"This document clears you of all responsibility for the failure of the spell. You played your part with commendable skill and accuracy. There was no way you or any of us could have known that the words you spoke were defective. My people have long been aware of the Old One's treachery, and this final manifestation of his guile should surprise none of us. You have shown yourself a good friend to my people. I regret that you have been made the Old One's tool."

"Your Majesty, I must object," the Vicar interrupted in considerable agitation. "The wording of a major spell is quite difficult. Even the greatest of wizards could make an honest mistake."

"You are to be commended for your loyalty," Oberon replied brusquely. "But be the mistake honest error or treacherous deceit, no blame for this catastrophe is to be laid to this man."

"The Old One never could stand me," the Puck muttered, digging his pointed toes into the ground. "It's obvious he did this for spite."

Oberon laughed. "Don't give yourself airs, Robin. The Old One would hardly go to so much trouble just to play a trick on the likes of you. You have been unwise to call attention to yourself. I am reminded that you have a score yet to settle here. Come before me."

The Puck obeyed reluctantly, watching Ian under his eyelids. Oberon spoke.

"This Puck of mine has attacked you without justice, Ian James, and has given you grievous hurt. According to our laws you are entitled to redress in kind, which you may administer with your own hand if you so desire."

An enticing proposition. Folding his arms, Ian studied the Puck for a long moment. There he was, the one living creature that he felt he would really enjoy thrashing, delivered into his hands. It was an opportunity not to be lightly passed over. The Puck met Ian's gaze with defiant bravado, but apprehension was fairly easy to detect beneath the brash mask.

"You meant to kill me, didn't you?" Ian asked softly.

The Puck lowered his eyes. "Yes, I did then. But I bear you no ill will now."

He was too proud to beg for mercy to save his skin, and Ian gave him credit for that. He had gone as far as one could expect a puck to go in the way of apology. Ian was satisfied and resolved to decline the offer of redress. Before he could communicate his decision to the King a small group of fairies hurried in, followed by Garumpta, leading the changeling girl. Her gown was torn, her arms scratched, her hair loose and matted. She kept her hands over her face.

"Let the changeling come before me."

Garumpta led her to the King and then retired.

"Uncover your face," Oberon commanded.

"No, please." Her voice was barely audible. Oberon

scowled and raised his staff threateningly. Ian sprang forward, took the girl's wrists, and forcibly pulled her hands from her face. She resisted as well as she was able and continued to keep her eyes hidden behind tightly closed lids. Ian held her hands firmly in his.

"You must do as he says, my dear," he urged her. "He is the King."

"Look at me."

Oberon kept his voice low and quiet, but the command inherent in it could not long be resisted. The girl slowly opened her eyes and raised them to meet her King's. He studied her long and keenly. She shrank from his penetrating stare. Ian gave her hands an encouraging squeeze.

"Don't be afraid, little one. No one here will harm you."

After studying the trembling girl for some time, Oberon turned to the Puck, who stood with his back to her.

"Look upon her, Robin. She is otherwise most fair."

"I have looked upon her, Master. She is hideous. I cannot abide her. I will not have her."

The girl gave a little cry, threw her hands once more over her face, and began to sob. Deeply moved, Ian put his arms around her.

"That is my prince?" she asked.

"I'm afraid so, dear."

"Mompen said he would be kind to me because I would be beautiful. But I am not beautiful. I am hideous, and he will not have me." She buried her face in the bloody remnants of Ian's shirt and cried.

"You are not hideous," Ian exclaimed indignantly. "You are very lovely, and I am proud to have had some part in the making of you. He is a great fool and never deserved to have you."

"But that is the only reason I came, to be his princess and save Mompen's people."

"I can force him to take you, if that is what you wish," said Oberon. "But I would not willingly make such a move, even to save my people. He is not by nature a kindly creature, and when thwarted, as this man will testify, he can become very cruel. Nevertheless, if it is your wish I will force him to take you."

The girl shook her head. "No, if he will not have me,

I shall not have him." She turned abruptly to face the King. "What, then, is to become of me?"

Oberon took her by the shoulders and looked kindly into her terrible eyes.

"I cannot return you to your own kind. I have not the power, perhaps no one living does, to reverse a major spell. You are one of us now and must share our fate. But as this man has stated, you have nothing to fear from my people. Most of us are of a gentler nature than your unworthy prince." He raised his voice to address the company. "Let the Fernlord come before me."

As Garumpta came into his presence and bowed, he turned the girl around to face him.

"Lord Garumpta," he announced. "I give this unfortunate changeling into your care. Take her into your tribe and show her honor and much kindness that in time she may come to regret a little less the move that brought her so futilely among us. Will you have her?"

"I shall have her gladly. So long as I am Lord of the Fernwood she will have warm hands and a full cup." He took the girl's hands in his. "You shall be our lastborn and sit in Mompen's seat."

Placing his arm around her shoulder, he led her from the circle. Aneelen joined them, proffering Miss Crawley's linen handkerchief.

"Let Ian James come before me."

The King raised his staff and lowered it slowly until the smooth, round tip rested on Ian's forehead. Its touch was cool and soothing.

"I hereby release you from your pledge of aid given Midwinter last, with gratitude for the help and friendship you have given my people. May the blessings of the land fall ever upon you."

Ian bowed. He felt no elation, or even relief at the removal of the mark that had at one time caused him such anguish.

"I am ever at Your Majesty's service and at your people's," he said. "I hope you will call on me again when my help and my particular abilities are needed."

"That is most generous," the King responded. "But we shall have little call for your peculiar talents, I fear. But you will be a welcome guest at our feasts all the same."

"But in the event of another exchange?"

"There cannot be another exchange. Such Powers are raised up only in necessity and then very rarely. We now know that we cannot count on the co-operation of the Old One; whether this disaster has come through error or design," he shot a sharp look at the Vicar, "it does not really matter. We dare not risk perhaps a worse outcome than we have seen here tonight."

"Then what of your people?" Ian cried. "What will become of your people?"

"We shall diminish slowly. We are not subject, as your sort are, to killing and debilitating diseases, and we age but little through many centuries of your time. When your bones have long returned to their origins, my people will yet be feasting in the woods. The time will come at last, though, when the final aged fairy will fall. Then for good or for ill, the people of your race will inherit the forests of this land."

"I would not have it so," Ian cried.

"That is nonetheless how it will be, and there is not a thing you or I can do about it."

Oberon looked once keenly at the Puck, who stood, back straight, head held high, the hunch of his shoulders emphatically repeating the condemnation he had pronounced upon his people. "I will not have her."

"Your Majesty," said Ian, "I accept with gratitude your offer of restitution for my injuries, which I shall be delighted to deliver personally, if that labor may be postponed until I am in better condition to perform it properly."

"That is a reasonable request," Oberon replied. "Will you be sufficiently recovered by tomorrow night?"

"Tomorrow night will do splendidly."

"Very well. Return here at midnight, and my Puck will be handed over to you. Deal well with him."

Chapter 13

A Bit of the Puck

The feast, like the one at Midwinter, took the form of a buffet. The guests were served from the long table, placing their food and drink on large wooden platters and then sitting around in a loosely formed circle on the ground. Unlike most other fairy activities, there seemed to be no ritual or protocol of any sort associated with the feast. The King and Queen sat at ease amongst the lowliest of their subjects. In spite of all that had occurred since the last celebration, the atmosphere as well as the form of his feast were remarkably similar to it. And just as in Midwinter Ian James found himself quite unable to participate. He took a roll and a mug of nectar and sat on a mossy mound a short distance from the group of feasting fairies, watching them in brooding silence.

As though he were replaying a scene, the Vicar rose quietly from the group, just as he had done on the previous feast, and carrying his mug, came and sat next to Ian. He laid the same reassuring hand on the younger man's knee (a gesture that by now had a familiarity of a mannerism) and spoke the same line.

"What do you say I take you home?"

But here the script was altered. This time Ian's response was negative.

"No, thank you, Vicar," he said. "I'm all right—physically, anyway. But I just can't accept it. The end of it all. Just like that."

He gestured toward the group of feasters, which was now wholly absorbed in an effort to cheer the little changeling. She sat, eyes lowered, between Garumpta and his lady, responding with shy gratitude to every gesture and offer of food and drink. Ian clutched his head.

"Seeing touch not," he muttered bitterly, "seeing touch not." He turned with sudden vehemence on his companion. "Come now, you don't really believe that was a mistake."

"I prefer to believe it was. Leave an old man what little he has, please."

"I'm sorry, Vicar," Ian exclaimed. "I didn't mean to say that. We all seem to be beating the wrong people tonight, don't we?"

"I hadn't any business getting you involved so deeply in this."

Ian did not reply nor make any indication that he had heard. He was staring straight ahead of him, suddenly alert. The change in his behavior made the Vicar somewhat nervous. The Vicar did not always know what to expect from this impetuous young man. Ian was rhythmically slapping his right fist aganst his left palm, a gesture that not only had the familiarity of a mannerism but the power of a sign as well. He was debating with himself about something, the Vicar knew, and perhaps was coming to a decision. He wished he had the skill to read the fellow's mind.

"I say, Vicar, are you doing anything tomorrow?"

"As a matter of fact, I'm not. I had rather planned on celebrating late tonight, so I left tomorrow free for recuperation. Why?"

"I just wondered if you would mind too much driving me down to Cornwall in the morning."

"What on earth for?"

"Well, suppose you're right, about it being a mistake, I mean." Ian spoke slowly, almost as though thinking aloud, tapping fist against palm with disturbing regularity. "Oberon claims not to have the power to change the spell. But what about old Merlin? If he made the mistake, mightn't he have the power to repair it? Or suppose the Puck is right, and the whole ghastly thing is nothing more sinister than an ill-considered practical joke? If he really is willing to help save the little people, wouldn't he be willing, if he does have the power, to make the matter right? And if the worst possibility should be the case—that he used me as his tool to condemn the fairies to extinction—what have I to lose by trying to change his mind? Garumpta has given me back my head, for what it's worth. I might just as well do something useful with it."

"It's more than your head you'll lose if you dare to propose such a thing," the Vicar exclaimed in consternation. "I doubt if anyone has ever presumed to suggest that the master modify or reverse any spell he has made. Do you really think he is going to confess to an error like a schoolboy in fear of the cane?" He tightened his grasp on Ian's knee. "I don't think you realize yet how narrow a squeak you had last winter. Don't risk his anger again, James. He could do anything to you."

"That's a chance I mean to take," Ian replied, gently removing the Vicar's hand from his knee and rising somewhat stiffly. "If you would rather not have anything to do with it, I understand. He is your master, after all. I'll see what sort of connections I can make by rail or bus."

"Listen to me. You haven't the least chance of gaining anything but your own destruction."

"What makes you so certain?" Ian asked, walking rapidly past the festivities. "I have surprised you and your master before. Perhaps I may surprise you again."

The Vicar seized his arm suddenly and dragged him into the midst of the startled feasters. He grabbed Mrs. Hubbard roughly with his other hand.

"Sybil, do something," he cried. "Maybe you have some influence with this madman. Talk to him, in the name of heaven."

"Why, what's the matter, Thomas?" Mrs. Hubbard cried, alarmed. "What's wrong with you?"

"Nothing's wrong with me, Sybil; he's the one," the Vicar said, pulling Ian around with a jerk to face her. "He thinks he's going to challenge the master and make him change the spell."

Ignoring the excited and shocked response this announcement brought forth, Mrs. Hubbard took both of Ian's hands in hers.

"Come now, my dear," she said. "We have all had a very rough evening, you more than any of us. Why don't you just sit quietly with us for a while until your head clears a bit? Then we can discuss this problem like reasonable people."

"My head is quite clear already, I assure you, Mrs. Hubbard," Ian replied. "I am not in the least bit delirious. I know what I'm doing. I know that I'm taking a great risk, that I have a very good chance of not coming out in my own skin. But I also know, as you may not, that I have just the merest chance of getting what I'm after. That's enough for me. I'm resolved to gamble on that one chance. So wish me luck, if you will."

"I wish you luck in all things, Ian. But I don't care to see you throw yourself away in such a hopeless gamble. You are too inexperienced to realize what danger you're putting yourself into. If there was anything that could be done about all this, you know we wouldn't hesitate to do it. But there's just nothing that can be done."

"It's no use, Mrs. Hubbard. I'm a fearfully stubborn fellow, and my mind's made up. I'm off for Cornwall in the morning." He dropped her hands lightly and turned to go. Garumpta blocked his way.

"I've changed my mind, Ian James," the Fernlord announced. "I'm entitled to your head, and I'm taking it. I shall give you a swift and decent death, which is more than you could expect from the Old One."

"I may yet have one more service to perform for your people, my lord," Ian replied. "Until I have at least attempted that, I will not willingly submit to you. If you want my head now, you must take it by force."

He spun around again so quickly that Garumpta was thrown off balance. Ian tried to push through the crowd that surrounded him. At a sharp command from Garumpta the circle tightened around him, and he found himself suddenly made prisoner in the center of a ring of grim-faced fairies, separated from his human companions. Garumpta confronted him.

"Have no business with the Old One," he said quietly. "I do not want to kill you, but I swear I will do just that as an act of kindness if you persist in this folly."

"A strange act of kindness, my lord, but one that you may be forced to perform."

Through the heavy silence that surrounded them, Oberon's voice broke sharply.

"A man of courage and power ought to be allowed to choose his doom."

The crowd gave way before the King and Queen, and Garumpta bowed reluctant obedience.

"You are determined to confront the Old One?" Oberon asked.

"I am, Your Majesty, in the hope of getting him to make good on the damage he has done and save your people."

"That is a faint hope on which to gamble your life. My protection cannot follow you there. I have never tested my power against his and would not care to attempt to now for fear of bringing a swifter doom upon my people."

"I do not ask Your Majesty's protection," said Ian. "This is my gamble, and I want no one else to share its danger."

"You will go alone?" Titania asked.

"Yes, Your Majesty. I must go alone." Ian paused a moment. "I ought really to have some witness, though, especially if things turn out badly."

A small, sly smile moved across his face. He addressed himself once more to the King.

"Could I presume upon Your Majesty's kindness to lend me your Puck for the day?"

"Oh no!" The Puck's shrill voice betrayed his position just beyond Oberon's left shoulder, where he had been watching the scene with amused interest. "You must think I am as great a fool as you are. I'll go to the devil for no man."

"Very well, Robin," Ian replied, "do as you will. But you would be wise to pray that I do come to a bad end, for on my return tomorrow night I have a debt to collect from you, and I mean to exact full payment."

The Puck turned away with a contemptuous shrug. But Ian was not done with him yet.

"I have the will now to deal with you as you deserve. By tomorrow night I shall also have the strength. I lack only a suitable cudgel." He glanced inquiringly around him, keeping the Puck in the corner of his eye. He approached the King with a deep obeisance.

"Could I ask a favor of Your Majesty?"

"I am prepared to grant you anything reasonable that it is in my power to grant. What is it that you desire of me?"

"On my return tomorrow night may I have the use of your staff for a few minutes?"

Ian was pleased to see the Puck blanch and turn to his King a look of silent appeal.

"An unusual request," said Oberon, studying Ian sharply. "But the position is unusual. I grant it."

"Master!" the Puck wailed.

"Silence, Robin. It is no more than you merit."

Ian approached Aneelen with a low bow. "I must beg your pardon, my lady, for having been such a poor guest again. If you can save some remnant of your splendid feast, when I return tomorrow night I hope to be able to do it justice."

"Stay and feast with us this night," she urged him. "Forget this foolhardy venture and be content that things are not worse than they are."

"I'm afraid I cannot do that, so you must save me some leftovers in the hope that I return."

Aneelen clapped her hands sharply. A maidservant appeared almost at once, carrying a large blown glass flask.

"Marian."

"Yes, my lady," Marian Crawley responded with a diffidence unusual for her.

"The good effect of my medication will wear off soon, and this man is going to need attention. You are to look after him for me. Do you understand?"

"Yes, my lady," Miss Crawley answered, placing the flask in her voluminous handbag beside the key case she had inadvertently taken from Ian's pocket. "I'll take as good care of him as I can."

Ian had paid no attention to this conversation, for he had noticed the little changeling hovering uncertainly on the periphery of the crowd near the Great Fire. He went to her and taking her face in his hands, gently forced her to look at him.

"Hold your head high, little one. You have every reason to be proud. You are Lastborn of the Firstborn, and that is a noble title." He kissed her eyelids. "No more tears now. With a bit of skill and a great deal of luck, I just might get you your worthless prince."

The crowd of fairies stepped aside in some awe as he started toward the entrance, his three human companions following.

"Wait!" The Puck ran to Ian and grabbed his coat sleeve. "If I go with you will you be easier on me?"

"If you go with me—and I ask no more than that you be present and observe what happens, you do not have to reveal your presence—then I shall consider your debt wholly canceled. You have my word on that. And if you do not go with me, you can expect from me on my return all the compassion you showed me when I was your prisoner last winter. Only don't think that I would punish you so severely for anything you've done to me. It is for your desertion of your own people that I would make you pay, and your shameful treatment of the bride I got for you."

The Puck stood a moment, nervously shifting his weight from one foot to the other.

"Well," Ian prodded, "are you coming or aren't you?"

"All right," the Puck gulped at last. "I'll come."

"Splendid, Robin," Ian took him warmly by the shoulders. "You will travel in my breast pocket, the favorite vehicle of a more worthy member of your race."

Ian regarded the little group near the banquet table with a wry smile.

"There's one thing I'll say for this Puck," he called. "He's the only one of the lot of you who thinks I just might be back here tomorrow night."

By the middle of any night, even the hottest of the summer, the borough of Elvinwood was fast asleep. The last streetlamp fluttered out somewhere in the vicinity of one o'clock, leaving the darkened town free to the stars and an occasional insomniac. But there were no insomniacs abroad that night to notice the four silent figures slip out of the forest along the path behind the housing estate and turn up Buckingham Avenue, and the stars showed no huddle near the corner of Churchill Lane.

"I'll pick you up at your flat around seven, then," one of them said.

"Oh are you going to take me down, after all?" another inquired.

The first speaker shrugged. "If you're determined to go to your doom, I might just as well drive you there. Besides, it will give me another chance to try to talk you out of this."

"That's a waste of effort, Vicar, and I think you know it. But I'll be glad for your company all the same."

After hurried farewells, the first figure turned down Churchill Lane and was soon out of sight beyond the lip of the dark hill. Another member of the group prepared to separate.

"Good night, Ian dear. Do get some sleep now and think things over in the light of day before you do anything rash."

"Good night, Mrs. Hubbard. Pray for me, if you will."

"I shall, dear, with all my heart. You look after him, Marian."

"I shall, Mrs. Hubbard. Don't worry," the fourth member of the group replied. "Good night, now."

The two that remained stood together for a few minutes gazing in silence at the large, dark, square shadow that was the next house.

"I do hope things went a little better for Mompen," one of them said, leaning rather heavily against the brick gatepost.

"Oh I imagine his end came off all right," the other answered, giving her companion a curious look. To an alert ear his voice sounded just a trifle strained and unsteady. She gripped his arm firmly. "Here now, I think it's about time we got you home."

He made a feeble effort to resist her.

"I believe you have that wrong, Miss Crawley. It is the gentleman in our society who sees the lady home."

"Circumstances alter custom, Mr. James."

She led him briskly across the street and up the deserted sidewalk of Southdown Road.

"Come along now. You know better than to argue with me. Suppose you took a notion to pass out again. I'm a mere helpless woman, hardly prepared to sling you over my shoulder like a sack of meal. I should be forced to leave you where you fall, and you would have quite a time trying to explain your condition to the local constabulary. I'm under orders to look after you, and that's just what I intend to do, whether you like it or not."

Half scolding, half urging him, she propelled him quickly past the rows of darkened houses and fragrantly dormant gardens. He made no more than a token effort at resistance, for in truth he felt none too sure of his ability to get himself safely home.

In a surprisingly short time he found himself standing at his front door.

"Well," he whispered, "thanks for the escort. Good night now."

Without replying she coolly reached into her bag and extracted his key case.

"Surely you don't think you're in any condition to go sailing up those stairs on your own."

Before he could object he was in the house and up the stairs. His persistent escort unlocked the door at the end of the hall, pushed him inside, and closed it behind them, turning the bolt with an authoritative click. Ian stumbled in the dark to the heavy oak desk that dominated his cramped lounge and leaned over it, resting his weight on his knuckles. Miss Crawley switched on the desk lamp.

"At the risk of appearing rude, Miss Crawley," Ian muttered through his teeth, "I shall once more wish you good night and ask you to excuse me if I fail to extend my hospitality. I am very tired and need rest."

"According to Aneelen it's more than rest you need. And from the look of you I'd say she was not far off."

"I'm only tired. Please go home so I can get a little sleep."

Miss Crawley laid her handbag on the desk with a thump.

"Although the Lady Aneelen speaks with a softer voice than her lord, she expects as much to be obeyed. She has ordered me to look after you, so as little as that prospect may appeal to either of us, I'm jolly well going to look after you. So be a nice, reasonable chap, now, and take off your coat so we can get on with it."

Ian sighed heavily. The last thing he wanted was to be cared for by anyone, but especially by this insufferable woman. He longed to be alone so that he could give in freely for the few hours that he had to the demands of pain and despair.

"Please don't think me ungrateful," he was really trying to control his rising irritation, "but there is absolutely nothing you can do for me that I cannot and would rather not do for myself."

Reaching into her handbag, the estate agent produced a very small brown-glass flask about the size of a piece of gravel.

"Along with your other talents, Mr. James, I was not aware that you were a contortionist."

She stood silent, arms folded, watching him. Ian supported himself by leaning heavily on the desk. Pain and fatigue were rapidly getting the better of him; he had to get rid of her before he collapsed wholly. She seemed to read his thoughts.

"I'm a stubborn woman, Mr. James, and quite accustomed to male resistance. Believe me, the quickest way to get rid of me is to let me have my way. If you stand there glaring at me long enough you're very likely to faint; then I can remove your coat myself."

"Oh very well, if you're so set on playing nurse, I give in to you," Ian said with a shrug (a singularly uncomfortable gesture, he discovered too late). "I hope you don't object to my having a spot of anesthesia first." He started for the kitchen.

"Not at all, if I am included," Miss Crawley replied. "This isn't my usual line of work, you know. A little fortification might well be in order."

It took some effort to locate two reasonably clean wineglasses. Ian was forced to rest for a while, leaning against the wooden cupboard where he kept his supply of port. He reached one hand blindly into the cupboard and drew out a bottle. When he set it on the counter in front of him, he saw that it was not the familiar Cockburn's ruby, but that fine Madeira he had bought on a whim right after his visit to Cornwall the previous winter. It was yet to be opened. He had been saving it for a special occasion. He started to reach for another bottle, then paused. Was he likely to have in his life a more special occasion than this night? He had flawlessly cast a defective spell, had been flogged by an enraged hobgoblin, had volunteered to beard the devil in his den, and now, most remarkable of all, he was entertaining in his rooms at nearly two in the morning a lady whose chief ambition seemed to be to get him out of his clothes. The cork came up with a smack.

"What is that?" a small voice queried from somewhere below his beard. The Puck was leaning on his arms over the top of Ian's breast pocket, a familiarity that Mompen would never have presumed to take.

"Man's potion," Ian snapped. "Very good." Moved reluctantly to a gesture of hospitality in remembrance of a more congenial guest, he unscrewed the cap from a bottle of HP sauce, rinsed it, half filled it with wine, and gave it rather ungraciously to the occupant of his pocket.

Returning to the lounge, he stopped abruptly in the doorway, nearly dropping the glasses he carried. Marian Crawley stood in the center of the room, facing him but unaware of his presence. She was breathing on the tiny flask she held in the palm of her right hand. She raised the hand suddenly in front of her and spoke in an intense whisper that, in spite of its discreet level of sound, carried in it the authority of command.

Increase, expand to fill this hand,
Hold full amount of man's account.
You are needed, give forth!

The flask slowly increased in volume like an inflating balloon until it did completely cover the upturned hand that held it.

"Enough, be still," Miss Crawley commanded, lowering her hand and grasping the now quite large flash by the neck. Ian breathed a low whistle.

"I say, that is rather good. I didn't know you had any power."

"I've damned little," Miss Crawley answered, accepting a glass of wine. "I couldn't have done that much without Aneelen's co-operation."

"You do it splendidly all the same." Ian raised his glass. "Since the exchange fell on its face, I don't know what to drink to."

"I shall drink only to the removal of your coat."

Ian shook his head. "I must say, Miss Crawley, that I am just as glad not to be one of your tenants. You must be a terror with an inventory."

"I am known, Mr. James, as a person who gets things done."

Ian set down his glass, still more than half full and, taking the Puck from his pocket, placed him on the desk next to it.

"Make yourself as comfortable as you can, don't get into my things, and mind your own business," he said.

It did not take the Puck long to find a convenient perch on the base of the desk lamp from which he could watch the activity in the sitting room. The woman was now helping the man to ease the jacket off his shoulders. It was neither an easy nor a pleasant task for either of them. When it was at last completed, with no little scolding from Miss Crawley ("I don't know why you put it back on, you've quite ruined the lining." "I always wear a coat when dining with royalty, Miss Crawley."), the Puck found himself faced with the ugly results of his violent attack on the speaker of the spell. He turned away, sickened. His cruelties did not usually take the form of physical violence, and his pride as well as his aesthetic sensibilities were injured by the sight of so much bruised and lacerated flesh for which he was responsible. Real, human pity for the suffering of another creature was an emotion quite beyond his capacity, but he did experience the closest feeling to remorse to be known by a puck.

"You may as well get rid of the shirt, too," Miss Crawley directed in the wholesomely brisk manner of an admitting nurse, revealing in her voice no trace of either revulsion or pity. "It's too bad, really. It was a handsome garment."

"I shall not further distress you by telling you what I paid for it," Ian replied with a strained laugh. The undressing procedure had finally done for him, and he sank without protest or resistance onto the sofa.

After a period the Puck got up enough courage to have another look. The tableau before him was certainly an unusual one. The man lay face down on the sofa while the woman, kneeling on the floor beside him, applied the aromatic contents of the flask to the wounded back and shoulders.

"Would you kindly stop holding your breath," she muttered crossly. "I am quite aware that I'm hurting you, so you might as well groan or whatever it is men do."

"Men hold their breath, Miss Crawley."

The Puck leaned back against the stem of the lamp, arms folded. He was starting to enjoy the little scene. In the dim light of the sitting room it all looked vaguely erotic. The woman's pale blue dress fell in a soft circle around her knees. Her long, well-manicured hands stroked the man's shoulder in a gesture that could have been taken for a caress. A strange, most remarkably puckish idea developed in his mind. Stealthily he took from a private pocket on the inside of his jerkin a small green-glass vial and rolled it between his palms. It was quite a temptation, just the sort of thing they always claimed he was doing. But hadn't he done this poor man enough harm already? He glanced around the cluttered lounge. Maybe he would be doing the fellow a favor, making up in a way for the beating. In any event, it was too good an opportunity for a puck to let pass. He ran quickly but very cautiously to the corner of the table where the two glasses of wine sat. Stretching on tiptoe he was barely able to place a drop of the liquid from the vial into each glass. One drop only; at their age and state of fatigue resistance would be low, and an overdose could prove disastrous. The mischief accomplished, the Puck recorked the vial, secreted it once more in the depths of his jerkin, and returned to his seat to watch the fun.

"Better now?" Miss Crawley asked as Ian sat up.

"Considerably, thank you. Despite my forebodings you've proved an excellent nurse."

"Let's give credit where it is deserved," she countered, bringing the glasses from the desk and seating herself demurely on the chair near the sofa. "It's Aneelen's medicine you should be thanking, not my clumsy attempt at doctoring. There are few living in her world or ours who have her skill with herbs."

"Then let us drink by all means to the Lady Aneelen's skill." He emptied his glass in one swallow. Not to be outdone by such a show of masculine braggadocio, Miss Crawley downed her wine in the same manner. The Puck hugged his knees and hunched his shoulders in silent glee. This promised to be an excellent show.

Miss Crawley cleared her throat. "Do you have any objection to my going along tomorrow?"

Ian frowned. "What do you want to do that for?"

"For Dr. Heaton's sake mostly." She gave him a slow smile. "I'm about to be encouraging again. Just suppose things do go badly for you tomorrow. He's likely to take it hard. He thinks the world of you, you know. He might attempt to rescue you or do something else equally desperate. It would be well to have a hardhearted wench like me along to keep things under control."

"That's very thoughtful of you," Ian murmured, looking at her in some surprise. He was beginning to suspect that he had badly misjudged this woman. A hardhearted wench she certainly was not. Her touch was gentle, and now she revealed that she possessed considerable sensitivity. Marian Crawley was, he began to realize, much more of a woman than he had supposed. He wondered now that he had thought her homely. Her features were bold, but they went well together; and he much preferred the open generosity of a wide mouth to the parsimonious tightness of a narrow one. And her hair. It was strange that he had not before noticed her hair. It was a warm, auburn color that picked up and softly reflected the light of the desk lamp. And for once it was not perfectly in place. Wisps of it had fallen around her cheeks, softening the lines that had begun to develop about the eyes. Ian smiled to himself as he recalled his landlady's assessment of the estate agent. "Not bad-looking, if a bit angular." Whatever her defects, he reflected, observing with no little pleasure the soft curves under the bodice of the dress, angularity was not one of them. Ian caught himself with a little jerk and rubbed uncertainly at his forehead. What on earth was the matter with him, gawking at the woman's breasts like a virgin schoolboy? He thought he'd put that sort of thing behind him years before. It must be the wine. It seemed to have hit him rather hard. He lowered his eyes in embarrassment, wondering what she might think of his staring at her so.

He might have set himself at ease on that matter. Marian Crawley was quite unaware of his gaze, for she was deeply involved in a problem of her own. It was not on the wine that she blamed her feelings, but that damned lock of hair that kept falling in his eyes. She wanted so awfully to smooth it back. Perhaps it was only a compulsive urge for neatness that moved her, but she didn't really believe that was it. Did it remind her of something, someone? Of course, Fremna's hair had fallen over his face like that. No, that wasn't right. Fremna's hair had curled close to his head, hadn't it? She wasn't sure now just how his hair had looked. That was impossible. His face had been before her mind's eye constantly for the past quarter century. She closed her eyes so that she could conjure up again his face as it had been, handsome and merry, his green eyes warm with laughter. But all she could see were the craggy features and mocking dark eyes of Ian James. Annoyed, she quickly opened her eyes. That was going a bit too far. She rose abruptly, smoothing down her skirt in a gesture of latent modesty.

"I really must be going now. We both need what rest we can get."

"What do you say to a stirrup cup?" Ian asked, starting to rise.

Miss Crawley considered a moment. "Well, all right, if you let me fetch. You're still my patient, you know."

"I should prefer that you didn't see my kitchen. It's in rather a jumble."

She laughed. "Oh I know what bachelors' digs are like. I let them, after all." Taking the two glasses she headed for the kitchen.

"Don't forget poor Robin," a small, wheedling voice reached her from the desk. The Puck stood smiling obsequiously, holding out the empty sauce cap.

"I'd like to forget you, you vicious little imp. Look at all the trouble you've caused."

The Puck grinned and struck a mockingly theatrical pose.

Gentles, do not reprehend,
If you pardon we will mend.

Miss Crawley snorted. "It's mending you'd need if I got a lick at you." She took the cap with her, though, into the kitchen.

She returned in a few minutes with the refilled glasses, pausing at the desk to give the Puck his ration. Ian watched her as she crossed the room, enjoying the easy movement of her hips beneath the clinging skirt. She was aware this time of his gaze but somehow did not mind. After handing him his glass, for no reason that she could give, she sat down on the sofa beside him rather than returning to her chair. He raised his glass to her with a gallant smile.

"I know now what to drink to. I drink to you, Marian,

for you are a remarkable and, if I may say so, a singularly attractive woman." He took a sip of his wine, smiling at her over the top of the glass with disarming shyness. "You won't be offended, I hope, if I call you Marian."

She suppressed an absurd temptation to giggle.

"Considering the time of day and your present state of undress, it strikes me as highly proper, Ian."

Only half aware of what he was doing, Ian put his arm lightly around her shoulder. She did not resist his touch.

"Do you still feel as you did—about men, I mean?"

"I don't really know," she replied slowly. "It's been so many years since I've been this close to a man."

"That is a great waste, Marian." He drew her slowly toward him, bending close to her face, enjoying the vague scent of rosemary that always seemed to surround her. She could feel the warmth and smell the odor of his body. There was another odor she got as well, one she remembered vaguely as belonging somewhere in her past. Then she recognized it, the strange, slightly pungent odor of male passion. She pulled away and sat erect on the sofa, pushing her hair back into place.

"I really must be going now, Ian."

He removed his arm at once, turning red with embarrassment.

"I'm sorry," he murmured. "Please don't be offended. There's no harm in me really. I'm only a weary old bachelor with a sore back."

She squeezed his hand lightly. "I'm not offended, Ian. I like you. Truly I do. I hadn't realized before tonight how much I really do like you. But the night is getting away from us. I must go now so you can sleep."

"I—I rather wish you wouldn't. I don't especially care to be alone tonight." He gave a little nervous laugh. "Now, that does sound childish, doesn't it?"

"Not to me. But it's rest you need all the same, not company. We both do. Here now, finish your drink and go to bed before it all wears off."

They rose and just looked at each other for an awkward moment.

"Good night, duck," Marian whispered, kissing him lightly on the tip of his beard. "You go on in. I'll find my way out."

"Good night, then, Marian."

He turned, dejected, and went into the bedroom, closing the door behind him.

Marian Crawley stood silent, her arms at her sides. It was strange how very empty the room seemed when he had left it. She shook her head, gathering up the glasses and returning them to the unkempt kitchen. She oughtn't to drink late at night that way; she wasn't used to it. As she started to put out the desk lamp she noticed the Puck still sitting on the base of it grinning at her. She snatched a throw cushion from the sofa and slapped it onto the desk.

"There's a bed for you, and here's a coverlet."

She pulled another linen handkerchief from her bottomless handbag and threw it to him.

"Now turn around and go to sleep."

"Are you sure you can find your way out?" he asked impudently.

She seized from the desk a paperweight folded in the shape of the Albert Memorial and brandished it threateningly. The Puck turned his back at once, settling comfortably on the cushion as she switched off the lamp. He lay quiet, listening. There was no sound for a while. Then there were footsteps; a door opened softly, then closed. The Puck turned just in time to ascertain that the door closed behind Marian Crawley was indeed the one that led to Ian James' bedroom. He settled once more on his cushion, thoroughly pleased with himself. He dropped off to sleep almost at once, murmuring in cadence, like a lullaby:

So good night unto you all.
Give me your hands if we be friends,
And Robin will restore amends.

Chapter 14

The Changeling

Mompen woke slowly from a sleep too heavy to be normal, the Queen's soothing voice still in his ears. He was conscious first of a singularly unpleasant sensation in the lower torso; then he became aware that he was lying not on his back, as he usually did in sleep, but on his belly. His cheek was pressed against a smooth, cold material, quite different from the mossy covering of his woodland couch. All around him was a vaguely familiar earthy odor. Reluctantly he opened his eyes to find himself in prison. He was surrounded on four sides by high wooden bars. Slowly he began to realize where he was and what had happened to him. He could remember nothing after his shameful breakdown before the King. Silently he cursed himself for his weakness. Oh well, in spite of him the thing had apparently worked. He was now imprisoned in the large, unmanageable body of a human child. The exchange had been accomplished. There was only one further question to be answered. With some difficulty he worked the pudgy, pink baby hands that were his new vehicles of sensation inside the layers of wrapping that now enclosed his critical parts. There he found the answer to his question as well as the source of the odor and the discomfort. He was female, and she was badly in need of a change.

The bedroom door opened a few inches, and a small blond head appeared around it.

"Yes, she's awake now. Let's go in and see her."

The door flew back violently against the wall, and two of the American children, Anne and Ned, danced in.

Mompen had a little difficulty identifying these quite normal-sized creatures with the giant children she remembered from her earlier visit. But she was more than glad to have them there. These violent changes in her life, she had found, were best weathered if they were as much as possible ignored. It was blessedly difficult to think, much less brood, in the company of this ebullient pair.

"We're going on the train today, Penny," Ned cried, chinning himself on the side of the cot. "We're going to London, going to London."

Anne dangled in front of the baby's face a small, woefully inaccurate replica of a rabbit with a silly-looking smiling face that seemed to be filled with dry straw. Mompen found the thing repulsive and pushed it emphatically away. Anne was taken aback.

"What's the matter, Penny?" she asked. "Don't you love Bunny anymore?"

Mompen winced inwardly. So. The test was starting already. If she hoped to successfully wear the mask of a human child, she was going to have to be more prudent in her responses. Resolutely she grasped the dreadful plaything. It didn't feel too bad once she had it close to her face and was no longer forced to watch it swaying from the rubbery string around its neck like a gibbeted corpse.

The mother now appeared in the doorway, red-faced and anxious.

"Good grief, Ned. Don't you have your shoes on yet? Go and get ready at once. What have you been doing all this time? Go downstairs right away and finish your breakfast, Anne. There'll be no London for you if you don't eat."

Once she had shooed the older children out of the room and quietly approached the cot, her manner altered.

"And are you awake now, little pet?" she murmured, gingerly lifting the baby from the cot and laying her on a nearby bed. "How would you like a nice change and a lovely bowl of porridge?"

Mompen attempted to produce an affirmative answer, forgetting the limitations that now lay on her powers of speech. However, the motions and noises that she did manage to produce pleased the mother surprisingly.

"Oh you are a little dear, aren't you?" she chortled, patting the baby's new cleansed buttocks with a heavily scented powdery substance. "Does my bright little Penny like to go choo-choo train?"

Mompen did not know how to reply to this query, as she had not the least idea what the human woman was talking about. The children had seemed enthusiastic about the day's excursion, so she dutifully indicated her pleasure and even made a not too bad attempt at verbalizing the odd syllables, "choo-choo." The mother was delighted, and Mompen submitted to a stifling embrace, quite pleased with her success. She was beginning to respond to the challenge of this queer masquerade.

"Look at the baby in the mirror," the mother urged, standing with the child in her arms before the looking glass that hung over the umbrella stand in the front hall. It was a devastating experience for Mompen, looking into that mirror, seeing in the mother's arms the baby, Penny, almost exactly as she had looked when the fairy Mompen had lived so perilously in the springs of her cot. A terror rose in her suddenly too great for even the releasing potion to counteract. Mompen, she realized, was a creature who no longer existed. Penny was a person she had not yet become. It was like looking into the glass and seeing no reflection at all. It was certainly worse than death, for the dead do not have to witness their nonexistence. Burying the face that was not her own in the neck of the mother that was not her own, she cried, giving expression to all her grief and horror in a ludicrous infant wail. The foolish sounds that came from her throat served but to increase her distress, and she cried all the louder.

"What's the matter?" "What's wrong with her?" "Did she fall?" "Is she sick?" The entire family rushed into the hall from various parts of the house to gather around mother and child.

"I don't know," the mother exclaimed. "She was fine just a minute ago. She might be teething again. I don't know."

The doorbell rang abruptly just above their heads, causing all to start, including the baby. The mother carried her into the lounge, joggling her up and down and murmuring, "Hush, hush," into her ear. The baby stopped crying almost at once, for the joggling motion made her seasick. The gambit worked. The instant she stopped crying the awful bobbing ceased. Mother and child were each quite pleased at finding the other so easy to control.

"It's Mrs. Hubbard, dear," the father called from the hall. The baby stiffened at the sound of a familiar name. It was indeed Mrs. Hubbard who now entered the room, the same Mrs. Hubbard whom the defunct Mompen had known as an honored guest in his father's halls. She smiled warmly at all the family but had a special, private greeting for the baby watching her over the mother's shoulder.

"I wouldn't have bothered you so early, but that I saw you were up, I have a bit more dundee cake on hand than I can hope to use before it goes stale. Perhaps the children would enjoy it."

She gave a paper-wrapped package to Anne, who was jumping up and down beside her. The children were so loud and enthusiastic in their gratitude that they were sent off at once to put the cake in the pantry. "And how are you today, sweet?" Mrs. Hubbard held out her arms to the baby. The mother was astonished to see the baby allow herself to be taken into another woman's arms with no hesitation and, in fact, with considerable eagerness.

"Aren't you becoming a little beauty, now?" the old lady cooed, turning her back momentarily on the adults in the room. "All went well in the Fernwood," she whispered hurriedly. The baby clung to her.

"I don't know what's the matter with Penny this morning," the mother was saying. "She doesn't seem herself at all."

"Oh they're all rather like that at her age. Storm clouds one moment and sunshine the next." Mrs. Hubbard carried the baby over to the large window that protruded into the garden. "Oh look at the birdies, dear." Bending once more close to the child's ear she whispered, "You are going to be all right now. Just carry on as you are, and it will all come easier soon enough."

"We're off to London for the day," the mother said. "We have to take an early train if we're going to see the Changing of the Guard."

"Oh splendid. Just the thing." Mrs. Hubbard handed back the baby. "Now, you will enjoy that, dear. A little change of scenery is just what you need." She started for the front door. "Well, I shan't delay you any further. Do have a pleasant day."

"Thank you, Mrs. Hubbard. Drop by again when there's time for a visit before we have to leave for home."

"Don't worry. I intend to see a great deal of you all." She winked at the baby. "Good-bye now, pet. Have a good time."

The Vicar had passed an uncomfortable night, what little there had been of it. Shortly before dawn he gave up the effort to force himself into sleep. He rose, dressed, and took a brisk walk in the refreshing early-morning air. It was a little cooler than it had been, which was a pleasant change, but walking did not calm him the way it usually did, perhaps because this was the first solitary walk he had taken in many months. Even as he paced in steady cadence along the deserted sidewalks he imagined that Ian James matched strides with him, hands in pockets, head lowered, repeating that damned formula over and over.

("Seeing touch not, seeing touch not." Come now, you don't really think that was a mistake.)

It was not yet half past six when he parked his dilapidated sedan in front of the large stone house on Southdown Road. He got no answer when he pressed the bell labeled "James." After waiting close to a minute he started to press the bell a second time, but then thought better of it. Why wake the poor chap if he could sleep? He'd said he'd call at seven, so seven it would be. He had turned and was starting back down the walk when a raucous buzz informed him that his summons was heard and the door was waiting to be opened. He entered and sprinted up the stairs at a pace that would have proved too much for many men half his age. The door at the end of the hall was opened by Ian James, who was hastily fastening the last button on his dressing gown. The Vicar got the distinct impression that he was wearing little or nothing under it. Ian seemed slightly nervous and ill at ease.

"Good morning, James. I'm sorry if I got you up. I am

early, I know, but I have been anxious to see how you spent the night."

Ian looked at him startled, went pale, and then blushed painfully. "Why I . . . we . . . You see, it just . . ." he stammered. Then he gave a nervous little laugh. "Oh I see what you mean. I'm quite all right, really. Fine, feel splendid, in fact. But then, you know, I've been very well taken care of." He blushed again and turned away abruptly. "I don't mean it that way. I mean, well, you know what I mean . . . I mean . . . Oh bloody hell!"

Throwing up his hands in despair he sat down heavily on the sofa. It was at this moment that the Vicar saw Marian Crawley's handbag lounging comfortably on the desk.

"Hmm," he murmured. "I see, I see."

The handbag's owner now appeared in the kitchen doorway, bearing a pot and three teacups on a tray, and looking not only tense and embarrassed but also slightly, attractively disheveled. Her dress was rumpled and loose at the neck. On her feet she wore large, soft men's slippers. Her hair fell untended around her shoulders.

"Could I put on an egg for you, Dr. Heaton?" she asked, rather unsteadily serving him his tea.

"Just toast for me, thank you, Marian," he replied, deftly returning to the cup the rather large amount of tea she had succeeded in sloshing into the saucer. He seated himself on the sofa beside Ian and cleared his throat. It was obvious that they expected him to comment on the situation.

"My dear children," he began, taking a long drink of tea. They looked at him and he at them. Then he smiled and finished his tea in another long gulp. He leaned back on the sofa and smiled again benevolently. "My dear children," he concluded. Marian turned quickly and fled to the kitchen. Ian sat staring into his cup.

"If it's an explanation you're after, I haven't got one."

The Vicar laughed. He couldn't help it.

"I'm afraid I fail to see where an explanation is necessary or, for that matter, even desirable." He paused, frowning. "However, it does occur to me that you might now want to change your, er, plans for the day."

"I don't think that has entered either of our minds," Ian said firmly.

"Did Ian tell you I'm coming along today?" Marian called from the kitchen. "Just for the ride, so to speak."

The Vicar scowled at Ian. "Do you think that wise?" he asked in a curt whisper.

"Do you think it's wiser to leave her here all day, wondering what's going on?" Ian replied. "No, Vicar, I shall feel much better about both of you if I know that both of you are well occupied keeping an eye on each other."

Marian brought the breakfast in to them on a large tray.

"You'll have to manage out here, I'm afraid," she explained. "I wouldn't allow you in the kitchen. It's a disgrace. You really ought to wash up occasionally, Ian, just for appearances."

"No time to domesticate him now, my dear," the Vicar murmured. "He's probably too old anyhow; you'll just have to take him as he is. So you're going along for the ride. Did your untidy friend here tell you how dangerous that can be?"

"I intend to go as far as you and no farther."

"I should prefer that you did not go at all," said the Vicar.

"You're wasting your time," Ian interposed. "She's a very stubborn woman. And a damn good cook. It takes a certain gift to make the perfect egg."

"I hate to rush you, children," the Vicar interrupted, "but it's going for seven and we've a long day ahead of us. No washing up, now, Marian," he added as she began neatly stacking the few dishes onto the tray. "You'll just have to add those to what's already here."

"Oh I say, I'd better be getting dressed, hadn't I?" Ian sprang up with an embarrassed laugh. As he turned he winced slightly. Hastily Marian set down the tray of dishes and snatched up the blown-glass flask still sitting on the desk.

"Not so fast, my dear. If I'm not mistaken you could stand a little medication."

"She fancies herself Florence Nightingale," Ian called over his shoulder as he was half pushed into the bedroom.

"I find the role very becoming to her," said the Vicar. He took up the tray and carried it to the kitchen. It was on his return that he noticed the Puck sitting cross-legged in the center of a puffy throw cushion like a miniature rajah, chuckling quietly to himself behind the scrap of lean bacon he was munching.

"What are you smirking at?" the Vicar asked crossly.

"I am reminded, reverend sir, of a line in a play I once saw: 'Lord, what fools these mortals be!' "

"The quote is unsuitable," the Vicar snorted. "I'll give you another more appropriate from the same source:

Lovers and madmen have such seething brains,
Such shaping fantasies, that apprehend
More than cool reason ever comprehends."

As the old sedan turned the corner at the intersection of Southdown Road and Churchill Lane, its occupants were surprised to see an elderly lady in a beige lace blouse waiting patiently at the curb like an expectant hitchhiker, a large, old-fashioned picnic hamper on the walk beside her. The car pulled in with a jerk in front of her, and the Vicar jumped out, scowling.

"What's all this now?" he asked gruffly. "Next thing someone will be hiring a police escort and a brass band."

"Oh don't be vexed, Thomas. I've been so terribly anxious. I thought it might be nice if you had a bit of lunch along. . . ."

"All right. The lunch goes, Sybil, but you do not."

"Why not indeed? I see you have already acquired Marian."

"I'm not the one who's acquired Marian," the Vicar retorted.

Ian, who had just come around the car and was lifting the hamper, went scarlet.

"Good morning, Ian," Mrs. Hubbard said. "How are you feeling?"

"Splendid, thank you, Mrs. Hubbard," Ian replied, hefting the cumbersome basket into the boot. "And in a far more cordial mood than my chauffeur." He held the rear door open for her. "Come now, we shall have your lunch and your company as well."

The Vicar shrugged and got back into the car.

"What's the harm?" Ian asked as they cruised along the A3 a bit faster than he considered comfortable. "We might as well make an outing of it." He chuckled. "You can all sit around telling one another tales like Chaucer's pilgrims while I tend to business."

"I went next door this morning on the pretext of taking the children some cake," Mrs. Hubbard said. "Everything seems to have gone well there."

"How is Mompen managing?" asked Marian.

"Roughly at present, but not too badly, considering. I gave him—her—the impression that the whole exchange has been successful. She has quite enough to handle without worrying about this business. They're going to town for the day. The diversion will probably help."

Ian sighed. He was relieved to know that some part of his spell had been successful, but he did not enjoy being reminded that the Mompen he had smuggled into the theater, had drunk with and had laughed at, no longer existed. He felt as though he had slain a friend.

At around one o'clock the Vicar pulled over into a layby that adjoined a small wooded grove. It was a relief to get out of the car and stretch awhile, for they were all stiff and cramped. The Puck, delighted to be freed from the stifling closeness of Ian's pocket, ran about the grass in circles. As the two younger people laid out a linen cloth and set upon it the dishes and cutlery neatly strapped to the inside of the hamper's lid, the Vicar struggled to light the ancient spirit stove.

"Oh dear," Mrs. Hubbard gasped as she watched Ian spin a dinner plate high in the air. Marian caught it expertly and placed it with exaggerated care on the cloth. They both laughed, easily, intimately.

"I must be getting old, Thomas," Mrs. Hubbard murmured as she prepared the teapot. "I see I have been missing something rather important."

The Vicar followed her gaze to the pair unloading the hamper, responding to each item, taking any excuse to touch and look at each other.

"No, Sybil, you haven't been missing anything. All this is a very recent development—as of last night, from all I can gather."

"I see." Mrs. Hubbard filled the pot with boiling water. "I don't think that's exactly what Aneelan meant by taking care of him."

"I can't say in all honesty that I'm unhappy about it."

"I would agree with you, Thomas, if I could be certain how things are going to work out today. Two affairs ending in tragedy might be a bit much even for a strong woman like Marian."

"Then why in the name of heaven doesn't she try to talk him out of it?"

Mrs. Hubbard started to reply but quickly lapsed into silence when Ian trotted over to see how the tea was coming on.

"My, what a grand little feast, eh, Vicar? Elegant yet homely. It rather puts me in mind of the finale to the first act of *The Sorcerer.*"

Carrying the teapot ceremoniously to the center of the cloth, he sang:

> *Now to the banquet we press;*
> *Now for the eggs, the ham;*
> *Now for the mustard and cress,*
> *Now for the strawberry jam!*

Happy for a chance to demonstrate his still-viable voice, the Vicar took up the verse:

> *Eat, drink, and be gay, banish all worry and sorrow,*
> *Laugh gaily today, weep, if you're sorry, tomorrow!*
> *Come pass the cup round—I will go bail for the liquor.*
> *It's strong, I'll be bound, for it was brewed by the vicar!*

"Now, there's a proper song for the occassion," Ian laughed. "Except that it is Mrs. Hubbard's brew that I'm for now. A little milk, yes, thank you. Our Vicar, I gather, deals in brews of a quite different sort."

The Vicar turned, his mouth open in anticipation of a wedge of cheese he was in the act of raising to it.

"Just what do you mean by that, James?"

"I mean only that I have wondered at times exactly

how much you've had to do with the concocting of the particular stew I keep finding myself simmering in."

The Vicar slowly laid the wedge of cheese back on his plate. "Surely you don't think I had anything to do with that ghastly business last night?"

"Oh no. Of course not," Ian assured him. "If we have been used by your master, you are obviously as much a victim as the rest of us. But you very well know that my involvement with all this didn't begin last night. It started last winter—at the pantomime, to be exact. You were carrying on a rather private conversation with Mrs. Hubbard in a rather public voice. I am not the sort of fellow who goes around listening in on private conversations, but I would have had to be deaf to avoid hearing that one. The invitation to go into the forest on Midwinter Night I received rather directly from you.

"The invitation to go traipsing down to Cornwall with you was even more direct. And you know I would never have looked into that damned globe if I hadn't been forced to. If my memory serves me correctly, it was you who pushed me into the chair. If I hadn't gone where in hell I went with that thing, I would not have agreed to cast the spell.

"Last night things got rather out of hand for you, didn't they? First the spell, and then me. Whatever it is you have been trying to seduce me into, it certainly doesn't include challenging your devilish master. Well, I'm for it all the same. And now, since I may not have the opportunity in the future to discuss the matter with you, I think I'm entitled to some straight answers. Just exactly what is this game you have been playing with me?"

"Ian!" Marian Crawley's shocked voice cut through his tirade. He looked around, taken aback a little by his own vehemence.

"Let him go, Marian," Mrs. Hubbard said. "It was bound to come out. After all, he has a right to know how things stand with him."

The Vicar sat staring at his plate. Ian reached across the cloth and gave the old man's knee a reassuring pat.

"Oh come now. Don't take it to heart. I'm sorry; I didn't mean to blow off like that. I'm not angry, only damnably curious. You must admit you haven't been completely honest with me."

"No I haven't, James. But I've had my reasons for that. I'm getting old, you see, older than you realize, and my health isn't what it used to be. The most important work of my life has been the study of the art you call necromancy. I've been hunting for years for a suitable person to pass my knowledge on to.

"You have no idea how long I've been watching you. I think it was your work in the theater that first attracted me. I could see that you had the imagination and the style to do splendid stuff. But I also found out when you consulted me once about some material on the Magi or some such that you are a thoroughly conventional fellow. I had to move very slowly and very carefully. I planted seeds, many seeds, and dropped scores of hints. The conversation at the pantomime was only one of these. And you're right to call them invitations. That's just what they were, and you were always free to turn them down.

"Now, as far as getting out of hand is concerned, you did that continually from the outset. I was telling the truth when I told Oberon that I didn't know how you got into Garumpta's halls. I had intended merely to pique your curiosity by letting you overhear our plans for the evening. It never occurred to me that you would dare to follow us. Believe me, I was horrified when you were caught, though I must admit I was delighted with the outcome of your capture. Here was the chance I needed to work with you closely without frightening you away. Why wouldn't I encourage you to go to Cornwall with me? You were free to turn down that invitation, too."

"And the globe? Was I free to turn that one down?"

"It summoned you. I think you're quite aware of that. None of us is free to turn down a call like that. The incident only confirmed my own evaluation of you. The Powers were as anxious to have you as I was."

"But old Merlin saw it differently, didn't he?" Ian said. "I think I took the globe away from him, at least for a while. He lost control of it and of me, and that is how I came to descend to the Pit. He is not my master, nor can he ever be. I flatter myself with the belief that he is just a little afraid of me. It's on that belief, if you must know, that I'm gambling today."

"You're not only mad, James," the Vicar said, "you're damned presumptuous. What gives you the fool idea that he's afraid of you?"

"He told you—ordered you, really—to drop me because I was too extraordinary, wasn't it, for his tastes."

The Vicar looked at Ian, his eyes glinting. "You have not been entirely honest with me either, I see. And you have become less scrupulous about listening to private conversations. You may also have noticed that I have made no move to drop you, nor have I the least intention of doing so."

Ian helped himself to dundee cake, dropping some large crumbs and an almond on the cloth next to him where the Puck sat contentedly cramming his mouth full of anything he could reach.

"I'm sorry, Vicar, but you might just as well drop me and put your time in on some other successor. I am not about to let your mantle fall on me. If I get out of this mess alive I'm retiring from sorcery permanently. I intend to become once more a thoroughly conventional fellow. Tea in the morning, port at night, *The News of the World* on Sunday afternoons. When I get hungry for adventure, I'll take the train for Bognor. I won't forget you, though. Whatever your intentions were, I have enjoyed your company these last months tremendously."

"As I haved enjoyed yours, my boy. If I hadn't liked you I would not have taken you on, no matter how great your talents." The Vicar smiled wistfully. "However, I haven't anyone else, nor do I plan on getting anyone else. You are my man, whether you want to be or not. If you won't take up my mantle, then it must lie."

Having done as much damage as they could to Mrs. Hubbard's abundant supplies, the travelers now proceeded to clear up the remains and repack the hamper. The turn of the conversation had left them all rather subdued. It was the Vicar who finally broke the silence.

"I'll gladly drop you, James, or do anything else you want, if you'll come back with me now and give up this absurd idea that you can scare the master into doing your will."

"I say, that's bribery, Vicar," Ian laughed. "I hardly expected you to stoop to that. Eavesdropping is one thing, but bribery!"

He wrapped the remaining cake rather clumsily and handed it to Marian.

"Oh dear, no," she scolded good-naturedly. "You daren't wrap it like that; it'll go stale. It must be made airtight. Like this, see?"

"What in the name of holiness ails you, girl?" the Vicar exploded. "Carrying on about stale cake when your man's on his way to damnation. You're the only one of the lot of us who might be able to stop him. Make proper use of your womanhood for once."

Marian finished wrapping the cake, slowly and meticulously, and filed it in its proper nook before she replied.

"The gentleman in question made sport of me once for my scruples; he may want to thank me for them now. I consider it unethical and wholly unacceptable to take that kind of advantage of his feelings for me. Besides, I agree with Oberon. A man of courage and power ought to be allowed to choose his doom, without some damned woman whining at his heels."

Ian burst out laughing. Marian looked at him in surprise and began laughing too.

"What a man! I take his part, and he laughs at me."

"I'm sorry, my dear. I am grateful for your defense and your scruples. But the picture of you whining at anyone's heels was more than I could handle soberly."

Together they carried the hamper to the car, taking the opportunity to exchange a few whispered endearments, Mrs. Hubbard linked her arm in the Vicar's.

"Come now, Thomas. Don't make things harder for them than they already are. It's no longer your responsibility. He's on his own this time. Wish him luck and let him go. I have a feeling he'll wear your mantle yet."

"If he survives today, Sybil," the Vicar said. "I'm prepared to wager my life on that."

Chapter 15

The Metamorphosis of Ian James

The quiet little Cornish village looked as old-fashioned and unassuming in the heavy heat of mid-June as it had in the mild chill of February. The old sedan spun around the corner by the inn and began climbing the hill.

"Pull over for a bit, would you, Vicar?" Ian asked suddenly as they drew alongside the little park. It was the first time he had spoken since lunch. He had been deep in his own thoughts, and his companions had sympathetically left him to them. Delighted with what he took to be a sign of hesitation, the Vicar parked at the side of the road. The four of them walked for a while along the edge of the stream, talking easily and casually of the beauty of the place. Two compatible couples on a day's outing. Mrs. Hubbard was pleased to discover a rare wildflower growing amongst the tree roots. She and Marian at once became involved in a close study of the undergrowth. A short time later the Vicar spotted a remarkable specimen of *Collybia radicata,* the rooting shank mushroom, an unusual find so early in the summer.

"Here, James," he called. "Come have a look at this."

There was no response. He knew before he turned to look that Ian had gone. He had to fight down the impulse to run after him. The ladies, still intent on their search for herbaceous plants, were unaware of what had happened. Well, perhaps it was best that way. The Vicar bowed his head and pressed his folded hands against his face in an attitude of prayer.

"Good luck, son," he whispered. "Try to keep your head, and don't do anything terribly foolhardy." He looked down at the mushroom with a sigh. It was a discovery he had very much wanted to share.

The little walk that led up to the front door of the old wizard's cottage was bordered now with pansies in a most astonishing variety of colors and textures. The circular flowerbed in the center of the front lawn contained a large and beautiful cluster of salmon-colored geraniums. The front door was closed, the curtains drawn. Ian James rapped on the door, three sharp knocks, a pause for a count of three, then two light taps. The door sprang open immediately, and Merlin stood before him dressed in a faded polo shirt and worn khaki trousers. His eyes were an ingenuous light blue and registered surprise on seeing Ian.

"Well, well," he cried. "If it isn't Tom's friend with the Celtic name. Mr. Ian, er, Ian St. John, isn't it?"

"James, Master. Ian James."

"Yes, yes, of course. Well, come in, whatever your mother called you, and tell me the news from the Fernwood."

Ian entered the little sitting room and accepted the chair offered him. The room seemed enveloped in shadow after the brilliant sunshine outside, but it was refreshingly cool. Out of the corner of his eye, Ian noticed that the door leading to the wizard's workroom was slightly ajar.

"Now," Merlin said, seating himself on the chair across the cold fireplace from Ian, "tell me all about your great exchange. How did it go?"

"Not well," Ian replied in an even tone.

"Dear me, don't tell me you botched the spell."

"The spell was botched before I received it, Master. It produced a changeling perfect in every aspect but one. She has Mompen's eyes."

Merlin chuckled in the depths of his throat, and his eyes turned several shades darker.

"Oh dear, dear. That must have been quite a shock for the Puck. How did he take it?"

"For a starter, he gave me such a vicious thrashing that I'm still feeling the effects of it."

The wizard seemed genuinely disturbed.

"I'm terribly sorry to hear that. Why did he take it out on you particularly?"

"The general assumption was that I had botched the spell, as you suggested. But I had no trouble clearing myself, since I had with me the paper on which you had written it."

Merlin lifted his eyebrows. "A wise precaution. I wouldn't have credited you with that much sense."

"Actually it had little to do with sense, just an actor's superstition. And so it is that you see me today with my head still intact, but not my mission. The Puck refused to accept his imperfect bride which, as you can imagine, rather put everything out of joint."

Merlin chuckled. "He wouldn't have her, eh? Just what you could expect of such a creature."

"Exactly. It was such typical behavior that most of the little folk assumed that you had foreseen it and had deliberately sabotaged the spell in the hope that he would react in the way he did, and so save you the necessity of condemning the fairies to extinction by doing so himself. The Vicar, being the splendid, loyal fellow he is, insisted that the whole thing was nothing more than an honest mistake. I don't think he realized how insulting his defense of you was. For myself, I find it hard to believe you capable of such a clumsy error. 'Seeing touch not.' It never sounded right, even to the ears of an amateur like me. How would it have gone, anyway, if it had been right?"

Merlin looked at him sharply, a dangerous orange light flashing in the depths of his eyes.

"Why do you want to know that?" he asked.

Ian grasped the arms of his chair in a sudden spasm of fear. He was going to have to put in the performance of his career if he was going to get what he wanted out of this sly old fellow and still avoid his own demise. He could not afford to appear eager. The only feeling he dared show now was casual indifference. He concentrated on his hands. They began to relax their grip. He feigned a careless shrug.

"Oh just curiosity. It's a rather frequent failing of mine.

It doesn't really matter, I suppose, unless you would be willing to consider correcting the mistake."

"I would consider what?"

The wizard's voice was shrill with sudden anger. His eyes turned brilliant red. He raised his forefinger as if preparing to make a pronouncement. Ian began talking very rapidly, never taking his eyes away from the threateningly upraised forefinger.

"There's no point, you see, in ruining the exchange now. I can understand your objecting to the abduction of the human child. I choked a bit on that myself. But it's done now, and Mompen seems to have come through quite nicely. The parents aren't even suspicious. So there's really no reason for messing with this end of the exchange. The little people ought to be given a chance to survive, don't you think? What possible threat could they be to you, diminished as they are in size and numbers? It would be a magnanimous gesture on your part to grant them this chance, perhaps to be reconciled with them after all these years. You've no real reason for wanting their destruction. Why not give the fool Puck his bride and see if he really can make a go of it? There. I've had my say. That's what I really came down here for. If you choose to do something awful to me for asking you decently to do a decent thing, I cannot prevent you."

Ian lowered his head and waited, for what he did not allow himself to think. After a long pause, Merlin spoke.

"Do something awful to you? I ought to; you've certainly been begging for it. I'll do you up proper if Tom Heaton weren't such a soft old ass. He'd be rather provoked with me, I'm afraid, and he's the only student I have left. But if you ever show your ridiculous face around here again, I swear I shall see to it that you have a very short but very exciting life."

Ian slowly raised his eyes. Merlin sat as he had before, hunched forward in his chair. But his finger was no longer upraised, and his eyes had turned greenish brown. There was yet in the depths of them a hint of subdued flame. But around the corners of his mouth was the suspicion of a wry smile.

"You can see no reason for my wanting their destruction," he continued quietly. "Well, I can see no reason for wanting their survival. They've been nothing but a plague to me, and they serve no useful purpose that I can discover. I see no point in contributing to their continued existence, and I'm certain you can give me no real reason for doing so."

"Haven't they the right to survive as much as any of us?" Ian cried, forgetting in his indignation the danger of provoking his host. "I fail to see where you get the right to decide who will live in this land and who will not!"

"I have the right of private ownership, my dear boy. These islands belong to me."

"That's preposterous! How can you own them?"

"They were a gift—from my father. Any other questions?"

Ian sank back in the chair and closed his eyes. No, he had abandoned that line of inquiry some time ago. He wasn't about to get pulled into it again.

"No further questions," he murmured. "So," he added, sitting upright in his chair, "I have done what I could. It was the one chance and I had to take it. There's nothing for me now but to accept what I cannot change, to thank you, Master, for sparing my life, and to leave you in peace."

"That would be just splendid."

Ian started to rise. Then he paused as if struck by a sudden thought. He sat again and leaned forward.

"At the risk of being translated into something unspeakable, could I ask one favor of you?"

"You seem to make a habit of taking risks. Well, what is it now?"

"I have never tasted in my life before, and I never expected to taste again, such beer as I drank in this room last winter. I consider myself something of a connoisseur, and I must say that to my thinking your brew surpasses any to be found on these islands. If your skill in brewing is also a gift from your father, then I honor him for it."

Merlin laughed. "You liked my beer, eh? That is fortunate. I should be hard put to translate anyone with a taste for good beer. I knew there was something about you I liked. However, if it's a glass you're wanting now, I'm afraid you'll have something of a wait. It will be necessary to tap a new keg."

"Oh I don't mind waiting. I have nothing to do now that this affair's settled." Ian threw the line away, lightly and easily. The old wizard, quite mollified and, if the truth be told, just a little flattered, disappeared at once through the double doors that led to the kitchen and eventually to the cellar.

Ian jumped from his seat and ran into the unguarded workroom, bolting the door behind him. The room was in better order than on his previous visit but was otherwise little changed. The sinister-looking black chair had been moved closer to the table. The globe, sitting uncovered on its pedestal, shifted patterns subtly as he entered. Ian seized it at once, spinning it on his fingertips. It flashed streaks of variecolored light, but then began to fade as he spun it faster. What was wrong? What had he done amiss? He gave the globe another spin. As it turned it flashed suddenly, throwing a fleeting beam of light on the conjuror's robe hanging on a hook on the wall next to the cooker. Replacing the globe carefully, Ian pulled the robe down and shrugged it quickly over his shoulders. The fit was just a little tight.

"Get me out of this! Get me out of this!"

The thin, small voice sounded like an echo of his own, but he realized at once that it was coming from the Puck who, pale with fear, was trying to climb out of his pocket.

"Oh I'm sorry, Robin." Ian removed the trembling Puck and placed him carefully on the table. "I quite forgot you were there. Here you'll be safe, I think, and in a much better position for witnessing."

"What are you going to do?" the Puck asked.

"Find out if I can cast a leek in a stewpot."

As the Puck watched from the farthest corner of the table, Ian raised the spinning globe above his head and rapidly intoned the usual invocation:

Powers of earth, of air, of sea,
Powers above, beneath, around,
Powers beyond all creature fear,
Hear and heed my voice!

He paused, head bowed, eyes closed, waiting for the Powers to possess him. Fortunately, they were prompt.

After only a few seconds he addressed them in a voice so low that the Puck was forced to strain to hear him.

"I seek the power to correct the changing spell, to change the eyes. Give me the right words and the power to use them. Quickly. I have little time."

He raised the ball higher over his head, spinning it so fast that it seemed to the Puck to be no more than a blur of color, mostly red and yellow.

Powers of darkness, Powers of light,
Powers of the highest, Powers of the Pit,
Fearsome Powers, dread of men,
Come, do my bidding, come!

The man's face was absolutely white, his mouth set, as if in resistance to pain or terror, his eyes staring into the depths of the globe, which he now held only a few inches from his face. His voice had dropped to a strained half whisper.

Powers that rule all creature spells,
Give me this spell, this spell is mine.
Hear me, heed me, come to my aid.
Tell me the words, give me the power!

He stopped speaking but continued to stare intently into the globe. His lips moved, silently forming words. "Yes," he whispered. "Yes." His eyes, still held by the spinning globe, were now bright with excitement, and his lips turned up in a hard triumphant smile. The Puck, cowering behind a large book on the table, feared him as he had never before feared any creature. He found he could no longer bear to watch and turned his face from the scene. A slight movement on the door caught his attention. The bolt was slowly turning by itself, and now drew back.

"Put it back, quick, he's coming!"

The door flew open with a terrible crash, and Merlin stood in the doorway, looking huge and powerful in his wrath, his eyes blazing a deep, hot red.

"Put that down!" he cried in a voice of thunder.

Ian gave the globe a wild spin. "Now, the spell! Give it to me now. It is mine. You are mine. Obey me!"

Merlin took a step forward, then stopped abruptly as though he had hit some sort of barrier. Ian did not look at him, but continued to stare into the spinning globe. He was no longer smiling, but his lips had begun once more to silently form words.

Merlin spoke again, in the quiet, firm, distinct voice of irresistible command. "Put the globe back."

"No. It is mine!" Great streams, fountains, and sprays of colored light flashed from the globe as Ian turned it faster and faster. But he did not flinch or back off from them.

"Speak," he continued to exhort the Powers within the globe. "Answer me! Answer me!"

Terrified by the supernatural fireworks display, the Puck threw himself flat on the table and covered his head with his arms. He almost wished he had braved the threat of Oberon's staff. Nothing could be worse than the terror of helplessly witnessing such a monstrous battle. The room had become quiet. Neither of these dreadful people had made a sound for some time. The Puck's curiosity got the better of his fear, and he slowly raised his head over the binding of the large book he hid behind. The globe was still spinning, and Ian James was still staring into it. His face was set and grim; he was breathing heavily. Merlin stood where he had been before, his right arm outstretched, the forefinger pointing to the globe. His face was expressionless, but his eyes, as intently fastened on the globe as his opponent's were, glistened black as coals. The little room was filled with the reverberations of the awful struggle that was going on between these two silent adversaries. The Puck was relieved to see that the great flashes of light were no longer shooting out from the globe, until he realized the significance of their absence. The colors within the globe were gradually fading, and it was not spinning as rapidly as it had been, although Ian's hands were turning it as fast as before. The man's eyes filled with tears.

"No," he cried in a choked voice. "You are mine. Obey me!"

"Be still." It was not the man that the Old One addressed thus, but the globe. It obeyed him, spinning more and more slowly like a waning top, until it stopped completely and lay on Ian's fingertips, a beautiful but quite dead thing. With a despairing cry, he raised it high above his head, as though to smash it against the floor.

"Be still."

At once Ian James was still, so still that the Puck feared he had been turned to stone. Merlin walked over to him.

"Give me my globe," he said quietly.

The man's arms lowered in uneven staccato movements, like those of a poorly worked marionette. Merlin removed the globe from his stiff fingers and returned it to its pedestal, covering it with a small, black veil. He appeared weary and moved with unaccustomed slowness.

"Now give me my mantle."

Ian's arms dropped to his sides; Merlin pulled the robe from his back. On his return to the table, he spied the Puck hiding behind a book.

"Aha," he exclaimed, snatching him up. "What are you doing here?"

"He forced me to come, as a witness," the terrified Puck whimpered. "He threatened to use the King's staff on me if I didn't come with him."

Merlin laughed. "That was resourceful of him, I must say. Well, you've no more reason to fear his hand now. As long as you are here, you may as well lend me some assistance in devising a suitable punishment for this foolish man's presumption. You're clever at that sort of thing. Let me see; suppose I diminish him to the size of a speck of dust. Then you could have the privilege of stepping on him, slowly, so that he would have to watch your foot approaching him. Or is that too obvious? If you prefer we could put him in a bottle and set it in the center of the dining table where he would be forced to watch us eat while we watch him starve. Or what do you say I turn him into a male spider of one of the less savory species and introduce him to a female in her season? That way he could enjoy the dubious pleasure of her favors before she devours him. Well, speak up, Robin. What would you have me do with this fool?"

The Puck looked at Ian, who stood staring before him as though he still held the globe. Only his eyes, and the tears that streamed down from them unchecked, revealed the terrible despair of defeat.

"In truth, Master," the Puck said at last, "I would have you spare him. He is a fool to be sure, but he is also a very brave man."

"You're getting soft, Puck," the wizard snorted, setting him back on the table with a bruising thump. But he did return the mantle to its hook before once more approaching Ian. Merlin stood then a long time looking into his defeated opponent's face. Finally he put his arm almost paternally around Ian's shoulders and led him to the chair.

"Sit down." Ian sank unresisting into the chair.

"You are released." Ian's limbs gradually relaxed. Covering his face with his hands, he bowed his head and gave in wholly to his grief. Merlin stood over him silently watching. The Puck also watched, still just a little frightened. It wasn't that he had not seen men weep before (even his own sort wept sometimes), but nothing in his past experiences with men, and with this man in particular, had prepared him for such a painful breakdown. Merlin left the room, returning with a tankard of beer. He patted Ian's heaving shoulders.

"All right. All right. It's over and done now. Here." He shoved the tankard under Ian's nose. "Get some of this into you. It might calm you a bit. I find it difficult to talk reasonably with a man who's turning himself inside out. It's very distracting."

Ian took the tankard but hesitated, looking up apprehensively at the wizard standing over him.

"Go on and drink. It's beer and nothing more, you can be sure of that. I never administer potions secretly." (The Puck winced a little, secretly.) "No doubt it hasn't occurred to you that even I have an ethic of sorts. There, that's better. If it's any comfort to you, you put up a damned good fight."

"It's no comfort," Ian whispered huskily. "I lost."

Merlin leaned back against the table in a half-seated position.

"So. My earlier impression of you was correct. You are a very dangerous fellow, indeed. Not that you are the first to attempt to usurp my power, but you probably came closest to succeeding. If I do let you leave here in one piece, and I am in no way guaranteeing that I shall, I advise you strongly never to return. If you do I shall be forced to dispose of you for my own protection."

"You have nothing to fear from me," Ian replied. "I don't want your power. I don't want any part of it. All I want is that spell fixed." He emptied the tankard and set it on the floor near his feet. He leaned back in the chair exhausted. It had been such a dreadful struggle; fighting against his own terror to call forth the fearsome Powers, then forcing them to submit to his will, only to be challenged at the moment of success by a stronger and more experienced will. His desperation had kept him fighting on far beyond his strength. But now that it was over, and the terrible gamble lost, he was far too weary to care what happened to him. His head ached horribly; the muscles of his abdomen were sore from the strain of heavy and prolonged weeping; and his back was starting to bother him again. But he still could not accept his defeat. He had one last, dreadful gambit to play, the one thing he had most feared and was most determined not to do. But now that it had come to the point he found that he didn't really care that much.

"You can have my soul, if that's what you want."

A low chuckle rumbled in the depths of the wizard's throat, gradually building into a roaring crescendo of laughter, the reverberations of which made the small room rock and echo.

"Do you hear that, Puck?" he gasped, holding onto the table for support. "This generous chap has offered me his soul. What does he suppose I can do with his bloody soul, stoke up the fire?" He took a while to calm himself and settle back once more against the table.

"I don't want your soul, thank you very much. I don't want anything you have to offer, except your absence. In fact, to show my magnanimity, I am more than willing to grant you what you want, if it really is what you want."

Ian sighed. He was in no condition to play games.

"You know quite well what I want. I want that spell reversed, as far as the eyes are concerned."

"Reversed? Just reversed? That's not so awfully difficult. I could arrange that for you, I suppose. Of course, it will be a bit of a shock to the parents of that child. As for Mompen, he's lived with the affliction for many centuries; another sixty years or so shouldn't prove too great a burden."

"No!" Ian cried. "That's not what I want."

"See? It's not so easy, after all. Just what is it that you do want, then? I very much suspect that you have overestimated my capabilities. I have the power of metamorphosis. The power of creation is practiced elsewhere."

"But you produced the spell that altered Mompen's appearance in other ways. Surely you can do the same in just one aspect."

"No, actually I can't. The spell has been used. I cannot alter it."

"You cannot or you will not?"

Merlin shrugged. "So long as I do not alter the spell, it is unimportant, is it not, whether I cannot do it or simply do not choose to? The only way to improve your changeling is through another, minor exchange. That I can do, and, more important, I am willing to do. But first of all I must have a pair of normal eyes to exchange with, eh? You have an enemy, perhaps, on whom you would enjoy taking a rather unusual form of revenge?"

Ian shook his head.

"No?" Merlin raised an eyebrow. "I might have guessed as much. Whatever the fellow's weaknesses he's hardly the vindictive sort. You'd know what to do with such an opportunity, wouldn't you, Puck? Ah well, then we'll just have to gamble a bit. Select a name at random from the London telephone directory. You need never know your victim and will probably never see him. Shall we give it a try?"

"No! No!" Ian cried. "That's horrible. I could never agree to such a thing."

"You are a very difficult person to satisfy, Mr. Ian James. I'm terribly sorry, but if you can't supply me with a suitable and available pair of eyes, there is absolutely nothing I can do for you."

Ian sighed heavily. So that's how it was to be. All that he had done and that had been done to him in the past six months, all the fear, triumph, powers, and potions, Oberon's ring and Garumpta's spikes, the taste of nectar and the scent of rosemary had been leading him just to this. It was for this that he had turned his back on the sleeping town and plunged into the forest of Midwinter Night. There was no question of his refusing to accept it. Having come this far he was hardly going to turn back. In a way he felt relieved, now that he knew where it was that he had been led. It was comforting, at least, to know that the Powers had a sense of humor.

"Come here, Robin," he said quietly. The Puck scampered along the tabletop and straddled the corner nearest Ian.

"Look at me, Robin. Look at my eyes. Do you like them?"

The Puck nodded, a little puzzled. "Oh they're all right, I suppose. Rather nice, really, when you're not glaring at me." He realized on a sudden the man's intention. He gasped, genuinely distressed. "Oh no! You don't want to do anything like that."

"Why not? They're my eyes, aren't they? I suppose I am permitted to do what I wish with them. Fortunately I am not particularly vain about my looks, not having any great reason to be."

Merlin stood back, stroking his beard.

"Well, well, it seems Tom was right. You are an extraordinary man. And I was right when I foretold that we would make a hero of you—a rather peculiar-looking hero, as it turns out. But you would do well to consider carefully what you are proposing. There will be no further reversing if you find you can't live with it."

"I can live with it, have no fear. Now, I have supplied you with a suitable and wholly available pair of eyes. Do you intend to fulfill your part?"

In way of reply, Merlin donned his robe and conical hat and began busying himself with a mortar and pestle at the cooker and the cupboard of jars and bottles, occasionally consulting a large book he had taken from the shelf, like a nervous cook working with an unfamiliar recipe. In a surprisingly short time he returned to the chair with a small gold cup.

"You are going to regret this, you know."

"I know."

Ian took the cup and raised it to the Puck.

"To Garumpta's grandchildren!" he cried and quickly drank the contents. Merlin took back the cup, placed it on the table, raised the globe, and set it spinning. As Ian reached out his hands to take it, Merlin suddenly drew back, a flash of red glinting in his eyes.

"No tricks!"

"No tricks. I swear before heaven or anywhere else you desire. I have no more need of tricks; I have got what I came for."

Ian took the globe and held it before his face.

"Tell me what you see."

"I see what I saw before. My own face."

But this time he knew that the trim face looking at him from the depths of the whirlpool was not an image, but his actual reflection. His mouth turned up in a slow, bitter smile, and the face in the maelstrom smiled back.

"Very good," Merlin said. "Now concentrate, bend all your will on the eyes in that face. Will the eyes away. With all your power will to be rid of them."

He began thumbing through another book rapidly, checking on the exact wording of a spell he needed. A page caught his eye in passing, and he turned quickly back to it, chuckling deep in his throat. "Look here, old chap," he called over his shoulder. "While we're about it, would you care to take a stab at the Holy Grail?"

Chapter 16

Oats, Peas, Beans and Leftovers

A clock somewhere in the town had just struck midnight on that shortest of nights when Oberon, King of Fairies, accompanied by his Queen and members of his court, descended upon the Fernwood and, preceded by his trumpeting guards, entered the thorn thicket that sheltered the scant hope of his people. The King stood awhile in silence before excusing the inhabitants of the thicket from their prostrate obeisance. He was counting heads. The little changeling's he recognized, her cornsilk hair bound by a wreath of violets. Next to hers he saw with relief and no little astonishment the head of his Puck. He then turned his attention to the humans who knelt just behind the Fernlord and his consort. There were four of them. Much encouraged, the King bade the company rise. He looked first at the changeling. She did not flinch from his gaze nor hide her face, but looked at him straight and proud with bright black eyes. The effect was striking, a dash of pepper to cut the richness of a too-perfect sauce. Oberon frowned. Those eyes were strangely familiar. He looked quickly back to the group of humans.

"So," he said. "So." Then he spoke in a warm, gentle voice, more a polite invitation than a command.

"Come before me, Ian James."

The man stepped forward, poised for his customary theatrical bow. The King raised his hand as if to restrain him.

"You are not to bow to me, Ian James, nor to any of my subjects. It is I who shall bow to you, who bear so much for the sake of my people." He stepped back as though he really meant to bend his knee.

"Oh no," Ian cried. "I beg Your Majesty. Don't do that. It would make me most uncomfortable to have the great lord of the first people of this land bow before such a queer-looking fellow."

Oberon smiled. "Very well. I should not want to make you uncomfortable. We are all so deeply in your debt that we can by no reward or gift hope to pay you. All I can offer you is the hospitality of all my people for as long as you live. There was a time when that might have been a very large gift indeed, but it is a meager one now."

"For me it is a great honor and pleasure, and it will be a larger boon in time, I think."

"I am prepared to grant you anything within my power."

"I am content, Your Majesty," Ian said. "I have done no more than fulfill my pledge. I have nothing to ask of you beyond the favor I requested last night: the use of Your Majesty's staff."

Oberon nodded. "That I freely give you, but I give it with a warning. It bears a powerful sting and will recoil on anyone who would attempt to misuse it."

"I am not so foolish as to consider misusing it," Ian protested.

Oberon offered him the staff. As he took it, Ian staggered back a little, as if momentarily overpowered by the weight or strength of the staff. But it affected him only for an instant. He straightened and turned slowly, holding the staff upright before him. The Puck had been too busy admiring his pretty companion to realize what was going on until a firm hand touched his shoulder.

"Might I have a word with you, Robin?"

The Puck looked up, startled. When he saw the staff in Ian's hand he jumped back and seemed on the point of bolting. At a hissed command from Oberon the two guards took up positions just behind his shoulders, cutting off any chance of escape. It was Midwinter Night reversed. The Puck showed signs of panic.

"You said you'd let me off if I went with you. You gave your word."

"So I did," Ian replied. "You took me at my word and

went with me. You behaved reasonably well for a puck, and, as I am a man of my word, I am letting you off. I completely and unconditionally pardon you your mistreatment of me last night. However, as your King has said, all of your people are deeply in my debt, you, I should say, more than any. Don't worry, I'm not going to try to make you pay that debt. I only want to ask you a few questions with some assurance that I shall get straight answers."

The Puck squirmed, shifted his weight from one foot to the other, and, fidgeting with the lacing of his jerkin, stared at his feet.

"I'll give you straight answers. You don't need to threaten me. What is it you want from me?"

"To begin with I want you to look me in the face."

The Puck bit his lip. "I would rather not, if you don't mind."

"You will do it all the same." The carved staff rose slowly over the Puck's shoulders. He lifted his head and looked with a grimace he could not conceal into his questioner's eyes.

"Well, Robin, are you satisfied with your bride now?"

"Oh yes," the Puck smiled with relief. "She's lovely, don't you think?"

"Quite. Will you have her, then?"

"I will have her gladly, if she will have me." He looked over at the changeling with a tender smile. She nodded, blushing, and shyly gave him her hand.

"Splendid," Ian exclaimed. "I am well satisfied. So, you are going to take a mate and settle down at last. I think you'll find the change from your former life rather pleasant once you get used to it, helping keep the house in order, playing with the children, perhaps later putting in a bit of a garden. . . ."

"Well, that wasn't exactly what I was thinking of doing."

"Oh? What were your plans, then? To take her flitting about with you, how is it:

> *Over hill, over dale*
> *Thorough bush, thorough briar?*

It sounds fun but is hardly the sort of life in which to raise a family. This girl is not given to you just for your enjoyment, you know, but for you to father children on. That, in case you have forgotten, is what the exchange was for. You are no fairy prince, my dear Puck; in truth a simple stud is what you are. Do you understand? Your function and your duty is to produce and bring up young to replenish your race. I can think of no safer or better place to do that than right where you now are. Don't forget that it is as the Lord Garumpta's lastborn that you take this changeling now. When you rejected her the Fernlord willingly took her in. It is not right that you should take her from him. No, if you will have her, you will have her here, where you will settle down as a member of the tribe, a good and dutiful husband and a puck no more. You will be ruled by her gentleness and her lord's justice." He laughed as the Puck cast a nervous glance in Garumpta's direction. "Oh yes, he can handle you. And he won't be alone, for I am at all times a welcome guest in these halls and plan to look in frequently to see how you're getting on. That may not be exactly what you had in mind, but that is just how things will be if you take this girl. Will you still have her?"

The Puck plowed a furrow in the ground with his toe. He looked at the girl beside him, at Garumpta, at Oberon, and finally at Ian.

"Yes," he said slowly. "I will have her, though I be made to darn stockings and peel onions." He turned to the changeling, took both her hands in his, and looked intently into her dark eyes. "She will be my playfellow and the mother of my children. And I shall be not her prince, but her servant. For surely I do love her."

Drawing her to him, he kissed her.

"Very nice," said Ian. "But before you go any farther with that sort of thing, I believe it is only proper and polite to present yourself to her lord, asking his permission to take her and begging his blessing on your mating."

"Yes, sir."

Pulling his bride along by the hand, Robin scurried over to where Garumpta stood. Ian watched with amusement the intense conversation that now developed between Robin and his new lord. The Fernlord was evidently driving a hard bargain. Yes, Garumpta would keep the scamp in line, that was a certainty.

In spite of the earlier admonition, Ian bowed deeply as he returned the staff to Oberon.

"I thank Your Majesty for this great privilege," he said.

The King allowed his staff to rest a moment on the man's bent shoulders. The touch transmitted to him a wonderful sense of peace, warmth, and serene strength. That touch alone was sufficient compensation for all he had been through.

"There is nothing more I can do for you?" Oberon asked.

"I have seen the successful completion of my spell and the fulfillment of my pledge," Ian replied. "I can see the hope of your people coming closer to reality. I am content. There is but one thing more I desire, and that is not Your Majesty's to grant."

"I have great power. Tell me what it is you wish."

"It was the middle of the day when I last ate, and I have labored hard since then. I am now most unbearably hungry. So I should like to ask the Lady Aneelen if I might prevail upon the hospitality of her table, now that I am in condition to do it justice."

Aneelen stepped forward and would have bowed to Ian had he not prevented her.

"You know," she said, "that I would rejoice to present you with the finest delicacies to be found in these woods. But we are not prepared to handle two feasts in as many nights. And now, when we have reason to hold the greatest feast of all, I have nothing to offer you but reheated leftovers."

"Do you know, my lady," Ian replied, "that I am uncommonly fond of leftovers?"

As it turned out, Aneelen had no need to apologize for her feast. It was excellent, and her guest of honor seemed determined to make up for those past feasts he had failed to take part in. A goodnatured rivalry developed as Robin attempted to equal or outdo Ian's capacity. The little changeling trotted happily to the serving table and back, filling and refilling her bride-groom's plate and cup.

Kicking off her pumps, Marian Crawley, with much merry raillery, began performing a similar service for Ian. The other guests looked on with considerable amusement.

"Well," Aneelen remarked to Mrs. Hubbard, "either age has finally gotten the better of me, or I am less wise than I think myself. I have been missing much that has been going on. I surely never thought to see Marian fetch for anyone."

Mrs. Hubbard laughed. "You are not the only one surprised, my lady. I had been under the impression that they rather despised each other. But then I suppose I am rather old-fashioned. My own courtship was quite different, and I certainly never fetched."

As the changeling passed on another trip to the table, Ian reached out and gently grasped her slender ankle.

"Here now, little one," he said. "You've trotted enough for this worthless scamp. Let him serve himself for a while. Come sit and talk with me."

He drew her down onto the ground beside him just as Marian returned with a mug of nectar.

"I don't hear you excusing me from trotting," she snapped.

"Then hear me now, my dear. Come join us and trot no more. I am quite satisfied anyway. If Robin wants the rest of the table, I surrender it to him."

"I'm certainly relieved to hear that," Marian responded dryly, seating herself on his other side. "I was sure you meant to eat yourself sick."

"You mustn't mind my Marian," Ian explained to the changeling. "She's a hardhearted wench, but she takes excellent care of me. Now tell me, are you happy in your new life?"

"Oh yes," she smiled, blushing a little. "Now that he will have me, I am happy. I know he isn't very nice, but I like him all the same." She looked up at Ian, then turned away quickly. "But," she whispered, "I'm so sorry you. . ."

"Nonsense," Ian snapped. "If I'm not sorry why should you be? Besides, my needs are not as great as yours, because my mate is not so bloody particular. She thinks it's funny. She just looks at me and laughs. Makes for a very jolly relationship."

The changeling giggled shyly.

"There," Ian cried. "That's much better. Now tell me how you like your lord and lady. Are they kind?"

"Yes, sir. But I am a little afraid of the lord."

Ian laughed. "Oh you must not be afraid of the Lord Garumpta. He growls like an ill-tempered beast, but his heart is very good. And has he given you a name?"

"No, sir. He calls me 'child.' "

"Oh dear. That isn't very satisfactory, is it? You ought to have a proper name." A mischievous light shone in his ungainly eyes. "He may choose for you what name he will, but I shall call you Tinkerbell."

Through the shocked murmur of the company came Garumpta's voice, cold with anger.

"Someday, man, you will go too far."

"Someday, perhaps, my lord," Ian replied. "But not, I think, tonight. Tonight I am privileged and may say what I please."

He winked at Marian and raised his cup.

"I should like to propose a toast. To Tinkerbell, and to all the chubby, jam-faced children who dutifully clap their hands for her, as well as to all the embarrassed adults who clap theirs secretly, under their coats. I have done my part to save her and insist on my right to drink to her."

Garumpta scowled but slowly raised his mug.

"To Tinkerbell, then," he said, and emptied the vessel in one swallow.

"Tinkerbell!" the members of the Fernlord's tribe cried out in chorus, clinking their mugs together with a terrible din.

Ian gently urged the blushing changeling to her feet.

"They're calling for you, dear. Take a bow, make a speech, sing a song."

The girl's black eyes widened suddenly, and she clapped her hands against her face.

"Ah-yo!" she cried. "I had forgotten. I promised Mompen I would teach his people Ah-yo."

"What is Ah-yo?" Garumpta asked, raising his hand for silence.

"Why it is—is—I don't know how to explain it, my

lord," she said in some confusion. Then she brightened. "But I can show you. May I?"

"Please, do, child."

She stood erect, hands at her sides, her head uplifted, and sang in a voice clear and delicate as a chiming bell.

Oats, peas, beans, and barley grow,
Oats, peas, beans, and barley grow.
Do you or I or anyone know
How oats, peas, beans, and barley grow?

She stood silent, her head bowed. Garumpta spoke in a hushed voice. "Mompen was right. This is a great and beautiful art. You will teach it to us."

Robin stepped forward and took his bride's hand in his. "In a far distance of time I knew this art. I remember it but vaguely now. Our people were once masters of it. I have heard it practiced by humans before, but their skill is no more than a shadow of what we are capable of. Come let us go through it together, that the forest may ring again with the beauty of the sound."

Their voices blended perfectly, like a pair of well-matched bells. She led him slowly through the verse. He stood in front of her, concentrating on the movements of her mouth, mimicking each movement, echoing each sound.

Oats, peas, beans, and barley grow,
Oats, peas, beans, and barley grow.
Do you or I or anyone know
How oats, peas, beans, and barley grow?

As they concluded, another voice rose, the light, confident baritone of Ian James.

Thus the farmer sows the seed,
Thus he stands and takes his ease,
He stamps his foot and claps his hands
And turns around to view his lands.

Bounding forward, Ian caught the changeling around the waist and drew her out into the open. As the Vicar led the entire company into the chorus, which by now even Garumpta was ready to attempt, Ian led his partner through the steps of a simple dance. She was naturally graceful and followed him easily. As the Vicar and Mrs. Hubbard started on the third verse, Marian Crawley, barefoot and woefully off key, pulled the delighted Robin onto the dance floor.

Waiting for a partner,
Waiting for a partner,
So open the ring and choose one in,
While we all gaily dance and sing!

There were but two couples on the floor; however, they made up in enthusiasm and energy for their lack of numbers. Garumpta tapped his stick in rhythm, and the Fernwood echoed with the joyous music.

"May I have the pleasure?" Robin seized the changeling from Ian's arms. Before he had a chance to object, he found himself dancing with Marian. They continued the round, panting slightly.

Now you're married you must obey,
Must be true in all you say,
Must be kind, you must be good,
And help your wife to chop the wood.

They had launched into the chorus again when Ian realized that he and his newly acquired partner were the only couple on the floor. Marian smiled at his questioning look.

"I informed the bridegroom of the whereabouts of a certain small and private chamber of my acquaintance," she explained with a sly wink. Ian spun her around once more at arm's length and concluded the dance with a courtly bow.

"I can always count on you, Miss Crawley," he said, "to say something encouraging."

She spread her skirt in a formal curtsy.

"I am known, Mr. James, as a person who gets things done."

Chapter 17

A Thoroughly Conventional Fellow

With the end of summer came the end as well of the American family's long visit. The baby understood the meaning of the bustle of packing and the to-do concerning tickets and passports, though she tried to avoid thinking about it. She was wearing her new skin fairly comfortably now, except when something—a glimpse of the forest, the odor of mushrooms cooking, the soft touch of moss—reminded her too keenly of her former life. She was moody and cried easily, but the family was too busy tying up the ends of their holiday to notice much.

For most of the year they had had few visitors. Their neighbors had been cordial but not oppressively friendly. Now, however, on the eve of their departure they were deluged with well-wishing callers. Mrs. Hubbard had dropped by for a short visit at least once a week since the middle of June. That interesting old clergyman they had met at Great Pond came twice to see them. Even the formidable Miss Crawley had been extraordinarily cordial and surprisingly lenient with the inventory. The baby seemed to enjoy company, and the company inevitably made a great fuss over her. And yet she was not really satisfied. There was one visitor she looked for who did not come.

Accounts were settled, trunks were shipped, farewells were said, and finally one late August morning, suitcases were set in the hall and a taxi was summoned to transport the baggage and the family that owned it to the station to catch the Southampton train.

The taxi stopped briefly in front of the office building on Station Street. The mother, baby on back, ducked out of the taxi and entered the door marked "M. Crawley, estate agent." The time had come for the final ritual of departure—the surrender of the keys.

Miss Crawley was sitting at her desk talking to a man wearing dark glasses. The baby became quite excited when she saw the man and reached her arms out toward him. While Miss Crawley kept the mother occupied with questions and comments about their impressions of England and the expectations of their journey home, the man in dark glasses talked to the delighted baby.

"Well, look what a lovely little creature you turned out to be." As he bent to plant a kiss on her head, she made a sudden grab for the unfamiliar spectacles. He caught her hands quickly. "Still a bit of a rascal, I see."

Observing that the mother was paying no attention to him, he began whispering rapidly.

"Did you think I could let you leave without so much as a good-bye? It's best you're going, you know. I'm sure you'll find it all a lot easier once you're away from here. Just think: you'll be seeing things I have never seen. I have never crossed the ocean on a ship or been to the land you are going to. You have many fine adventures ahead of you. Here, don't hold my fingers so tightly. It's high time you let loose of everything, even of me. You're not going to make a go of it if you don't. Be what you now are, a human child, and a charming one at that, and in the name of heaven have a good time."

He backed off abruptly as the mother rose to leave.

"Here, let go, you little scamp!" he laughed, shaking his hand free of the baby's grasp. He offered it then to the mother.

"Have a pleasant voyage home, Mrs. Pierce. I must say I'm going to miss seeing your little crowd taking over the front row in the auditorium."

"Thank you, Mr. James. I'm afraid we're going to miss being there, but we have to go. Good-bye, then. Say bye-bye, Penny."

The baby struggled determinedly with her unco-operative tongue and pronounced the required sounds in a high-pitched sing-song.

"Bye-bye."

Ian James clapped his hands in delight.

"Splendid, splendid! Bye-bye to you, my dear. Go and enjoy yourself."

The last she saw of him as she looked back from the street, he was standing just inside the office door, his arm around Marian Crawley's shoulders, waving. Blinking back tears, she raised her hand in an awkward wave. "Bye-bye!" she called. She ducked her head as the mother squirmed into the taxi. They pulled out into the street and turned toward the railway station.

The ocean voyage was good for the entire family, serving as a period of limbo when they could get used to the idea of returning to the land of their labors. The children took delight in the ship's playroom and game decks, all but the baby. She hated the playroom and wailed vigorously whenever she was left there. Now that she had been forced to release the last remnants of her former self, she clung to her adoptive mother. She was going through a phase, her well-read parents concluded, and chose to ignore her behavior in the hope it would go away.

The baby did like the ocean, though. It was so different from anything she had known in her life that she really began to feel that she was living in another world and was, indeed, another being. Her greatest delight was to ride on her mother's back as they walked the decks in the evening after dinner to watch the sun set over the endlessly moving water. By their second day out she could say "ocean." Before the week's voyage was over the memory of that grotesque little creature Mompen had all but died, and the only mother and father she recognized were the ones who now carried her through the ship's dining room, set her in a high chair, and offered her samplings of exotic food from their plates.

One night the father offered her a piece of sautéed mushroom. She did not like it at all and spat it onto her plate. She felt an inner twinge of regret, as if she had lost something valuable, but she did not know what it was. She was quite irritable that evening and refused to go to sleep. In desperation her mother administered a healthy swig of the Cockburn's port she had in the stateroom. The baby drank it, smiled contentedly, and dropped off to sleep at once.

The customs officer who was in charge of passengers from N to R was a slight, cheerful man with a keen eye for smugglers. He certainly had no suspicions of the family he was now clearing, despite the vastness of their paraphernalia. He felt sorry for them; they were having such a rough time. First there was the frantic search for a missing trunk; then a lock stuck. As he had suspected, there was in the end nothing to declare, nothing of value; clothes painfully mussed from too tight packing, a reproduction from the British Museum, uncountable guidebooks and theater programs, a deflated soccer ball. Nothing of interest to United States Customs. After stamping the two large trunks, three suitcases, canvas bag, shopping bag, radio, camera, and portable typewriter, the officer, in a whimsical mood, planted a stamp on the tip of the wide-eyed baby's nose. There was general laughter as the family passed through the heavy gates into their native land. No one, not even the people bearing it, was aware of the unprecedented contraband that was smuggled in that day stamped with the blessing of the Customs Service itself.

The sedate little community of Elvinwood settled comfortably into autumn. Coachloads of bird watchers regularly invaded Great Pond; the square-faced maidens of the Oak Haven School marched down the hill to the church two by two every Sunday. Mushrooms and chestnuts were abundant in the forest, allowing the Fernlord to replenish his hoard—and well he might, as there would be more celebrations required that season. September had not ended before the official announcement confirmed the rumors that had been circulating around the thorn thicket for weeks: little Mistress Tinkerbell, the lastborn of the tribe, was already with child. Abundant harvests of more than chestnuts could be foreseen for the people of the forest.

An Australian family with three adolescent boys moved into the brick house on Buckingham Avenue. They were neat and efficient, which pleased Miss Crawley, but not very friendly, which displeased Mrs. Hubbard.

There was a slight, discreet sensation in early October when Ian James began appearing in public without his dark glasses. No one said anything, of course, not even anything solicitous. That would have been considered bad form. However, things did get a bit tight when he showed up at tryouts for the pantomime, which that year was *Peter Pan*. In the conflict that ensued among the producers torn between loyalty and aesthetics, loyalty won out by a very close margin. It turned out to be a fortunate decision, for it soon became apparent that whatever Ian may have lost over the summer it was not his talent. His theatrical powers had, if anything, increased. There was general agreement amongst those who attended the performances that his Captain Hook was the best in living memory, sinister and at the same time ludicrous. And children by the hundreds clapped their hands wildly to save poor Tinkerbell, while a gratifyingly large number of their parents applauded surreptitiously under their coats.

The comparatively mild weather of March was interrupted by a freak cold spell that froze pipes, raised the price of coal, and did much to discourage early-blooming crocuses. It lasted only a few days but, being unexpected and unprepared for, it caused considerable damage. The first day that the weather returned to something like normal, a group of shivering Boy Scouts ventured out onto the moor that surrounded Great Pond on a prescheduled hike that they refused to postpone. They found beside a footpath leading from the pond the frozen body of an elderly man in clerical attire. A notice of the discovery was placed in the local paper. It had hardly been out an hour when a proper-looking old lady made her appearance at the police station offering to identify the body. The police did not like subjecting a person like that to such an ordeal, but, as she insisted and they had no other leads, they were forced to acquiesce. She was subdued but quite calm as she viewed the body. Yes, it was, as she had suspected, her old friend Thomas Heaton, the former vicar of Wensley. He had no living relatives, she assured them. Since she was the closest thing he had to a family, she offered to see to his interment. It was a simple solution to a rather touchy problem, so the authorities agreed.

The following day the three surviving human members

of the Midsummer conspiracy sat together in Mrs. Hubbard's parlor. The large armchair near the window was empty, and a simple urn sat unfamiliarly amongst the bric-a-brac on top of the piano. In a far corner near the sofa were piled three large cartons of books. Ian James sat in his usual chair staring morosely at his hands.

"He's taking it hard," Marian whispered to their hostess.

"I expect he would," Mrs. Hubbard murmured sympathetically. "They became very close in such a short time."

Ian looked up sharply. "Well," he challenged Mrs. Hubbard, "can you explain to me why a man in his right mind would go out on the moor alone on the coldest day of the year?"

"He was tired, Ian," Mrs. Hubbard explained, laying a gentle hand on his arm. "When you are older you will better understand. Thomas was very old, you know, older than he let on. And he has been in increasingly poor health. He made sure you were never aware of that. He lacked the patience to tolerate a long illness. I imagine he sensed the distant approach of death and chose to meet the fellow halfway."

"He did it deliberately? But why didn't he say anything to me? Why, I was out on that damned moor with him little more than a week ago."

"What would you have done if he had told you, dear? You would have tried to talk him out of it, wouldn't you, and ruined that final walk together. He knew, I suspect, that you would be hurt in any event, but that it would be easier on both of you, if he just made a run for it when you were looking the other way."

"Did you know what he was up to?"

"Yes, I was suspicious when he brought those things over last week." She indicated the cartons of books. "He said he wanted to be certain that they didn't fall into the wrong hands if something were to happen to him. He wouldn't say any more, although I pumped him mercilessly."

"Why didn't you warn me, at least?"

"A man of courage and power ought to be allowed to

choose his doom," Marian interrupted, "without having to suffer the well-meaning interference of his friends."

Ian clenched his hands. He knew the truth of what they were saying, but he still found the reality hard to accept. His grief was bitter, and he could find no comfort.

"To have let you know," Mrs. Hubbard went on, "would have been to betray his confidence. I did for you and for him what I could. I got to the police first and so spared you the cold ritual of filling out forms and signing releases. But now the worst of it's over with, I feel that it's only right that you, his dear children, should have some say in the disposition of his remains."

They all sat silent for a while. Ian wiped his eyes with the back of his hand. Marian offered him a linen handkerchief from the recesses of her handbag.

"He wouldn't want any fuss made," she said. "He always despised that sort of thing. Perhaps it would be best simply to scatter his ashes over the moor."

"He's probably had his fill of the moor," Ian snapped. He rose and stood looking out the window. The red-faced Australian boys were kicking a football around the garden next door. They were quite skilled at it. On an impulse, Ian bent his power on the boy who was now kicking. The ball went wild, spinning insanely, and crashed through the kitchen window.

"You'll have to send a glazier over next door in the morning, Marian," he called over his shoulder. "One of your prize tenants has just broken a window." The gesture gave him some satisfaction and eased a little the tightness in his throat.

He turned to the window facing the front of the cottage. It looked out over the rose garden, neatly pruned and hibernating in its carefully laid blanket of mulch. Suddenly he bolted out the door, making for the little shed behind the house, from which he took a trowel. Kneeling in the damp grass at the edge of the rose bed he began slowly to work the soil loose around the naked bushes. When he had prepared the bed to his satisfaction, he looked up to find Marian standing beside him, the urn in her hands. Taking it from her he carefully worked the ashes into the mulch, dust to dust, in the ritual act of interment by which a man resigns himself to putting the period onto the sentence of a life, so that he may lay it aside and accept it as completed. After he was done, Ian remained awhile on his knees in the chilly afternoon sun. At length he rose, dusted off his trousers, and with a relieved sigh let go the tightness that had bound his throat.

When they had returned to the house they found that Mrs. Hubbard had laid out tea, an abbreviated version of her usual repast: just bread and cheese, with a few biscuits in a cellophane packet for sweet. While she poured, Ian crouched beside the carton of books. Many of them looked to be ancient and quite valuable. He knew that the Vicar had possessed a library in his chosen field that would have been the envy of Faust himself. He picked up one of the books and thumbed through the heavy, closely written pages. They were filled with elaborate and exotic symbols. The text appeared to be in English, but he could make no sense of it.

"What's to be done with these?" he asked.

"He wanted you to have them, dear," said Mrs. Hubbard.

"Oh really? That's very touching, but I'm afraid they wouldn't be of much use to me; I can't even read most of them. I say, what's this?" He drew from the bottom of the carton a garment of some sort and held it up. It appeared to be a loose-flowing robe of fine gray silk.

"Why, it's his mantle," cried Mrs. Hubbard, almost dropping the teapot.

"He wanted me to have that as well, I suppose, the old fox."

"I didn't know it was there," Mrs. Hubbard protested. "Truly I didn't."

"The old fox," Ian murmured, running his hand along the soft folds of the robe. It put him in mind of the shirt he had worn at the exchange. It shimmered seductively as he moved it in the soft afternoon light. "The wicked old fox." He turned, protesting, to the two smiling women. "It's not playing fair, doing it like that. I wouldn't have thought him capable of such a perverse trick."

"Then you didn't know him so very well, after all," said Mrs. Hubbard. "Of all of us, Thomas was the least troubled with scruples, especially when it came to getting his own way. He told me once, Ian, that he was prepared to wager his life that you would take up his mantle in the end."

Ian looked at the beautiful garment now resting across his arm. He resolved to put it down but found that he could not bring himself to do so. Perhaps later, when the edges of grief had worn a little smoother. Slowly, hardly aware of what he was about, he shrugged his arms into the flowing sleeves and pulled the robe over his shoulders. It fit him perfectly, which was surprising, since the Vicar had been both taller and broader than his reluctant disciple.

"Are you sure he actually wore this?" Ian asked. "I should have thought he couldn't get into it."

"Garments of this sort fit those who are meant to wear them," Marian explained.

"Oh, I see." The robe felt good on him, light in weight yet exuding a pleasant warmth. He could sense the presence of power in it. As he looked admiringly at it, he noticed that the material was intricately patterned, like fine damask, with the sort of embellishments one might find on old church windows—doves, roses, and the disembodied wings of angels intertwined with endless mazes of leafy vines. Rarely had he seen anything so beautiful. He stood lost to himself, warm tears slowly rising in his dreadful eyes.

"Come now, dear. Your tea is getting cold."

Ian James removed his master's robe, folded it with reverent affection, and laid it on top of the carton of books. As he sat down, Marian solicitously offered him a cup of tea and a slice of bread. He looked at her keenly.

"Well, what in hell am I supposed to do with all that?"

She smiled. "I'm sure you'll think of something, dear."

Chapter 18 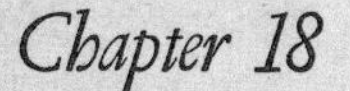

Reprise: La Belle Dame sans Merci

The London-to-Portsmouth train stopped briefly at Elvinwood, letting off a single passenger, an attractive, blue-eyed girl, perhaps in her early twenties. She looked about her curiously as she emerged from the station, carefully placing the return portion of her day ticket in the change pocket of her slim handbag. So this was the town. It didn't look a great deal different from other English towns its size: narrow, curving streets bordered by shops and offices interspersed with the brick-and-stone cottages of workingpeople, the private treasury of their gardens protected by walls and high hedges. An occasional road led off the main thoroughfare toward the more gracious and more generous estates of the well-off. The girl looked questioningly up some of these lanes, checking their names on signs, if she could find any, but she was unable to locate the street she wanted.

Turning a corner, she glanced at the street sign above her: Station Street. That had a familiar sound. She began walking up the street. There was the post office, there the police station, and now directly across the street from her was a slightly shopworn-looking brick building. The bulletin board attached to its wall identified it as Elvinwood Auditorium and announced the next event to be held in it: the Elvinwood Choral Society's autumn concert. The society, to judge from the sound filtering out of open windows, was at present in rehearsal. The girl leaned against the wall of the building across the street and listened. She loved music with all the passion she seemed unable to feel toward men. When she closed her eyes and allowed herself to be possessed by the music, she became lost to herself, her surroundings, her problems, her reason (if she had any) for coming to this place. It was only at times such as this that she was free for a while from the constant undercurrent of restlessness with which she had somehow learned to live. She recovered from her reverie slowly, coming gradually to the realization that the rehearsal had been over for a while, that most of the people who had come from the auditorium had left by car or on foot. It had occurred to her to ask directions of one of these people, for it was getting late. Now only one old man remained, standing with his back to her, examining a notice on the bulletin board. She hurried across the street before he also had a chance to escape.

"Excuse me," she said rapidly, for she was embarrassed talking to strangers. "Could you please tell me how to get to Buckingham Avenue?"

The man turned and looked at her. She gave a low cry and shrank back. Nowhere outside of a nightmare had she seen such a face. The man smiled apologetically.

"I'm sorry I startled you," he said.

"I—I'm sorry," she murmured, forcing back tears of humiliation.

"You've no reason to be. You're a stranger. People get used to me after a while. I shall be very pleased to show you Buckingham Avenue. It's the street I live on, and I'm on my way home."

He began walking up the street, and, not knowing what else to do, she walked beside him. He resumed their conversation as he walked, assisting himself with a fine-looking walking stick.

"It's just a residential street, you know, hardly the sort of place to interest visitors."

"I know," she said. "You see, I lived there once."

The man turned on her, scowling. He really looked dreadful when he scowled. Her blue eyes widened in apprehension. What had she said to make him look at her so?

"Hmm," he murmured, tapping the pavement sharply with his cane. "This wasn't recently, I take it?"

"Oh no," the girl replied. "I was just a baby. I don't remember anything about it. That's why I thought it might be fun to see what it all was like."

"You don't remember anything?" the man asked.

"No, I don't. I was just a baby."

"You don't remember me, then?"

"No, sir. I'm afraid I don't."

He gave her another sharp look as though trying to see into her soul; then he smiled. It was better when he smiled; he merely looked comical, like Mr. Punch.

"I say, that doesn't seem right. I remember you quite well. You rode about town on your mother's back, much to the scandal of the local ladies, and your name is, let me see, Penny. Right?"

"Right."

"And my name is Ian James. Does that mean anything to you?"

"No, Mr. James, it doesn't. But I'm glad to meet you all the same."

He stopped in front of a small office building, and, taking her arm, he escorted her through the door.

"Come, you must meet my wife."

A severely neat, white-haired woman sitting at a desk looked up as they entered.

"You'll never guess who this is, Marian," the man said.

"Probably not, dear," she replied in a tone of well-worn patience. "Who is it?"

"You remember the American family that lived in the house on the hill when we were first acquainted? Well, here is the baby, all grown up."

The woman gasped and raised one hand to her mouth.

"She doesn't remember anything." The man's voice underlined each word in dark pencil.

The woman rose at once and went to the girl, holding out her hand.

"Welcome back to Elvinwood, my dear. What brings you to us again after all these years?"

"Curiosity, I suppose, Mrs. James. I've always felt somewhat cheated because I was so young when the family came here. I'm on a student tour right now. We got a free afternoon during our stay in London, so I slipped down here to have a look at what I missed."

"She wants to see the house," Ian James explained. "I have an idea. It's getting late, so why don't we close up shop and all go up together? Perhaps Miss Penny would consent to take tea with us before she returns to her tour."

"Why, that's very kind of you," Penny said. "But I don't want to put you out."

"Oh you wouldn't be putting us out, my dear. We live in the house next door to the one you lived in. We more or less inherited it from your neighbor of the time, Mrs. Hubbard. Before you return home you should certainly have the pleasure of a genuine old-fashioned English tea."

As the three of them walked up the hill, Penny found herself being subjected to a rather close interrogation. She was in her third year at a state university, she told them, studying her two great passions, theater and music. She was neither engaged nor involved with any man. As a matter of fact, she volunteered, astonished at her own candor, her real purpose in taking this tour was to escape for a while the unwanted advances of a persistent suitor.

They stood at the corner of Churchill Lane and Buckingham Avenue. Ian James directed the girl's attention to a square brick house surrounded by a gigantic hedge.

"That's it, Penny. And that," he pointed with his stick to an upstairs window, "was your bedroom. I believe the cot was next to the window."

The girl looked up and shuddered.

"Gee," she said. "It would be a long way to fall, wouldn't it?"

The man frowned. "Are you quite sure you don't remember anything?"

"Yes, I'm sure. Anyway, I didn't fall, did I?" She laughed a slight, nervous laugh. "You mustn't mind me, Mr. James. I have a terrible fear of high places."

She was glad she had decided to stay for tea. It was such a pleasant little meal. She was beginning to like these people very much in spite of all the questions they asked her. She felt more comfortable with them than with anyone she could recall.

"You two seem so happy together," she mused, looking through the window at the garden next door. "I envy you that. I think you love each other very much. That's my problem, you know. I just don't seem to be able to really love anyone. This current boy isn't the first I've driven off. I don't know what's wrong with me." The kindness and sympathy of these strangers seemed to open in her a tightly sealed chamber of secret fear.

"Do you know what I sometimes feel?" she went on. "I feel that I'm not human at all, that I'm some sort of alien creature that doesn't belong in the skin of a normal human girl. Isn't that weird?"

She stopped talking suddenly, for her host had risen from his chair and was now standing with his back to her, head bowed, clenched fists pressed against the lid of the upright piano.

"I'm sorry," he said in a choked voice. "I wanted you to be happy. All this time I just assumed that you were happy."

"Ian, please," his wife exclaimed. "Be careful."

The girl looked from one to the other in confusion and distress. "Oh dear, I've upset you, and you've been so nice to me. I didn't mean it, really. I'm happy. Of course I'm happy. Why wouldn't I be? I'm just a little moody sometimes. Please don't let my silliness spoil such a pleasant afternoon."

"That's all right, my dear," Mrs. James assured her. "My husband is also subject to strange moods. I suppose you just hit each other in the right spots. Could I give you some more tea?"

"No, thank you," Penny replied. "It's getting late. I'm afraid I'll have to go now if I'm going to get in that little walk in the woods beyond the housing estate before I take the train back."

"Oh no," Marian James cried in alarm, as if suddenly seized by the strange mood that had been circulating around the parlor. "You mustn't go into the forest."

"Why not?" the girl asked. "Is it haunted or something?"

"It—it's, well, not really safe, especially so near nightfall. You could easily get lost, and it's a frightening place after dark."

"I'm afraid of heights, Mrs. James, but not of the dark. I feel more comfortable, actually, in the dark. I won't go far if it worries you, but I'm really anxious to see the forest."

The other woman caught her arm as she started for the door.

"Please, dear," she begged, on the verge of tears. "Humor a superstitious old woman's whims. Be content with what you have seen and leave it at that."

"Let her go, Marian." The man's voice—low, steady, a little grim—cut through the soft afternoon shadows of the room. "If she is that strongly compelled to go into the forest it may be because she is meant to." He turned to the girl. "Do you know how to get there?"

"Yes," she replied. "My brothers gave me directions. The footpath is behind the housing estate."

"Go, then," he said, "with my blessing. But won't you please share a little drink with us before you go, to put a nice top on the day?"

He took from a low cupboard near the door leading to the kitchen a bottle and three glasses. She watched as he carefully poured out a dark, reddish liquid. When he had filled one glass he raised it slowly to the level of his face, breathed on it, and whispered some words over it. Then he handed the glass to her. The others he poured out without ceremony. After giving one glass to his wife, he raised the other in the manner of a toast.

"To your happiness, my child."

"Thank you, sir. And to yours."

She sipped at the liquid experimentally. It was rich, sweet, and warming. She emptied the glass in one swallow.

"Very good," she said.

The man turned away.

"Wait," he cried suddenly. "I have something for you."

He hurried into another room. On his return he pressed something small and thin into her hand.

"Take this with you," he instructed her. "If you find yourself in a tight place, especially a very small tight place, show it and say that it was given to you by Ian James. All right? Now I have given you as much protection as my power allows, and that is considerable. Go into the forest if you feel you must. Do not be afraid, but let whatever will happen to you happen. We shall probably see one another again in any event."

He kissed her gently on the forehead and escorted her to the door. Walking down the path she looked at the thing he had placed in her hand. It was small and made of wood—looked, indeed, something like a toothpick—but as she held it up in the vaguely pink light of the setting sun she saw that it was covered with minute and intricate carving. She looked back as she passed the high hedge of the house she could not remember living in. The last she saw of him, he was standing at the window with his arm around his wife's shoulders, waving. She waved back.

She liked the forest. It was cool and serene in the soft evening air. And she was cool and serene as well, more at peace with herself than she could remember ever having been before. She did not know whether it was the atmosphere of the twilit forest that had so strongly affected her or the power of the drink she had accepted from her strange host. Whatever it was, it had made her feel wonderfully free and light. She walked on, hardly aware of her feet, going farther into the woods than she had meant to. As darkness increased, she began to experience some difficulty in keeping to the footpath. Then the path she was following narrowed gradually until it had become nothing more than a thin rabbit trail disappearing into a large, dense thicket of thorny blackberry vines. It was then that she realized that it had become quite dark, and she wondered if she would be able to find the main path again. For the first time since she had entered the forest she sensed a twinge of fear. Turning back in the direction in which she believed the path to be, she began singing to keep up her courage, a song of her childhood that came uninvited to the head.

Oats, peas, beans, and barley grow,
Oats, peas, beans, and barley grow.
Do you or I or anyone know
How oats, peas, beans, and barley grow?

Something struck her smartly on the ankle. She turned, really frightened now, ready to run. But Ian James had told her not to be afraid, but to let whatever happened to her happen. She knelt on the ground and picked up the thing that had struck her, which still lay beside her foot. It was a chestnut. She laughed. All that to-do over a common chestnut. But before she could rise again, she heard a small, clear, faraway voice answering her song.

Waiting for a partner,
Waiting for a partner,
So open the ring and choose one in,
While we all gaily dance and sing!

The voice drifted away into the thicket as though seducing her to follow it. Still clutching the chestnut, she threw herself on the forest floor and began searching eagerly in pursuit of the song and its singer.